NEW

JAMES I. ROBERTSON JR.

STANDING LIKE A STONE WALL

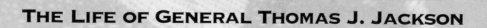

THE LIFE OF GENERAL THOMAS J. JACKSON

ATHENEUM BOOKS FOR YOUNG READERS

NEW YORK * LONDON * TORONTO * SYDNEY * SINGAPORE

Atheneum Books for Young Readers
An imprint of Simon & Schuster Children's Publishing Division
1230 Avenue of the Americas
New York, New York 10020

Book design by Julietta Cheung.
The text of this book was set in Bembo.

Printed in the United States of America
2 4 6 8 10 9 7 5 3 1

Library of Congress Cataloging-in-Publication Data
Robertson, James I.
Standing like a stone wall : the life of
General Thomas J. Jackson / by James I. Robertson Jr.—1st ed.
p. cm.
ISBN 0-689-82419-X
1. Jackson, Stonewall 1824-1863.
2. Generals—Confederate States of America—Biography.
3. Confederate States of America. 4. Army—Biography.
I. Title.
E467.I.J15 R6 2001
973.7'3'092—dc21
[B] 00-036253

✳ Table of Contents ✳

ACKNOWLEDGMENTS

No historian works alone. Many unselfish people give aid and encouragement all along the path in the making of a book. This one was no exception.

Easing the pain of research and writing costs were funds made possible by the late J. Ambler Johnston and Frank L. Curtis. Personnel in Virginia Tech's Photographic Services could not have been more helpful in converting old, faded illustrations into sharp, publishable images.

I am indebted to Macmillan Publishing USA, especially to Senior Editor Jill Lectka, for permission to reprint maps that originally appeared in my earlier biography, *Stonewall Jackson: The Man, The Soldier, The Legend* (1997).

Beth R. Brown, Lou Long, Joan Nunnally, Beth G. Robertson, and Kimberly Willison enriched earlier drafts by reading them with the careful eye of the mothers and teachers they are. My appreciation is deeper than they can know.

To the twenty-two undergraduates in a senior seminar at Virginia Tech, I owe a genuine expression of thanks. Each of them prepared research papers on aspects of General Jackson's life. They pointed out trees while I was gazing at the forest. This was another occasion when a professor learned from his students.

Vice President and Associate Publisher Jonathan J. Lanman at Atheneum was enthusiastic from the start about this project. He expertly guided the study from ideas to a printed reality. He has my gratitude, as does the editorial staff at Atheneum, for polishing hard copy into a smooth, finished text.

James Rogers of Frederick, Maryland, was the first person to suggest *Standing Like a Stone Wall* as the title for this book. He gets the prize in the contest—as well as my personal thanks.

My wife, Libba, whose love for children surpasses my own, urged me to undertake this study. She then left me alone while I worked. Her enthusiasm in the face of neglect is one of the things that makes her so special.

While this book can serve as an adult's introduction to the life of one of Virginia's most famous sons, it is primarily aimed at America's citizens of tomorrow. Hopefully, from learning their history, they will come to love their country even more.

—James I. Robertson Jr.
Virginia Tech

INTRODUCTION

"You May Be What Ever You Will Resolve to Be"

Early in 1863, a British newspaperman spent the night at the headquarters of Confederate General Thomas J. "Stonewall" Jackson. The reporter noted: "He is tall, handsome and powerfully built. . . . The General, who is indescribably simple and unaffected in all his ways, took off my wet overcoat with his own hands, made up the fire, brought wood for me to put my feet on to keep them warm while my boots were drying . . . With the cares and responsibilities of a vast army on his shoulders, he found time to do the little acts of kindness and thoughtfulness which make him the darling of the army."

So impressed was the London correspondent that he considered enlisting in the Confederate army.[1]

Jackson's life is one of the most inspiring in all of history. It is the story of an orphan who knew more about loneliness than love. He grew up in the mountainous wilderness of northwestern Virginia. Shy and silent by nature, poorly educated, he had no reason to expect to go far in his narrow world. Yet Thomas Jackson built a brilliant career on determination and faith. He never stopped believing that "you may be what ever you will resolve to be."[2]

By such willpower he graduated from the finest military school in America. He went straight into a war and became one of its real heroes. Ten years as a professor at the Virginia Military Institute brought him a reputation as a devoted teacher with odd habits. The death of his first wife and child continued the hard knocks that life seemed to hold for him. Jackson survived because by then he had dedicated his life to God and found a faith he could call home.

In 1861 the explosion of civil war across the land transformed the little-known college professor into a soldier of unflappable courage. He gained the most famous nickname in American military history in the Civil War's first major battle. His 1862 campaign in Virginia's Shenandoah Valley was instantly recognized as a masterpiece of planning and execution. For eleven months thereafter, "Stonewall" Jackson and General Robert E. Lee were a military team that gained one spectacular victory after another against heavy numbers.

He so mystified the enemy that he seemed to be everywhere at once. A Massachusetts private stated: "His name was terror in the union army, and with us expressed more fear than all other names put together."[3] Every Jackson success produced "a panic in the Northern states."[4] Northern women were known to warn disobedient children that if they did not behave, Stonewall Jackson would come after them in the dark of night.

Suddenly, in May 1863, it all ended. Jackson was accidentally shot by his own soldiers in the confusion of battle. He calmly died a week later with the words "Let us cross over the river and rest under the shade of the trees."[5]

Success is something everyone desires. The harder it is to prosper, the more one appreciates the prosperity. Thomas Jackson was the fulfillment of a rags-to-riches adventure. In his thirty-nine years he went from a lonely little boy who would not accept failure to the most famous general of his time. And throughout that climb to fame he insisted that he was but a servant of "an ever kind Heavenly Father."[6]

Jackson was brilliant yet shy; he was widely praised but strangely unique; he was heroic but humble. His genius in the field was as obvious as the faith deep inside him. Few men have done more to shape the course of events than "Mighty Stonewall." Jackson would have wanted to be remembered simply as "The Christian Soldier." Yet his life—and his death—were major turning points in the course of our country's history.

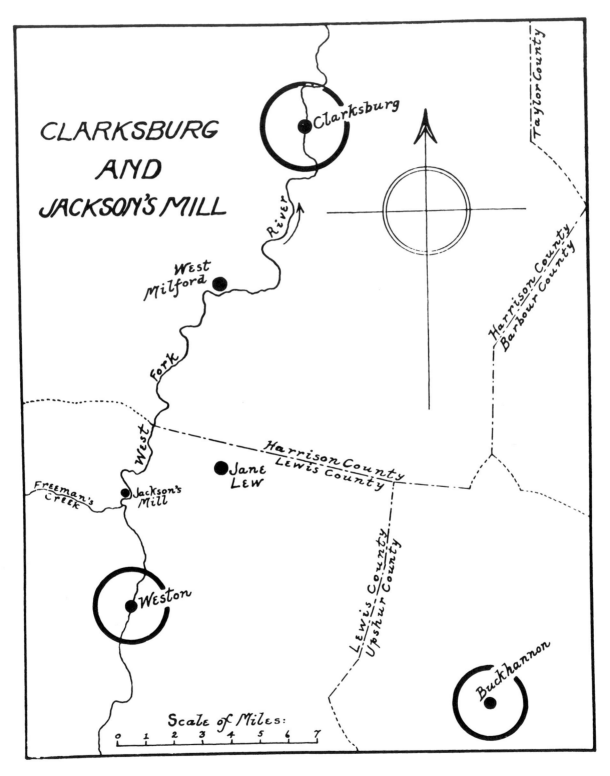

CLARKSBURG
AND
JACKSON'S MILL

Taylor County

Clarksburg

River

West Milford

Fork

Harrison County
Barbour County

West

Harrison County
Lewis County

Freeman's Creek

Jackson's Mill

Jane LEW

Lewis County
Upshur County

Weston

Buckhannon

Scale of Miles:

0 1 2 3 4 5 6 7

*This drawing shows the mountainous region where
Tom Jackson was born and spent his youth. The family property
at Jackson's Mill is now a West Virginia state park.*

✹ Chapter 1 ✹
Life as an Orphan

The little boy peered out from the shelter of leaves, brush, and vines that he had carefully built in a clump of white poplar trees. His homemade structure was small and flimsy, but it was the lad's refuge—his safe retreat from the stings of the world. A few feet in front of his lean-to was the curving West Fork River, whose swift waters always provided a cool breeze. On the other side of the river was the bustle of farm and milling activity that marked daily life at Jackson's Mill. The estate was the largest farming property in Lewis County, and the wealthiest.

Tom Jackson lived there, but it was not really home. He had only dreams and a faint memory of a real home. For the young orphan, life and loneliness were one and the same.

What knowledge Jackson had of his family was very limited. Only later would he learn that the American branch of Jacksons began with nothing. It rose to high prominence in the mountainous frontier of Virginia before family members began falling on hard times.

His great-grandparents had traveled across the Atlantic Ocean from England under the worst of circumstances. In the late 1740s John Jackson and Elizabeth Cummins had both been convicted in a London court of grand theft. Robbery was then punishable by death, but the two felons were among scores of other criminals banished to America for seven years of forced labor. Jackson and Cummins met as the boatload of prisoners made its way westward. They were in love by the time the vessel docked in Maryland.

The two married after completing their sentences. In the spring of 1758, the couple and their two small sons migrated west into the untamed Allegheny Mountains. They eventually settled near the hamlet of Buckhannon and amassed land holdings of more than ten thousand acres. The father and his sons all served as soldiers in the American Revolution. Afterward John Jackson gained election first to the Virginia General Assembly and then to the U.S. House of Representatives. For Jackson, America was indeed a land of great opportunity.

His youngest son Edward struck out on his own shortly after the Revolution. Edward Jackson moved twenty-five miles deeper into the mountains and was one of the founders of the town of Clarksburg. An accomplished surveyor, land broker, and civil engineer, he was a man to whom wealth and power came easily. Edward Jackson built a two-story log home eighteen miles south of Clarksburg at a place he called Jackson's Mill. The Jackson property consisted of several thousand acres including a large horseshoe bend in the

West Fork River. Fertile river bottomland stretched to hills densely covered with hardwood trees. The plantation became a community center for timber, milling, farming, and livestock production. To insure his influence, Edward Jackson laid out streets five miles away for a town. It was called Weston and in time became the governmental seat of Lewis County.[1]

Two generations of Jacksons had demonstrated that they had the basic characteristics of Scotch-Irish stock: They were brave, ambitious, self-reliant, and independent-minded. On the other hand, they displayed little attention to either culture or religion.

Edward Jackson fathered fifteen children by two wives. All lived at least to middle age. The father made the mistake of sharing the family fortune equally with each of them. The siblings naturally differed in ability and personality. While some sought to preserve the family reputation, others did not care. One of the worst abusers of the father's kindness was the third child, Jonathan Jackson.

Born in September 1790, Jonathan studied law under a well-respected uncle and began a career as an attorney in Clarksburg. He was a small man, with a ruddy complexion and cheerful nature. Practicing law on the frontier did not earn much money, so Jonathan began selling real estate and countersigning loans for friends. He had little ability as a businessman but a great talent for drinking and gambling. It did not take long for him to get deeply in debt. This forced him to sell large sections of the Jackson land he had inherited. Debts still continued to mount.

In 1817, in the midst of his troubles, Jonathan married Julia Neale of Parkersburg. Her family were Irish pioneers who had done well as merchants along the Ohio River. Jonathan was twenty-seven at the time of his wedding. Julia was nineteen and apparently so blinded by her husband's charms that she could overlook his business weaknesses.

A miniature likeness of Jonathan Jackson, Tom's father. He died when Tom was two years old and left the family without money or means.

The couple settled into a small, one-and-a-half-story brick home in the center of Clarksburg. A daughter, Elizabeth, was born in 1819; a son, Warren, joined the family two years later. Meanwhile, marriage did little to make Jonathan Jackson more responsible. He was soon borrowing money by putting up as collateral livestock, household furniture, and even the family bed.[2]

In that bleak atmosphere, during a bitingly cold night, Dr. James McCalley went to the Jackson cottage to deliver a third child. The physician thought that birth

In this simple cottage, across the street from the courthouse in Clarksburg, Virginia, Tom Jackson was born. The side of the house faced the main street.

occurred just before midnight on January 20, 1824. Family members insisted that the child was born in the early hours of January 21 and observed that birth date. The baby was a boy with his mother's brown hair and father's blue eyes. He was christened Thomas in honor of his maternal grandfather.

Family problems came to a crisis two years later. Elizabeth fell ill with typhoid fever. Jonathan Jackson had to care for his daughter because his wife was in the final stages of another pregnancy. Mr. Jackson also contracted typhoid fever. Within the space of three weeks, the daughter died, the father died, and the mother gave birth to a girl who was named Laura.

Thus, a twenty-eight-year-old mother was left alone with three small children and a mountain of debts. The family moved into a sparsely furnished hut. Mrs. Jackson did some sewing and occasionally taught school in order to earn a few dollars. Such efforts were not enough. Clarksburg citizens began donating funds to clothe and feed the family. Tom Jackson never forgot those years. What his father taught him most of all was the shame that comes from selfishness, laziness, and a lack of responsibility.

A child grieves by seeing others grieve. Little Tom had a sweet face, but few smiles ever passed over it. He watched the mother he adored struggle in vain to care for three ragged children. Too small to help, he became more quiet and withdrawn. In many ways, Tom Jackson was never a child. There was no room in his narrow existence for the joy and carefree ways that a normal childhood brings.

He was seven years old when the greatest blow fell. His mother married Clarksburg attorney Blake Woodson. She did so over the objections of the Jackson and Neale families. A widower with eight children scattered in every direction, Woodson was much like Jonathan Jackson: fond of good living but never quite able to support a comfortable lifestyle. Why Julia Jackson married an undependable man old enough to be her father was clear: Woodson offered a possible escape from the poverty she and the children had endured for four years. By then her health was failing. Jackson's mother had fallen victim to fatal tuberculosis.

Woodson's true nature emerged all too soon. The stepfather began complaining that his income could not support such a large family. He verbally abused the three children by blaming them for his own financial problems. More than once, Woodson asked Warren, Tom, and Laura (none of whom had reached the age of ten) to leave and find homes elsewhere. Meanwhile, Jackson's mother had become pregnant.

In 1831 Woodson accepted the position of clerk of court for Fayette County. The new home was far to the south in untamed mountain wilderness. Weeks were required to make the one-hundred-and-twenty-five-mile trip over rough mountain roads and along crude Indian trails. Finally the Woodsons reached their destination: a cluster of shacks known as Ansted. By then, Julia Jackson Woodson was ill to the point of being an invalid. She never recovered. That is why she could make but feeble protests when Woodson decided that her three children would be sent to live with relatives. Warren was to join the Neales in Parkersburg; Tom and Laura would go to Jackson's Mill to be with aunts, uncles, and cousins they had never met.

Telling his mother good-bye was the hardest task Tom had ever faced. On the day he was to leave, he hid in the woods until nightfall and came out only after his mother begged him to do so. His uncle, Cummins Jackson, and a slave placed the lad on a horse. As the animal moved slowly away, a sobbing mother with outstretched arms stumbled along the road. It was a sight no young boy could ever forget.

The journey through the mountains and valleys to Jackson's Mill took a week. It seemed endless to two children who were now orphans. Tom and Laura had been in their new surroundings only three months when a message arrived. Their mother had given birth to a son but had taken a turn for the worse. She was dying. Tom and his young sister made the long trip back to Ansted. They got there in time to receive Julia Jackson Woodson's last "farewell and blessing."[3] She died a month after the children returned to Jackson's Mill. Tom was never able to find her grave.[4]

Brokenhearted, without parents or a future, the youngster spent the next eleven years at Jackson's Mill. The fifteen-hundred-

Jackson's Mill, with the family home in the background. Here Tom Jackson lived for eleven years—the longest stay he ever had in one place.

acre estate stretched as far as the eye could see. It was also a beehive of activity. Tom found plenty to keep himself busy.

In time he knew how to fell trees, drive oxen, plow and harvest crops, work at a grist mill, care for livestock, produce maple syrup, fish in the West Fork River, sheer sheep, and transport wool to market. He became good at carpentry, worked in the foundry, and mastered the details of the machines on the farm. Tom built a canoe for riding in the river. At an early age he became a jockey at horse races his uncle staged at Jackson's Mill. In all things, the boy was an eager learner and hard worker. No one ever called him lazy.

This especially pleased his guardian, the man who presided over the Jackson's Mill domain. Cummins Jackson was well over six feet tall and weighed more than two hundred pounds. The uncle was an uneducated, rough, and quick-tempered bachelor. He allowed nothing to stand in his way on the road to success. He was incapable of loving anything. What his nephew thought was affection was only family friendship. Cummins Jackson was not so much a father figure as he was a big brother to his ward.

Slowly the uncle dirtied the family name and dragged down both its high standing and himself. In the mid-1840s (after Tom had left the family estate), greed and dishonesty became the downfall of Cummins Jackson. He was brought to trial on charges of counterfeiting. Jackson escaped from the courthouse and fled to the goldfields of California. He died shortly after reaching the west coast. On hearing of his uncle's passing, Thomas would say: "This is news which goes to my heart. Uncle was a father to me."[5] Although hardly so from Cummins' point of view, such was all the paternal kinship Jackson was to know.

An even deeper personal loss had come to Jackson earlier, after four years at Jackson's Mill. Tom's sister, Laura, was two years younger than he was. They shared a love made more deep by the bonds of orphanage. The two were comfortable only when each knew the other was nearby. By 1835, however, all of the female Jacksons at the mill had died or else moved elsewhere. The uncles thought it best to send Laura to live with her mother's family in Parkersburg, eighty miles away. Tom and Laura would seek to keep in touch by letter and an occasional visit. Yet the separation was an enormous personal loss for a lonely boy who knew little of the past and did not understand the present.

Years spent at the mill molded Tom into the man he would become. He never overcame the shyness that often sent him across the West Fork River to sit alone in thought amid the companionship of the trees. His silence and difficulty in making friends were lifelong traits. Dependability became his strongest virtue.

Tom came to find a certain contentment at Jackson's Mill because there was always something to do. Good training in many jobs gave him a confidence and a self-reliance he never lost. During the childhood years everyone at the mill treated him as being older than he was. To act less than an adult was misbehavior. A neighbor remembered: "Tom was always an uncommonly well-behaved lad, a gentleman from the boy up, just and kind to everyone, never controversial, but doing his duty right and left, in a devoted, dreamy sort of way."[6]

His sense of honor, too, developed in those early years. The best example is the now-famous "fish story."

By the age of nine, Tom was an excellent fisherman. He began supplying fresh catches to merchant Conrad Kester in Weston. For every pike over twelve inches in length, Kester paid Jackson fifty cents.

One day the lad came walking down Weston's main street toward the Kester store. In his arms was a pike over thirty-six inches long. Colonel John Talbot, a local resident, called out: "Hello, Tom! That's [a] fine fish you have. I will give you a dollar for it."

Without halting, Jackson answered: "Sold to Mr. Kester."

Talbott then offered a dollar and a quarter for the pike. Jackson looked back over his shoulder. "If you get any of this pike, you will get it from Mr. Kester," he said.

Jackson arrived at the store and placed the big fish on the counter. Kester wanted to pay twice the normal price. "No sir," came the reply. "This is your pike at fifty cents, and I will not take more for it.

*An early biographer had this sketch done
showing Tom and his brother, Warren, selling wood to steamboats
on the Mississippi River.*

Besides, you have bought a good many fish from me that were pretty short."[7]

Only once did Tom leave Jackson's Mill for an extended length of time. He had just turned twelve when his brother, Warren, three years older, visited the mill. Warren was a schoolteacher in one of the counties to the east. He was on his way to spend some time with Laura and his mother's family, the Neales, in Parkersburg. Warren invited Tom to go with him. The brother jumped at the opportunity.

Cummins Jackson raised no objections to the youths striking out on their own.

The Neales opened their homes and their hearts to the boys. Brothers and sister had a loving reunion. Yet the lure of the great Ohio River soon overwhelmed Warren and Tom. Uncle Alfred Neale was making a nice income from selling wood to steamboats on the river. Warren convinced Tom that they could do the same by going downriver and setting up a similar business.

In the spring of 1836, the two lads

made their way down the Ohio to its junction with the Mississippi River. They continued southward on the Mississippi to an island with a deserted cabin. There, through the summer and autumn, the boys cut wood for sale to passing steamboats. The work was hard, food scarce, insects constant, and income small. The undertaking came to an end when Warren and Tom both contracted malaria.

Weak in body and broke in funds, the two boys started home. Tom made his way back to Jackson's Mill, poorer but wiser for his experiences. Warren never fully recovered from the disease of malaria.

A desire for education became the most important thing in Tom's thoughts. He realized that only through education could he improve himself and have a chance of getting ahead in life. Yet increasing his knowledge of things was difficult. Uncle Cummins had no interest in matters of education or religion. He also did not conceal his belief that Tom was the dullest of his brother Jonathan's children. In addition, rural schools of that day were small, primitive in facilities, and open only in the winter months so as not to interfere with farming chores. Teachers were usually young men seeking a better job somewhere or boys with special skills in a single subject.

Somehow Tom convinced Uncle Cummins to allow him to begin a formal education. The guardian hired a Lewis County man to organize a small school for boys at Jackson's Mill. Later Tom attended occasional classes in nearby Weston. From the first day that young Jackson encountered

"book learning," his enthusiasm was constant. He could not get enough education. Arithmetic came easily to him. Each other subject was a challenge that he faced eagerly. A family friend noted that Tom "was by no means . . . brilliant, but was one of the most untiring, plain, matter-of-fact persons who would never give up an undertaking until he accomplished his object."[8]

The youth read rapidly but learned slowly. Sometimes he would master one subject at the expense of the other. Writing correctly was always a problem. Years later he would tell a niece: "If a person commences reading before learning to spell well, he will not be apt to ever learn much about spelling, because reading is more pleasant than spelling. . . . Still I am mortified at my spelling words wrong."[9]

In 1838 Tom acquired a close friend. The Benjamin Lightburn family moved from Pennsylvania to a farm only an hour's walk from Jackson's Mill. Joseph Lightburn was eight months younger than Tom. (In adulthood, he would become a farmer, Baptist minister, Union general, and member of the West Virginia legislature.) Joe and Tom quickly developed a special bond because each loved to read. The Lightburn family had a large library. They made all the books available to the quiet but likable boy who lived up the West Fork River.

Joe Lightburn unknowingly changed the course of Tom's life by introducing his fourteen-year-old friend to the Bible. A whole new world suddenly opened for young Jackson. He studied all of the military campaigns narrated in the Old Testament and the dozen other ancient biblical chapters known as the Apocrypha. In the New Testament he found promises of love and hope he had never known.

The Bible became the most exciting book the teenager had ever encountered. Lightburn family members encouraged this new interest by inviting Tom to accompany them to services at a nearby Baptist church. The lad gained additional inspiration closer to home. Granny Nancy Robinson was an elderly slave at Jackson's Mill and extremely devout. She read and explained the Bible to Tom on many occasions.

Religion thus entered his life at an important stage of learning. Tom responded with serious concentration. Sometime before 1841, he began praying nightly. Soon afterward, his letters to Laura were containing references of love for "Almighty God" and "an all-wise Providence."

For a time he even gave thoughts to entering the ministry. Tom told an aunt: "The subject of becoming a herald of the Cross has often seriously engaged my attention, and I regard it as the most noble of all professions."[10]

Tom soon abandoned the idea. He did not belong to an organized church, his education was limited, and he was very uncomfortable whenever asked to speak in public. Still, he maintained deep respect for ministers, and he continued to seek a religious faith he liked well enough to join.

Some other activities away from Jackson's Mill had given the lad a broader view of life. In his thirteenth summer, Tom worked as an engineering assistant on the turnpike being built through the mountains to connect Parkersburg on the Ohio River with Staunton in the Shenandoah Valley. Later he accepted a job as a schoolteacher in Weston. For four months he shared what knowledge he had with five poor children almost as old as he was. The teacher approached his job with determination. In one schoolbook Tom wrote this warning for his students: "A man of words and not of deeds is like a garden full of weeds."[11]

Jackson was an active youth who spent much time in hard work outdoors. Yet at fifteen he became ill with a sickness that would bother him off and on for twenty years. The problem was in his stomach and involved digestion of food. In that day, the condition was called dyspepsia. No standard cure existed. Physicians in Lewis County suggested that Jackson would get better if he applied hot mustard plasters to his chest and did much horseback riding. Jackson followed instructions, but improvement was slow when it came at all.

By his seventeenth birthday, Tom was giving much thought to what he wanted to do with his life. He had no hope that his uncle would ever put him in charge of the Jackson's Mill operations. By then, too, Cummins Jackson's shady business practices were slowly bringing the estate to ruin. Tom had advanced as far up the family ladder as he was going. His future lay somewhere else.

At that point, an opening occurred for a new constable in the West Fork district of the county. Such a position usually went to an adult with much experience. That did not stop young Jackson from seeking the job.

A constable carried out orders from the county court. He was a police officer who served court papers, hunted down people with outstanding debts, and performed other duties requested by the judge or the sheriff. The salary was good; the job was permanent. Traveling on horseback through the vast region of Lewis County would be interesting. It might also help Jackson's stomach problems. Neighbors and friends supported his bid for the position. In June 1841, the teenager received the appointment.

Tom quickly discovered that being a constable was not fun at all. He had to ride far afield in all kinds of weather and in country where wild animals outnumbered people. Even worse, the job thrust an innocent youngster into company with dishonest men who often used violence rather than words to settle differences. The new peace officer did not flinch. To the surprise of many people who knew the modest and reserved youth, Tom became a success at the job.

In one instance, Tom displayed real talent in apprehending a fugitive.

A local resident named Holt had owed ten dollars to a widow for a long time. She appealed to the court for help. Constable Jackson was assigned to collect the money. He went to see Holt, who agreed to meet Jackson on a certain day in Weston and settle the debt. The man failed to appear. Jackson paid the widow from his own pocket and said nothing more about the matter.

Some days later, Holt rode into Weston and hitched his horse near the blacksmith shop. Jackson learned that the man was in town and went searching for him. When Holt saw the constable approaching, he leaped upon his horse for safety. A common law of that age prevented a man from being dismounted by force but Jackson was ready. He grabbed the reins and led the horse toward the blacksmith shed. The entrance was not high enough for the mounted Holt. Jackson intended to "scrape off" the rider, if necessary. Holt jumped from the saddle and paid Jackson the overdue bill.[12]

Later that year, Warren Jackson died. Tom was with his brother at the end. Now the only other surviving member of his immediate family was his sister, Laura. She was frail and somber, but she had the advantage of love and contentment with the Neales in Parkersburg.

January 1842, brought Jackson's eighteenth birthday. He was approaching manhood in both outlook and appearance. Taller than most boys his age, Tom stood almost six feet and weighed close to one hundred and seventy pounds. Large blue eyes dominated his face. He had a high forehead, curved nose, and thin lips. He wore his brown hair short because it tended to curl. Outdoor life had turned his skin a natural tan. While he stood erect and was muscular, his feet and hands were larger than normal. His health was good except for occasional attacks of dyspepsia. Jackson's usual expression was a mixture of bashfulness and thoughtfulness.

The young constable had been on the job ten months when he received unexpected news. Congressman Samuel Hays would shortly interview candidates for an appointment to the U.S. Military Academy at West Point, New York. Jackson saw this opening as the answer to all of his hopes. West Point would give him one of the finest educations available in America. It also offered a good lifetime career in the U.S. Army. Certainly the honor of being a graduate of the academy would go far in restoring dignity to the family name.

Jackson wished for the appointment more than anything he had ever sought. He met the basic requirements of being between sixteen and twenty-one years of age, at least five feet tall, reasonably healthy, and unmarried. Being chosen to go there was the major hurdle.

Four local youths emerged as candidates: Gibson Butcher, Johnson Camden, Thomas Jackson, and Joseph Lightburn. The two strongest were Jackson and Butcher, a deputy court clerk in Weston. Jackson was the superior athlete and better in the important subject of arithmetic. Butcher had more

formal education and excelled in grammar. Congressman Hays came to Weston and interviewed the two finalists. In April, he made his decision. Butcher received the appointment.

The announcement fell heavily on Jackson. Not going to the military academy was the final blow in a childhood full of despair. His ambitions seemed useless. Neighbors would always talk about the "orphan child" that Jackson was and all of the good things in life he never knew. It was difficult for him to give love because he was a grown man before he knew what love was. Long afterward, his wife would declare: "In his after years, he was not disposed to talk much about his childhood and youth, for the reason that it was the saddest period of his life."[13]

From those barren early years came the stern personality Tom Jackson had in adulthood. This was natural. As English poet John Milton once noted: "The childhood shows the man, as morning shows the day."[14]

✹ Chapter II ✹
West Point Experiences

Gibson Butcher's stay at West Point lasted one day. The demands and the grimness of the place were more than he could bear. Butcher left without even informing authorities. Just before reaching his home in Weston, he stopped by Jackson's Mill and announced what had happened.

Suddenly Thomas Jackson had a second chance at a West Point education! His dream might come true after all! Letters of recommendation had to be gathered and forwarded at once. Jackson visited every man of influence he could find in the area and asked for written support.

The toughest test came with Jonathan M. Bennett, the leading businessman in Weston. Bennett responded to Jackson's plea with a series of stern questions. Jackson's hopes began to fade. Downcast, he stared at the floor. Then Bennett asked if Jackson thought his limited education was enough to get him through West Point.

Jackson raised his head, looked Bennett in the eye, and responded: "I know that I shall have the application necessary to succeed. I hope that I have the capacity. At least I am determined to try, and I wish you to help me to do this."[1]

Bennett smiled and agreed to do whatever he could.

Everyone was of the opinion that Jackson should make his case in person to Congressman Hays. The youngster packed his belongings in two saddlebags and left the mill. By horseback, stagecoach, and train, he traveled to Washington, D.C., Jackson appeared at the congressman's office unannounced. Hays learned from Jackson of Butcher's abrupt departure from the military academy. Before the Lewis County representative could say anything, Jackson handed him a packet of letters.

Hays was impressed by what he read. Neighbors praised Jackson as "a meritorious young man . . . quite a smart youth in every respect for his age and opportunity." All things considered, one writer concluded, "a better selection could not be made, west of the mountains." No one was more deserving, thirteen citizens said in a petition. "Mr. Jackson's ancestry are mostly Dead . . . and he is a destitute orphan."[2]

The Democratic lawmaker immediately nominated Jackson for the vacancy. Two anxious days passed as Jackson awaited a final decision from Secretary of War John C. Spencer. It came on June 19, 1842. Jackson was appointed to the military academy.

Jackson politely declined Mr. Hays's invitation for a sight-seeing tour of the national capital. The deadline for reporting to West Point was but two days away. Moreover, his appointment was only conditional. Jackson would not be a real cadet until he passed the physical and oral examinations given in the first week.

*Laura Jackson Arnold, Tom Jackson's younger sister.
The two orphans grew up as each other's best friend. Yet the Civil War produced
a permanent estrangement between brother and sister.*

The trip to New York was one of excitement and dread for the eighteen-year-old. Jackson enjoyed the all-night train ride to New York City. Then he boarded a packet boat and watched spellbound as the vessel made its way up the wide Hudson River. Several hours later the boat came around a slow bend in the river. There, on high bluffs to the left, stood the U.S. Military Academy.

If the school looked awesome to Jackson (and it surely must have), he looked odd to the cadets who watched him walk alone with long strides up the winding path from the boat landing. The tall young man with big hands and feet was dressed in gray homespun clothing. Weather-beaten saddlebags were slung over his shoulders. On his head was the large felt hat he had worn as a constable. Walking rapidly, with head down as if he was lost in thought, Jackson appeared to be exactly what he was: a farm boy entering a brand-new world.

That world had a spectacular setting for the mountain lad. West Point stood on forty acres of flat ground high atop a cliff overlooking the Hudson. The campus offered a beautiful view of the winding river surrounded by majestic mountains laced with sharp little valleys. Thick woods covered the entire countryside.

In the middle of the high plain were a dozen buildings. Some were tall, some were gray, and all were sinister-looking. Together, they formed the national military academy. The school had been established forty years earlier by act of Congress. West Point had steadily risen in quality to become not only the best military school in America but also the leading engineering and scientific university in the Western Hemisphere. Graduates of West Point were designing and building the nation's major roads, harbors, and forts. In the 1830s, President Andrew Jackson had proudly called the academy "the best school in the world."[3]

Jackson's grim look of determination on entering the gates caught the attention of a group of cadets. "That fellow looks as if he has come to stay," Cadet Dabney Maury stated. When Maury learned that Jackson was a fellow Virginian, he introduced himself and offered to be of help. Shyness and uncertainty led Jackson to mumble a stiff reply. Maury felt insulted. Jackson "received me so coldly," he snarled, "that I regretted my friendly overture."[4] This was but the first instance at West Point of the reserved nature that prevented Jackson from making many friends.

The entire freshman class—fourth classmen, or plebes, they were called—consisted of one hundred and twenty-three boys. Each had been selected either by a congressman or named "at large" by the president of the United States. West Point officials had nothing to do with appointments.

Their responsibility was to educate the students, once they had been found qualified.

A trio of physicians administered the physical exams. Jackson exposed his teeth, chest, joints, and feet to the stern gaze of a doctor. To test eyesight, the physician held up a dime at the far end of the room and asked whether it was heads or tails.[5] Jackson easily met the physical requirements.

The oral examination was something very different. Jackson was painfully aware of his lack of formal education. He had no hope of answering all the questions correctly, but could he respond sufficiently to pass? Actually the entrance examination was not as severe as commonly believed. The applicant had only to be able to read distinctly, write a legible hand, and solve a mathematical problem at the blackboard. Thirteen army officers formed the examining committee.

Jackson's turn came. He stepped forward to the blackboard, perspiration dripping from his face. He wiped it away with the cuff of his coat. For the next few minutes he struggled with chalk and eraser. Everyone in the room watched the anguish and intensity in the tall youth. Jackson responded to each question as if his life depended on the answer. He was covered with sweat and chalk when he finished the mathematical problem. An exhausted Jackson returned to his chair with the same serious expression. Yet every member of the examining board, it was said, "turned his head away to hide the smiles which could not be suppressed."[6]

The following afternoon, the commandant of cadets posted the names of those applicants who had been found "duly qualified." At the very bottom of the list was "Tho. J. Jackson."[7] He had gotten into West Point "by the skin of his teeth," Jackson admitted.[8]

Over thirty boys failed the entrance examinations. This meant that more than a fourth of Jackson's original classmates were dismissed from the academy before classes began. The orphan from the Virginia mountains had passed a major hurdle. He was now a fellow student with sons of some of the most rich and powerful men in the country.

A major aim at West Point was to instill in every cadet the necessary ingredients of discipline and instant obedience to orders. The first stage in this program came from upperclassmen who constantly shouted at and belittled the plebes. Jackson escaped much of this hazing. He was older than a majority of the cadets. More importantly, he carried out every command with such seriousness that upperclassmen spared him from much of the traditional bullying.

For the next three months the plebes lived out-of-doors. Home was a flimsy tent; bed was the ground. Extremes of heat and rain did not change the routine. From dawn to darkness, fourth classmen learned the fundamentals of soldier life. Proper uniforms, how to use a musket and bayonet, the correct way to cook field rations, guard duty, fatigue details, and constant inspection were part of every day.

The worst aspect of this new life

for Jackson was drill. Cadets had formal drill twice a day. They marched in cadence wherever they went. At first the plebes shuffled like a mob, bumping into each other or stepping on one another's heels. Jackson, with his oversize feet and lack of coordination, became one of the worst cadets for making mistakes at drill.

The academic year began in September. Fourth classmen left their outdoor encampment and moved into drafty, cold rooms in stone barracks. Two or three boys occupied each room. Furnishings included a cot, desk, chair, wall pegs for hanging clothes, fireplace, kerosene lanterns—and little else. A well outside the barracks provided water, which cadets carried to their rooms in buckets.

Class enrollment was based on academic standing. The smartest students were in the first section, as classes were called. At the other end of the ranking were the "Immortals," the cadets with the lowest averages. Jackson was a member of the "Immortals." All too quickly he learned how demanding college life in a military school could be.

Nine or ten hours per day were spent in study and classroom recitation. Another two or three hours were devoted to drill. Cadets in Jackson's day were required to do passing work altogether in ten different subjects. The first year's courses were in only two areas: mathematics and French. (French was taught at military schools around the world because the greatest soldier of that age was Napoléon Bonaparte and the better military manuals were written in that general's native tongue.) The two subjects were an agony for Jackson.

His knowledge of English was average at most. A new language such as French left him bewildered for weeks. And while Jackson had always excelled in basic arithmetic, he now encountered algebra, geometry, and trigonometry all taught at one time.

The subject matter was difficult enough. Jackson fell even further behind in every class because he refused to skim over a point. When any part of a previous day's assignment remained unclear, he would not move to the next lesson until he felt he had finally mastered the earlier snag. Such faithful dedication often left him unprepared for a recitation. Professors dutifully recorded low grades. Yet Jackson refused to take shortcuts of any sort. He did not absorb knowledge easily, a sister-in-law later declared, "but his mind never lost a fact or idea once committed to its keeping."[9]

Concentration became one of his pathways to success. He made it a rule when reading to sit stiffly with his back to the door and to speak to no one who entered the room or sought to start a conversation. Jackson might stare at a wall for as much as an hour while straining to memorize facts or figures. A roommate said in awe: "No one I have ever known could so perfectly withdraw his mind from surrounding objects or influence, and so thoroughly involve his whole being in the subject under consideration."[10]

Even more than concentration, the determination that would mark the rest of Jackson's life was evident in the first,

nightmarish year at West Point. He refused to let overwhelming homework, lack of comprehension, and low grades get the best of him. Nor would he bow to the rigid life at the academy. Food was plain and tough. The wake-up call came at 5 A.M. in summer and 6 A.M. in winter. Drum beats signaled every activity of the long day. This included required chapel service, where students sat in silence and listened to High Church Episcopal sermons that Jackson also had difficulty in understanding. [11]

The day ended at 10 P.M. For Jackson, however, lights-out usually meant more—and more difficult—studying. He would lie flat on his stomach and memorize his lessons by the dim, flickering light of the little fireplace in his room.

Cadets had little time to themselves. The more the upperclassmen hazed them, and the more the professors demanded of them, the closer the cadets grew to one another. Teamwork and reliance on friends were regarded as lessons just as important as those learned in the section rooms. The system worked well. Jackson began to make a limited number of friends in spite of his total attention to studies.

Throughout the year, the academy was a local showplace. Visitors and dignitaries were always on the campus. Young ladies flocked there to see friends, watch parades, or attend dances. Military balls were extremely popular with cadets. Jackson was never in attendance. Sports, group swims in the Hudson, campus organizations, informal conversations with fellow cadets, had no appeal to Jackson. Being uncomfortable around strangers, he avoided all social events. He never remembered even speaking to a lady during his entire stay at West Point.[12]

One of his favorite pastimes was to hike up nearby Mount Independence to the remains of Fort Putnam. It had been a key defense on the Hudson River during the American Revolution. By Jackson's time, the fort was a pile of stones partially covered by underbrush. Yet Jackson found peace of mind in the quietness. Fort Putnam became his haven from the cares of life—just as the little hut across the West Fork River had been his refuge in childhood.

Perhaps it was there, in the stillness high above the military academy, that Jackson began writing in a small black book the rules of life he intended to follow. "Through life let your principal object be the discharge of duty," said one. Another read: "Sacrifice your life rather than your word." Under the heading of social behavior he made this observation: "It is not desirable to have a large number of intimate acquaintances." Indeed, he had at most only a half-dozen friends at the academy. No immediate family awaited him back in Virginia. He knew that what he achieved in life he must make on his own. Into his book of private thoughts he wrote what became the most famous of his maxims: "You may be what ever you will resolve to be."[13]

Jackson spent the summer of 1843 reading in preparation for the coming term. The second year at the academy was easier for those who had kept pace with the instruction. No outdoor encampment or upperclassman bullying interfered with classroom work.

As a third classman, Jackson encountered a variety of courses in different fields. He continued his study of the French language, and also took advanced courses in mathematics as introductions to other fields. Geometry led into the study of calculus and surveying, which in turn gave cadets a foundation for the scientific and engineering classes that dominated the final two years at West Point.

In his first college-level work in English composition and grammar, Jackson did surprisingly well. His grades improved significantly by the end of the second year. The number of demerits he received had decreased as well. Jackson's best marks were mathematics and English, his worst in French and drawing (important for preparing building plans, maps, and the like). By the end of the school year, he ranked in the middle of his class.

A nine-week leave of absence at the end of the second year was the only vacation a cadet got in four years at the academy. Late in June 1844, Jackson returned to Virginia. He went first to see his sister.

Laura was then eighteen and living with relatives in Beverly, some fifty miles east of Jackson's Mill. Brother and sister shared happy hours in their first reunion in almost three years. Jackson was only two years older than Laura. Still, a relative commented, Jackson "felt a fatherly as well as a brotherly interest in his sister."[14] The two orphans were as close as siblings could be.

From Beverly, the proud cadet proceeded to Jackson's Mill to visit uncles and slaves. Jackson could not help noticing how shabby the home place had become. Saddened by the situation at the mill, Jackson stopped briefly in Weston to say hello to acquaintances. He told a cousin how difficult getting an education was for him. The kinsman asked if Jackson had any thought of quitting. The cadet answered with conviction: "I am going to make a man of myself if I live. What I will to do I can do."[15]

The third year of study at West Point concentrated on sciences. At the heart of the curriculum was a wide-ranging course known as natural and experimental philosophy. There students received huge chunks of such subjects as physics, astronomy, and mechanics. Jackson did no better in his drawing course. Horsemanship likewise was a challenge for him. As a child, Jackson had been a jockey at his uncle's racetrack. Riding with stirrups high and bending far over the horse's neck was a far cry from all the rigorous movements in cavalry training. Jackson was "awkward and uncomfortable to look at upon a horse," one cadet wrote. "We used to watch him with anxiety when his turn came . . . he seemed in imminent danger of falling headlong from the horse."[16] Another cadet stated: "When he advanced to riding at the heads, leaping the bars, etc., his *balance* was truly fearful." Jackson would not give up the effort. "No man in the riding-house would take more risks than he," a classmate declared, "and certainly no one had our good wishes more than he."[17] Not even in his years as a general did Jackson's posture in the saddle appear graceful.

High grades that third year, notably in mathematics and behavior, elevated him several steps among his classmates. During the 1844–45 term, Jackson led the entire corps of cadets in conduct. He did not receive a single demerit.

A rare bit of family news came in February when he learned that his sister had married Jonathan Arnold in Beverly. Jackson quickly replied with heartfelt congratulations. He also displayed his growing religious faith when he added: "My sincere desire is that you both enjoy all the blessings which a bountiful Providence can bestow. I think that if happiness exists in this world, matrimony is one of the principal factors."[18]

The senior year at West Point was usually the most enjoyable. First classmen were campus leaders. They also studied the most popular courses. Instead of concentration on a few subjects, senior cadets received instruction in geology, constitutional law, logic, and moral philosophy. More importantly, these soldiers-to-be got a heavy dose of military topics.

Hours were devoted to infantry tactics and artillery drill. The highlight of the year was the science of war course taught by world-famous Professor Dennis Hart Mahan. Under his guidance, cadets studied the genius of Frederick the Great and Napoléon, battle planning, how armies were placed in combat, the secrets to military success. Mahan taught West Pointers that boldness and daring, tempered by common sense, were the real keys to military success. Some cadets, like Jackson, never forgot those principles.

Throughout his years at the academy, Jackson made a habit of taking long walks. One reason was a growing belief that his health was failing. Jackson's physical condition became a real concern during this period. In his first letter to his sister from West Point, he reported good health. By his third year Jackson feared that he was a victim of several ailments. "My constitution has received a severe shock," he solemnly reported at one point.[19]

He became convinced that one arm and one leg were heavier than the other limbs. Therefore, his cadet friend William Edmonson Jones wrote, Jackson would sometimes "pump his arm for many minutes, counting the strokes, and feeling annoyed beyond measure whenever his companions interrupted him in his count."[20]

For the next fifteen years, Jackson would be "under a habitual fear of some chronic and fatal disease."[21] Many of his ailments were real; others were not. When things were not going well, Jackson felt terrible. If times were good, so was his health. Jackson never surrendered to sickness. He fought to recover with the same determination that marked every other challenge he faced.

At his June 1846, graduation from West Point, he was in good health as well as good spirits. Fifty-nine cadets had completed all requirements at the academy. Jackson ranked seventeenth among his classmates. Faculty and students alike felt that if the course of study had lasted one more year, the quiet, serious lad from the Virginia wilderness would have finished at the top of his class. Jackson's climb from rock bottom to near top was one of the most remarkable performances by any cadet in West Point history.

He had done it on his own, by sheer determination. All of his thoughts and energies centered on doing his duty. Such stern dedication made Jackson appear to be older than he was, which explains why cadets nicknamed him "Old Jack." But despite being aloof, withdrawn, and "bookwormish," Jackson won the admiration of many and the close companionship of a few. A former roommate observed that while many cadets outdid Jackson "in intellect, in geniality, and in good-fellowship, there was no one of our class who more absolutely possessed the respect and confidence of all."[22]

He left the military academy with the brevet (temporary) rank of second lieutenant in the artillery branch of the army.[23] Jackson would go straight into war, but he was ready for it. In one of his final letters written from West Point to his sister, he stated: "Rumor appears to indicate a rupture between our government and the Mexican. If such should be the case the probability is that . . . the next letter you receive from me may be dated from Texas or Mexico." Jackson concluded with a personal thought to Laura: "I shall continue to love you with a brother's love."[24]

✦ CHAPTER III ✦
HERO IN MEXICO

WAR BETWEEN MEXICO and America had been building for a long time. In the mid–1830s, Americans living in the Mexican province of Texas had fought for and won their independence. Mexico refused to recognize the free state. Hard feelings on both sides grew more intense. By 1846, President James Knox Polk wanted to obtain other Mexican lands, notably the California and New Mexico territories. At the same time, a new and strongly anti-American government in Mexico City wanted to regain the land that had been lost.[1]

At its head was General Antonio López de Santa Anna. He was then in his early fifties. Santa Anna had gained fame and lost a leg while fighting the Spanish and the French for Mexican independence. One writer described him as "a tall, handsome scoundrel, with broad shoulders and slender hips, who loved fine uniforms, women and money and spent much of his enormous energy in their pursuit." He was also more "show than substance"—a brave man but lacking in the mental qualities to be a successful general.[2]

Americans considered the Rio Grande River as the boundary with Mexico. Santa Anna insisted that the border was the Nueces River, some fifty miles to the north. Polk dispatched an "Army of Observation" to occupy vital points along the Rio Grande. In command was sixty-one-year-old Zachary Taylor, a headstrong and powerful Virginian.

A sketch showing Mexican emperor Santa Anna in the most favorable light.

The real Santa Anna was paunchy, moody, and lacking in military skills. The loss of a leg further hampered him in the war with America.

Mexicans viewed the presence of Taylor's army as an outright invasion of their land. Sharp fighting occurred in the disputed area, resulting in more than one thousand casualties. American bloodshed could not be overlooked. On May 13, a month before Jackson graduated from West Point, Congress declared war on Mexico. President Polk ordered a huge buildup of the U.S. Army. For the first time, America would invade a foreign neighbor and conduct military offensives. For the first time, too, a new professional officer corps from West Point would be in the thick of the action.

To new officers like twenty-two-year-old Thomas Jackson, war meant the chance for battle, winning praise and promotion, plus gaining the admiration of the whole country. Jackson "burned with enthusiasm" while impatiently awaiting orders.[3] He spent two weeks in Beverly with his sister and her family. Laura's husband, Jonathan Arnold, was a prosperous landowner and attorney. But what held Jackson's attention throughout the Beverly visit was a child born to the Arnolds a year earlier, a boy named Thomas Jackson Arnold. Jackson showered his nephew and namesake with affection.

The hoped-for orders from Washington finally came. Jackson was to proceed at once to Fort Columbus, New York, and join Captain Francis Taylor's Company K of the 1st U.S. Artillery. Taylor was a Virginian, nineteen years older than Jackson. He quickly proved to be a friendly officer as well as a valuable adviser. By mid-August,

when Lieutenant Jackson joined his unit, it had already received orders to proceed to the Mexican theater of operations. The trip southward took thirty-six days. Following a march of four hundred miles to Pittsburgh, Jackson's section boarded a boat for the voyage down the Ohio and Mississippi Rivers to New Orleans. The final leg of the trip was by boat to Point Isabel, Texas, at the mouth of the Rio Grande River. It was the base of operations for General Zachary Taylor's army.

Captain Taylor's company consisted of four guns, seventy-eight men, and eighty horses. It was described as "flying artillery" because the cannons were smaller than regular fieldpieces and could be moved more quickly from place to place.

On the day Jackson arrived at the village of Point Isabel, Zachary Taylor's forces seized the provincial capital of Monterrey in the Mexican interior. Yet Taylor found himself isolated deep in enemy territory, with high casualties and low supplies. He agreed to an eight-week armistice. The Mexican army withdrew from Monterrey and prepared to fight again.

President Polk, upset by an eight-week truce that Taylor had accepted, urged his general to resume operations. Taylor then started an advance to the mountain stronghold of Saltillo. Jackson hoped to see action when the Americans reached their goal. However, Mexican forces abandoned the town before Taylor's arrival. The next city target of any size was two hundred miles to the south over rugged terrain. General Taylor decided to stay where he

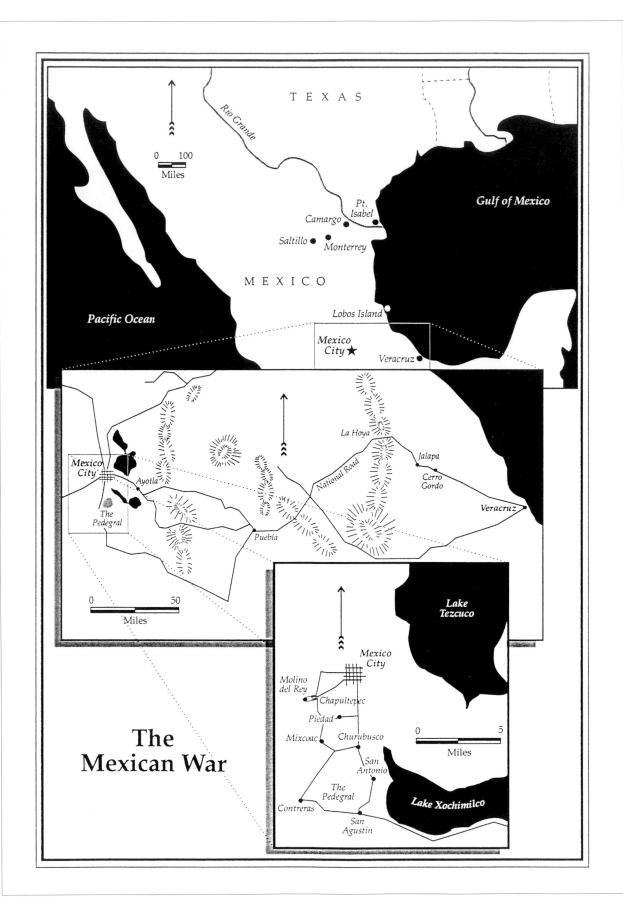

TEXAS

Rio Grande

0   100
Miles

Gulf of Mexico

Pt.
Isabel
Camargo
Saltillo   Monterrey

MEXICO

Pacific Ocean

Lobos Island

Mexico
City ★
Veracruz

La Hoya

Jalapa

National Road

Cerro
Gordo

Mexico
City
Ayotla

The
Pedegral

Veracruz

Puebla

0   50
Miles

*Lake
Tezcuco*

Mexico
City

Molino
del Rey
Chapultepec
Piedad
Mixcoac   Churubusco
San
Antonio
The
Pedegral
Contreras
San
Agustin

0   5
Miles

Lake Xochimilco

The
Mexican War

was. Such inactivity disappointed Jackson. A battle now seemed far in the future.

However, unknown to the young lieutenant, a major change took place in army leadership. Polk named General Winfield Scott to take overall command of military operations in Mexico.

The two highest ranking generals in this war were as different as their nicknames. "Old Rough and Ready" Taylor was a plain, rumpled soldier who rarely wore a uniform. He chewed tobacco, sat on his horse with a leg crossed over the pommel of his saddle, and cursed loudly when things were not going right. Strategy and battle preparation bored Taylor. A gallant charge and intense fighting were the things he liked and did best.

"Old Fuss and Feathers" Scott was a giant of a man, standing almost six and a half feet tall and weighing more than two hundred and fifty pounds. Half of his sixty years had been spent in the army. Scott wore fancy uniforms and surrounded himself with eager young aides. He was a walking textbook on military subjects. At the time of the Mexican War, Scott was the nation's leading soldier because he planned

At the time of the Mexican War, General Winfield Scott was America's leading soldier. "Old Fuss and Feathers" looked the part, standing six feet five inches tall, and weighing 250 pounds.

operations with great care and fought battles with brilliant precision.

Scott took charge with his own ideas of how to win the war. His plan called for an army-navy undertaking. A new and larger American army would move by boat down the coast of the Gulf of Mexico. At the naval fortress of Veracruz, ships would bombard the city while army units attacked the beach. Once that key port was in American hands, Scott would lead the army westward on Mexico's best highway. The National Road ran two hundred and sixty miles straight to Mexico City. It was the enemy's capital and the key to victory in this war.

Jackson still waited for his first taste of battle. One afternoon early in 1847, he was taking a solitary walk along the beach near the mouth of the Rio Grande. Lieutenant Daniel Harvey Hill of the 4th U.S. Artillery was visiting his friend, Captain Taylor. The two were discussing the war when Jackson came into sight. Taylor asked Hill if he had met the young lieutenant. "No," Hill replied.

"I taught him at West Point," Taylor said. "He never gave up on anything and never passed over anything without understanding it."

Taylor ended the discussion by adding: "Jackson will make his mark in this war."[4]

The captain introduced Jackson to Hill, who had graduated from West Point the year before Jackson arrived. As the two lieutenants walked along the beach, Hill at first found his new friend shy and awkward. Then, to his surprise, Jackson began a series of questions about battle: what one felt in combat, how different it was to lead men under fire, and the like. "I really envy you men who have been in action," Jackson remarked. "I should like to be in one battle."

When Jackson said that, Hill noticed his face light up and his eyes sparkle with enthusiasm.[5]

Taylor's Company K was part of the 13,500 men that Scott placed on transports for the new campaign. The boats moved down the coast. At Veracruz on March 9, Scott directed the first amphibious landing in American history.[6] Company K was in the third wave to go ashore in surf boats packed with soldiers and rowed by sailors. Soldiers cheered as each line of boats touched the beach. Bands played and flags snapped in the breeze as long lines of Americans conducted the invasion. Jackson thought it one of the most thrilling spectacles he had ever seen.[7]

Scott laid siege by surrounding Veracruz and sealing off all roads. Day after day American batteries pounded Veracruz with heavy fire. Santa Anna failed to send reinforcements to the besieged garrison. On March 27, Veracruz's defenders surrendered. Scott had won a huge victory. American forces were now firmly in control of the war.

Jackson's battery took an active part in the Veracruz bombardment. He must have been surprised by his own coolness under fire. Seated on a box and using his cot as a desk, Jackson wrote Laura about the campaign. His first battle action filled him with excitement—as well as exaggeration. The seizure of Veracruz, he wrote, "has thrown into our hands the strong hold of this republic and . . . must in my opinion excell any military operations known in the history of our country." He then wrote in an almost casual way: "While I was at the advanced batteries, a cannon ball came in about five steps of me."[8]

Scott was anxious to keep the enemy on the run and push toward Mexico City. More was involved than pressing his advantage. It was now spring, the season when dreaded yellow fever descended on the Mexican lowlands. Unless he got his army into high country fast, a plague of death would strike it. The National Road would be his route. Yet the road had long been neglected and was in wretched condition. The American commander did not know where Santa Anna and the main Mexican army were. Just as bad, many places along the National Road were ideal for an ambush in force. One American officer told his wife that "the Mexicans are quite hostile and are getting brave since the return of Santa Anna." Yet, he added, "their policy is to let us alone & the Country will use us up."[9]

On April 8, Scott's units began their

Jackson was not in the April 17–18, 1847, Battle of Cerro Gordo. However, he noted, his battery "came near enough to give the retreating column" of Mexicans "a few shots."

advance. The weather was hot and dry. Bugs (especially fleas) seemed to swarm everywhere.[10] The highway was so broken and steep in places that soldiers had to move cannon by tying ropes around trees and using them as pulleys.[11] Jackson gave little thought to the hardships. He had just received official word that he was no longer a brevet or temporary officer. He had been promoted to the permanent rank of second lieutenant.

The opening battle on the march to Mexico City came at Cerro Gordo, a mountain pass fifty miles west of Veracruz. Some twelve thousand Mexican soldiers had prepared strong defensive lines along rocky ground on both sides of the road. Scott carefully surveyed the Mexican position. He decided to attack simultaneously in front and on the enemy left flank. Late on April 17, Americans gained a toehold on part of the Mexican line. The next morning, after three hours of tough fighting, Mexicans fled the field.

At Cerro Gordo, Jackson was involved only in the pursuit of Santa Anna's routed forces. "We followed close on the retreating column," he told Laura, "and came near enough to give them a few shots from the battery."[12] However, Jackson's first sight of a mangled dead soldier "filled me with sickening dismay."[13]

Another day's march brought the Americans to Jalapa. This beautiful city, high up amid lush mountains, resembled the Garden of Eden to many of the soldiers.[14] The scenery was breathtaking, Jalapa's citizens were friendly, and the city streets were clean and inviting.

Jackson enjoyed his first three weeks there. He took daily rides and likened the countryside to "our own favored Western Virginia." The Spanish language intrigued him enough to begin studying it. In a rare attempt at humor, Jackson announced to his sister: "There are many pretty ladies here but you must not infer from this that you will have one of them for your sister-in-law, for such is not my intention at present and not theirs I hope."[15]

General Scott by then needed men and supplies. In a daring move he determined to advance over two mountain ranges to the city of Puebla. That would put him 185 miles from his major supply base at Veracruz but only seventy-five miles from Mexico City. Puebla was the country's second largest town. There Scott would await reinforcements before beginning the final push on the Mexican capital. Jackson looked forward to continuing the offensive deeper into Mexico; but to his surprise, Scott ordered Company K to remain at Jalapa on garrison duty.

Most soldiers would have welcomed a quiet assignment in a city as lovely as Jalapa. Not so with Jackson. Staying there meant no opportunity for battle. He was so "mortified" at not accompanying the army that he turned to heaven for support. "I throw myself into the hands of an all wise God," he wrote Laura, "and hope that it may yet be for the better." He suspected that God was keeping him in Jalapa as a way of "diminishing my excessive ambition."[16]

Jackson did not love war. Yet if there had to be conflict, he wanted to be in the thick of the action. To rise above his empty youth and become a man of distinction were his goals. Recognition, and glory, came from battle.

Jackson soon learned of the formation of some new artillery batteries. One of them would be Company I of the 1st Artillery Regiment, with Captain John Bankhead Magruder in command. Magruder was a dashing soldier who seemed always to be where there was fighting. He was also a hard-drinking and demanding officer. At the moment Magruder needed two second lieutenants in his battery.

Jackson was willing to overlook the man's faults if he was a fighter. He became the first applicant for one of the vacancies. In July he received orders to join Magruder's battery in Puebla. Jackson and a small escort were winding through the mountains when they were ambushed by a large band of Mexican guerrillas. The Americans held their own in the short fight. Jackson reported his men "killing four of the enemy and taking three prisoners, together with a beautiful sabre and some other equipment."[17] This was Jackson's first direct contact with enemy soldiers, but he treated the episode as nothing unusual.

As soon as he reached Puebla, Jackson gave total attention to helping Magruder organize the new battery. Jackson became second-in-command and the leader of a two-gun section. The explosive Magruder did not particularly like his new and uncommunicative lieutenant, but he did admire Jackson's skill at organization. In quick time, Magruder would praise what he called Jackson's "stupid bravery."[18]

General Scott gathered together ten thousand and seven hundred men at Puebla and took up anew the advance on Mexico City. Jackson tended to his guns as the American forces wound over mountains as high as ten thousand feet. One day the route led through a shallow pass. Down below, the Americans for the first time could see their objective. Twenty miles away, in a great valley, lay the sprawling capital of Mexico. It had been the goal of the Spanish conqueror Cortés and the seat of Montezuma's empire. Scott gazed down on Mexico City and exclaimed: "That splendid city soon shall be ours!"[19]

Soldiers under Scott's command were not as certain of that as they were of real fighting now close at hand. Santa Anna's army outnumbered Scott's by three to one. The Mexican general posted troops in strong fortifications east of Mexico City because he assumed that Scott would attack along the National Road from Puebla.

Instead, and again displaying the value of moving around the end (flank) of the enemy's line, Scott swung his forces in a wide arc that put him in a position to attack the capital from the south. The move knocked Santa Anna off-balance for the moment. He recovered in time to place ten thousand men and twenty-two heavy artillery pieces inside strong entrenchments in foothills near the village of Contreras. The Americans also learned that a second Mexican force was bearing down on them from the opposite direction. If Scott was to get to Mexico City, he had to attack at Contreras.

On the afternoon of August 19, Magruder's guns and another battery wheeled into position at an advanced point and opened fire. So did the Mexican cannon. One of Magruder's other lieutenants fell mortally wounded when a shell ripped off his leg. Jackson leaped forward and began directing the fire of three cannons he had placed amid large boulders for protection. It was no use. His light fieldpieces could not reach the enemy. Meanwhile, longer-range Mexican cannons were raining shells down on Jackson's position.

The battle continued for three hours until darkness and rain brought a pause. Only then did Jackson cease his part in the one-sided action. That night, American forces slipped around behind the entrenched Mexicans. Scott's men attacked at dawn in a fight that lasted only seventeen minutes. Panic seized Santa Anna's soldiers. One American officer thought the Mexicans ran from the field "as though each man had been summoned to the other world."[20]

Magruder was quick to call attention to his lieutenant's valor. Jackson, he wrote, had advanced to the fight at Contreras "in handsome style, and kept up the fire with equal briskness and affect." In his official report, Magruder continued the praise of Jackson. "His conduct was equally conspicuous during the whole day, and I cannot too highly commend him to the Major-General's favorable consideration."[21]

Such gallantry brought Jackson two quick promotions. One was to the permanent rank of first lieutenant, the other to the rank of brevet captain. Promotion meant less to him than the chance to prove himself under fire. Years later, Jackson was asked how he felt in his first major battle. He answered: "Afraid the fire would not be hot enough for me to distinguish myself."[22]

Magruder's guns suffered heavy damage in the Contreras fighting. Jackson was helping to obtain new cannons when Scott on August 21 soundly defeated the other portion of Santa Anna's army at Churubusco. Mexican losses in the two battles were four thousand killed and wounded, plus three thousand captured. Scott's casualties were barely one thousand men. He was now five miles from Mexico City.

Another armistice went into effect while an American peace commissioner tried to convince the Mexican government to surrender. Santa Anna illegally used the time of quiet to strengthen his forces for a new campaign. When Scott learned of this violation, he angrily put his army in motion for the final drive on the capital.

A day's march brought the Americans to the most imposing roadblock yet in their path. Two miles from Mexico City, a lone hill jutted two hundred feet into the sky. Atop it was an enormous stone building three-quarters of a mile long and a quarter-mile wide. With walls four feet thick and twenty feet high, it was the strongest fort on the American continent. It was also the very symbol of Mexican resistance.

The huge castle had once been the summer residence of Aztec conquerors. Since 1833 it had served as the National Military School—Mexico's West Point. Guns bristled from the fort's walls; outside earthworks made any approach difficult. An invading army could not bypass it because the place guarded the two main causeways leading into Mexico City. The stronghold was called Chapultepec.

By the time Scott's forces arrived in front of it, however, Chapultepec was not as strong as it looked. At least two thousand soldiers were needed to man its defenses. Thanks to Santa Anna's clumsy planning, only eight hundred and fifty Mexican soldiers were inside the fort. That number included fifty teenage cadets.

Scott and his generals were not aware of how poorly defended Chapultepec was. "We shall be defeated," General William Worth said at the final council of war. Scott himself confided to an aide: "I have my misgivings."[23]

Artillery began shelling the fort on the morning of September 12. The bombardment continued for fourteen hours. Scott's next move was a two-pronged attack. One American column would approach from the southeast; the main assault would charge from the west. To prevent Mexican reinforcements coming from Mexico City, Scott deployed two infantry regiments to block the pair of causeways between Chapultepec and the capital. Jackson's battery provided artillery support for the two regiments.

Shortly after 8 A.M. on September 13, storming parties advanced under fire from two directions. Overall progress was good. Jackson's situation was not. Magruder sent him forward with two guns to cover the advancing American infantry. Jackson's little six-pounders (so-called because of the weight of the balls they fired) had a very limited range. All too soon, Jackson found

himself "in a road which was swept with grape and canister [shells], and at the same time thousands of muskets from the Castle itself above poured [bullets] down like hail" on his position.[24]

Jackson placed his guns in a ditch for protection. That did not work. All of the twelve horses in the section were killed or wounded. His men abandoned the guns and fled for cover. Most of the American infantry disappeared. Jackson refused to accept defeat. By himself, he tried to move one of the cannons out of the ditch and across the road to a new firing position. He got the piece halfway on the road but could do no more.

Paying no attention to the shells exploding around him and musket balls

Victory in the war—and Jackson's third promotion for gallantry in Mexico—came with the American seizure of the fortress of Chapultepec. Occupation of Mexico City followed the next day.

bouncing off stones and trees, the young officer walked up and down the highway while pleading with his men to return to their guns. "There is no danger!" he shouted. At that moment a Mexican cannonball skidded between his legs. "See!" Jackson exclaimed. "I am not hit!" (He later admitted that this was the only lie he ever knowingly told.)[25]

His men stared at him in wonder. The lieutenant appeared to be fighting the whole Mexican army by himself. He was taking fire from some of the largest cannons the enemy had. A sergeant stepped forward through the battle smoke to help with the gun. From a safe vantage point, General William Worth stared at the spectacle in disbelief. He ordered Jackson to abandon the gun and fall back to safety.

No, sir, Jackson replied. It would be more dangerous to withdraw under fire than to maintain his position. "Go back yonder!" he shouted over the battle noise to the courier. "Tell Colonel Trousdale to send men forward! Tell him with fifty men we can overrun the battery ahead!"[26]

Reinforcements did not come, but Captain Magruder galloped down the road. Jackson and his sergeant were blazing away with their one gun against several enemy batteries. Magruder's horse fell dead from a shell just as the captain reached Jackson. Magruder helped get a second gun into position. Once-frightened artillerymen, taking heart at such bravery, rushed to the guns.

Jackson was the very picture of a soldier as his two cannons fired angrily at the enemy. The shoot-out continued until General Worth sent an infantry brigade charging against the Mexican breastworks in Jackson's sector. Americans overran the lines and raised loud cheers of victory.

Already the hero of the hour, Jackson was not finished. Santa Anna was struggling to get a large number of his soldiers in front of the gates of Mexico City. Quick action by the Americans would break through the confused Mexican ranks and bring control of the capital. Jackson found some horses, quickly hitched his guns and ammunition chests (caissons) to the animals, and raced across the causeway toward one of the city gates. Soon he had outrun Scott's entire army.

Jackson met a small detachment of American soldiers along the causeway. The two groups merged into an "army" of forty soldiers and two guns, then moved forward another half-mile. Suddenly, fifteen hundred Mexican cavalry came charging toward them.

Such an attack by so many soldiers should have meant the end of Jackson's little force. Yet the horsemen had to gallop two or three abreast because of the narrow causeway. Jackson saw them coming. He speedily unlimbered his guns and opened a point-blank fire. Shells tore huge gaps in the Mexican ranks before the cavalrymen turned and rode frantically back to the city.

Jackson's repulse of the mounted assault was one of the final actions of the battle of Chapultepec. The next morning, September 14, 1847, Scott's army filed into Mexico City. Some six thousand dirty and

A drawing of General Winfield Scott reviewing his troops after the fall of Mexico City. Jackson would have been one of the horsemen behind the general-in-chief.

ragged soldiers took possession of a capital of two hundred thousand residents. The unstable Mexican government collapsed. Drawn-out peace negotiations began. While diplomats talked, Scott's forces became an army of occupation.

The Mexican War was history. For Jackson, it was a good deal more than that. He was widely hailed as one of the real heroes of the contest. Praise came from all quarters. Magruder declared: "If devotion, industry, talent & gallantry are the highest qualities of a soldier, then [Jackson] is entitled to the distinction which their possession confers." General Gideon Pillow referred to "the brave Lieut. Jackson" who, "in the face of a galling fire from the enemy's position, did invaluable service." General Worth reported how the "gallant" Jackson "continued chivalrously at his post with noble courage." Even General Scott singled out the young Virginian as one whose "spirited affairs against superior numbers" had "gained merited praise."[27]

Elevation to brevet major came swiftly. Jackson had earned three battlefield promotions for heroism. No other American officer in the Mexican War gained more. Jackson had been in the field barely a year, and the twenty-three-year-old had won universal acclaim and respect. Former West Point classmates were stunned at what the shy and reserved Virginian had done.

The greatest compliment came to Jackson a few days after the occupation of the Mexican capital. General Scott hosted a reception for his officers. Jackson was anxious to meet the man the Duke of Wellington was calling "the greatest living soldier" of that age.[28] The young officer patiently made his way through the reception line. At last the introduction sounded: "Lieutenant Jackson!"

Scott instantly drew himself to full height and placed his hands behind his back. In a loud voice he declared: "I don't know if I will shake hands with Mr. Jackson!"

The hall suddenly grew quiet. All eyes turned to Jackson. He stood in front of the general. Blushing and confused, he could only stare at the floor. Scott thundered: "If you can forgive yourself for the way in which you slaughtered those poor Mexicans with your guns, I am not sure I can!"

Jackson's shoulders sagged with embarrassment. He wanted to run from the room. Then he saw Scott's huge hand extended to him. He looked up at Scott's smiling face and realized that it was all a joke. Applause exploded through the hall as the army commander warmly shook Jackson's hand. Another lieutenant in attendance observed: "No greater compliment could have been paid a young officer for courage and zeal."[29]

Always a serious student of warfare, Jackson learned many military principles from the campaigns in Mexico. The care needed in handling volunteer soldiers, the importance of drill, and the necessity for discipline were all unforgotten lessons. Jackson saw the rewards that come from scouting terrain in preparation for battle. Surprise attacks had the best chance for success. More than one engagement convinced him that flanking movements were an easier road to victory than blind assaults against fortified positions. The side with the best artillery was the side most likely to prevail in combat. And once a foe had been driven from the field, press him hard to turn simple defeat into smashing destruction.

Most of all, Jackson now knew himself. He liked the discipline and sense of duty in army life. In battle, he had met crisis with courage. Unruffled behavior under fire stamped him as a true soldier. The military would be his home. His childhood had been filled with uncertainties. He could now face adulthood with confidence.

✻ CHAPTER IV ✻
LEARNING LIFE IN THE PEACETIME ARMY

Brevet Major Jackson spent nine months on occupation duty in Mexico City. For the first time in his life, he had days to relax—to learn more about life in general and social graces in particular. He gave himself to what he termed "the mere delight of living."[1] Long horseback rides showed him new sights and activities. After tasting tropical fruit, Jackson maintained a lifelong love for every known fruit.

Dinner invitations at the homes of Mexico's wealthier families introduced the officer to good manners and correct customs. Everything in the Mexican capital had appeal for Jackson: the buildings, the language, dances, young ladies. In one letter to his sister, Jackson hinted at a future romance. "I think that probably I shall spend many years here and may possibly conclude (though I have not yet) to make my life more natural by sharing it with some amiable senorita."[2]

In December 1847, Jackson was happy to transfer back to Captain Taylor's artillery company. Taylor was as close a friend as Jackson had. The two men spent hours talking about a wide variety of topics. Increasingly the discussions turned to religion. Taylor was well-known as "an earnest Christian who labored for the spiritual welfare of his soldiers."[3]

He appealed to Jackson's sense of duty by emphasizing that the pursuit of religion was an obligation every man had. Jackson, eager to learn, began a serious study of Christian faith. Daily prayer and Bible reading became important parts of his life.

The stay in Mexico ended in mid-July 1848, when Jackson departed by boat for New Orleans. He spent three days in the South's largest city. The only thing of note he did there was have photographs made. The image was that of a uniformed officer clean-shaven and confident. Soft eyes offset a stern expression. Jackson appeared to be exactly what he was: a proven warrior with sensitive feelings.

His duty base for several weeks was Fort Columbus on Governors Island, New York. In the autumn he received a three-month leave of absence. Jackson automatically went to see his sister, Laura. At her home in Beverly, the army officer found himself the subject of hero worship from his three-year-old nephew, "Little Tom" Arnold. It was an affection that touched Jackson deeply. Arnold remembered that his uncle "walked & sat very erect & my Mother from that time forward made me do likewise."[4]

One of Jackson's cousins was also struck by the soldier now present in the young man. Isaac Brake recalled that although Jackson "wore civilian clothes on his furlough home, he maintained a natural military bearing." What Brake did not find

This first photograph of Jackson was taken in 1847 in Mexico,
probably Mexico City. It shows the twenty-three-year-old officer
fresh from valor in Mexico. A hand inside the uniform coat
was a typical pose of soldiers of that day and
was modeled after a stance always made by
French emperor Napoléon Bonaparte.

surprising was Jackson's deep modesty. He "was not much to talk about his exploits but conversed freely about the war and the heroism of others in the conflict."[5]

Jackson declined an offer to join a law firm in Weston. The military was his life. "If there is another war, I will soon be a general," he declared. "If peace follows, I will never be anything but Tom Jackson."[6]

Upon return to New York, his new duty station was Fort Hamilton. Located on the east side of the entrance into New York harbor, the granite structure was one of the army's most impressive posts. Downtown New York, but eleven miles away, offered relief from dull peacetime duties. In addition to drill and court-martial service, Jackson was also quartermaster and commissary officer for his artillery company. That meant attending to a constant flow of paperwork.

Health soon became Jackson's major concern. His weight had fallen from 164 to 140 pounds. This convinced him that none of his organs was working properly. He worried about his eyesight, hearing, throat, digestion, liver, kidneys, blood circulation, nervous system, and joints. The physicians Jackson consulted suggested that he stop "confining his mind" to a few subjects.[7] He should exercise and mingle more in social circles.

Jackson found such treatments unsatisfactory. Hence, as was his habit, he attacked the problem with hard study and grim determination. Self-cure would be the avenue he would follow. A search began for books and articles on human anatomy.

Jackson dosed himself with every pill, liquid, and application that held any promise of relief.

The answer, he concluded, lay in rigid discipline. He arose without fail between 5 and 6 A.M., and he was always in bed by 10 P.M. Next came major changes in his diet. Breakfast and supper were snack times; lunch was the main meal of the day. Even then, Jackson gave up most foods. "I have so strictly adhered to my wholesome diet of stale bread and plainly dressed meat," he informed Laura, "that I prefer it now to anything else."[8]

Occasionally Jackson would eat potatoes, beans, or a vegetable. Spicy foods, elaborate salads, desserts, coffee, and tea were not part of his diet. When he discovered that he liked bread better with butter on it, he gave up butter. The best food had the least taste, he felt.

The one exception Jackson made to this rule was fruit. He insisted that any fruit was good for a person's health. Many myths arose after Jackson's death about his supposed love of lemons. In truth, his favorite fruit was peaches, followed by apples and berries of any kind.

Jackson tried to get his sister to follow the same strict regimen. Yet he was quick to give her this warning: "If you commence on this diet, remember that it is like a man joining a temperance society: if he afterwards tastes liquor he is gone."[9]

A friend noted that Jackson "ate, as he did everything else, from a sense of duty."[10] He never strayed from his monk-like diet.

If invited to a dinner party, Jackson would show up with his own meal—usually a small bag of cheese and crackers.[11]

Equally intense were the rules of exercise he adopted.

He walked or rode five miles a day when weather permitted. Other outdoor activities were almost violent. Jackson developed a series of jumps, hops, arm-swingings, and the like that gave the impression of a man having some kind of seizure. Unaware how strange these actions looked, Jackson performed them regularly.

Sometime during this period, he met several of his West Point classmates. The group was engaged in conversation when Jackson began thrusting an arm into the air. "What is the matter?" an astonished friend asked. Jackson replied that "one of his legs was bigger than the other, and that one of his arms was likewise unduly heavy." He jerked the arm up and down so that "the blood would run into his body and lighten it." That convinced one classmate: Jackson was "the most remarkable character I have ever known."[12]

Jackson followed the custom of many young army officers of growing a beard in the quiet months following the Mexican War.

Another health care he embraced was the popular pastime of going to water resorts, or spas. These warm springs, with their heavy, often foul-smelling water, were supposed to be helpful for any ailment. Jackson became a strong believer in "water cures" and later made visits to spas a regular summer vacation.

Despite the multitude of treatments he attempted and endured, Jackson's health improved. His weight climbed to 166 pounds, the heaviest he had ever been. Eventually his complaints decreased in number to rheumatism, weak eyesight, and dyspepsia. How real and how serious they were cannot be determined. When Jackson was busy, he felt good. When he was bored, physical problems appeared. The three years of dull garrison duty after the Mexican War were a time when his health was at a low stage.

In time, Jackson came to feel that his improvement, and his cures, came from one source: God. The most important change in his life, having taken hold in Mexico City, was now fully underway. His letters to Laura shifted from health statements to the power of his Heavenly Father. Jackson saw a connection between the two. "My afflictions, I believe, were decreed by Heaven's Sovereign . . . and have probably been the instrument of turning me from the path of eternal death, to that of everlasting life."[13]

By April 1849, Jackson felt comfortable enough to make a formal declaration of faith. He was baptized in a local Episcopal church. Now, Jackson felt, God would surely tell him where his path of faith was to lead.

Carefree life in the New York area ended with Jackson's transfer in October 1850, to Company E of the 1st U.S. Artillery. That reorganized unit, manned largely by recruits, barely numbered fifty soldiers and needed a senior lieutenant with experience. Jackson was not pleased with the assignment for two reasons. Not only did it mean ending the close relationship with Captain Taylor; the transfer also meant serving under Captain (Brevet Major) William H. French.

Jackson had first met French in Mexico. The Baltimore native had graduated from West Point nine years ahead of Jackson. French won brevet promotions for gallantry in the same Mexican War battles as did Jackson, although French's conduct under fire was not as outstanding. Since then, the two officers had served in the regiment but were little more than acquaintances. French was a stickler for discipline, anxious for advancement, yet lacking in personality. He was testy while Jackson was courteous. French enjoyed fine wines and the

good life. Jackson preferred simple things and solitude.

In November 1850, Jackson's new company departed for duty in Florida. There was little to make the assignment pleasant. The weather was a welcome relief from the frigid winds of New York. Yet Florida was a wilderness, with the only settlements of note being along the winding coast.

For the past twenty years, the U.S. Army had been waging war off and on with small bands of Seminole Indians who refused to give up their native lands. They continued to make occasional raids on isolated farms and villages. The army had posted seventeen hundred men in tiny garrisons across Florida in an effort to keep an estimated 120 Seminoles in check.[14]

Jackson found himself in one of the worst of these stations. Fort Meade was an outpost only a year old. It was fifty miles from the closest settlement. Despite its formal name, Fort Meade was little more than a collection of wooden buildings clinging to the high bank of the Peace River.[15] Open ground immediately in front offered a field of fire against attack, but soldiers never knew what lurked in the distant woods and marshes.

The Fort Meade garrison also had much to worry about on the inside. Swampland was a breeding ground for mosquitoes. They in turn spread malaria and "intermittent fevers" that crippled any unit on duty.

Captain French appreciated Jackson's skill at organization. He appointed his lieutenant as both company quartermaster and commissary. French also expected Jackson, as his second-in-command, to act as such in all things. Jackson soon found himself the busiest man on the post. French was full of ideas. Thus, there were always things to be done.

Scouting missions were part of outpost life. Jackson often led small detachments in search of hostile Indians. Rarely did they encounter them—a failure that sent French into dark anger. The post commander wanted headquarters to know how he was fighting to maintain the peace.

Tensions began to mount as French became demanding in other ways. Soldiers had to wear spotless uniforms, despite the tropical wilderness in which they lived. French levied punishments for the smallest offenses. He ordered a building program to improve Fort Meade's facilities. That project brought a head-on collision with Jackson.

As post quartermaster, Jackson was in charge of the construction. French became

Major (later General) William H. French was the only U.S. Army officer with whom Jackson ever had a major disagreement. French was greatly responsible for Jackson leaving the army and going to the Virginia Military Institute (VMI).

irritated at Jackson making decisions without consulting the post commander. Jackson became irritated at what he considered French's interference. Mrs. Carolyn French's arrival eased tensions for the moment at the troubled fort. The captain's wife was a charming hostess. She was friendly to one and all, especially to the reserved Jackson.

However, the pleasant atmosphere shortly disappeared. Both French and Jackson sent letters of complaint about each other to department headquarters in Tampa. Relations grew more strained, which was almost natural. The isolated marshlands of the Florida interior offered no diversions or recreation. Hence, little things became crises.

All of these things combined to make this the low point of Jackson's adult life so far. Once again his health began to fail. In March 1851, Jackson reported himself too ill to perform normal duties. Digestive problems had returned; his vision was so impaired, he could not read. Only Christian faith offered any degree of relief.

Those beliefs caused the Jackson-French feud to explode with a noise heard all the way to the War Department in Washington. Jackson became convinced that French's actions were destroying all morale at Fort Meade. He thereupon filed court-martial charges against his superior. French in turn drew up court-martial papers against Jackson.

One or more messy trials loomed on the horizon. A discouraged Jackson began to see no future in remaining in the army. He was aware that promotion came strictly by seniority, not by ability.[16] No retirement policy existed in the army. This meant that high-ranking officers tended to remain in service until they died. Jackson faced the likelihood of serving under French for as long as the two were in the same regiment.

An unexpected opportunity offered Jackson an escape. In February 1851, Superintendent Francis H. Smith of the new and still small Virginia Military Institute (VMI) sent a letter to Jackson. The military school was seeking a professor to teach natural and experimental philosophy. A Mexican War acquaintance of Jackson, D. Harvey Hill of Washington College in Lexington, had recommended Jackson for the faculty position. Smith wrote Jackson to inquire if he might be interested in the job.

The unhappy lieutenant far away in Florida found the offer flattering. He wrote Laura: "I consider the position both conspicuous and desirable." Furthermore, in Lexington he would be only 150 miles from the Beverly–Jackson's Mill area.[17]

Because of disappointments he had endured trying to achieve other goals in life, Jackson tried not to dwell too much on the prospects of going into academic life in his native state. Jackson's only previous teaching experience had been in his teenage years and to a group of poor children. How well he might do as a professor teaching college students was a lingering question.

On the other hand, Jackson would be in a military atmosphere without the dullness of army routine, poor pay, and uncertain duty stations. Teaching would challenge his own mind to study old as well as new subjects. Living in a community rather than inside an army post would help him acquire good social behavior. Three months of vacation in the summer would give him much opportunity to travel and enjoy a stimulating life.

Late in April, at the height of the feud with French, Jackson received another letter from Superintendent Smith. He had been selected for the teaching position. Happiness swelled through Jackson. He had already applied for a furlough in order to get away for a while from Fort Meade and French. Jackson had used his health problems of impaired vision and painful dyspepsia as reasons for wanting a leave. Now he could depart Florida and the army.

Someone asked Jackson if he did not think it wrong to accept the VMI position while in poor health. "Not at all," was his reply. "The appointment came unsought, and was therefore providential; and I knew that if Providence set me a task, He would give me the power to perform it. So I resolved to get well, and you see I have. As to the rest, I knew that what I willed to do, I could do."[18]

On May 21, 1851, twenty-seven-year-old Jackson started for Virginia. His sense of duty, self-confidence, and Christian principles had become strangely twisted in the five months at Fort Meade. The result was one of the most unpleasant episodes of his life.

❧ Chapter V ❧
Professor and Presbyterian

The Shenandoah Valley of Virginia is one of the most beautiful and bountiful regions of North America. It lies between the two easternmost ranges of the Appalachian Mountains. Harpers Ferry and the Potomac River were its northern point; the town of Lexington marked the southern boundary. "The Valley," as Virginians have always called it, separated the aristocratic planters of the central piedmont and eastern tidewater sections of the state from the plainer folk in the mountains to the west.

Grain fields and orchards stretched across the Valley floor and up the hillsides. Herds of cattle, sheep, and horses grazed in lush pastures. Scotch-Irish and German settlers who had flocked to the area after the American Revolution dominated the population. Hardworking, freedom-loving, and devout, they were solid citizens in every respect.

Thomas Jackson liked what he saw from that moment in July 1851, when he arrived in Lexington. The Rockbridge County seat was larger and more sophisticated than Weston had been. Townspeople seemed open and friendly. Yet Jackson's overriding interest that summer day was to see the school to which he had dedicated his services. It certainly looked impressive: a four-storied barracks with turrets and towers (battlements), surrounded by a few small stone buildings,

The Virginia Military Institute was barely twelve years old when Jackson went there as a new professor. His classroom was on the second floor of the turret on the right end of the main building.

and all clustered on high ground overlooking the Maury River and the main road through Lexington. Jackson, ever the student, wasted no time learning what he could about the Virginia Military Institute.

The complex began in 1816 as a state arsenal for thirty thousand muskets left over from the War of 1812. When the threat of Indian attacks ceased with the passing years, Lexington officials urged the state to convert the arsenal into a military and scientific school patterned after West Point. In November 1839, the Virginia Military Institute began operations.

Although much like West Point in many ways, upon graduation, VMI seniors were not eligible to receive appointments as army officers. The Lexington school strove to prepare teachers and to elevate the standards of science. Even though VMI cadets were unlikely to see military service, they were "as carefully trained as if each private was someday destined to become an officer."[1]

When Jackson first saw the campus, six weeks remained before the 1851–52 school term began. Dyspepsia still bothered him. Jackson decided to make a quick visit to New York in hopes that a physician in the large city could help. He was in luck. The physician who did him the most good proved to be Dr. Lowry Barney. Jackson's condition was due to stress, Barney insisted. Continue to diet and exercise, he told Jackson, but stop worrying about things. Learn to play, and consider getting married. All but the last-named treatment seemed workable to Jackson.

Major Jackson of the VMI faculty, 1851. Note the sideburns fashionable in that day.

In September he began his duties as a major on the VMI faculty. Jackson's uniform was a double-breasted blue coat, white trousers, black boots, and white gloves. Every article of clothing looked too big for him. Since Jackson always stood stiffly erect and walked with long, rapid strides, he instantly seemed different from the other institute professors.

At the head of that group of a half-dozen faculty was Colonel Francis H. Smith. Almost thirteen years older than Jackson, Smith was the institute's first superintendent. Thin and bespectacled, he was both a commanding officer and father figure in the VMI "family." He established the still-unbroken custom of presenting each graduate with not only a degree but also a copy of the Bible.[2]

Among the first professors to meet Jackson was Major Raleigh Colston. The French instructor was disappointed in his

"The Father of VMI," Colonel Francis H. Smith was superintendent of the Institute for fifty years. Here he is shown in the uniform of a Confederate general—a rank Smith never acquired.

new colleague. "There was nothing striking about his exterior," Colston said of Jackson. "His figure was large-boned, angular and even ungainly for his hands & especially his feet were very large. . . . He wore at that time the old-style 'side-whiskers' . . . This gave to his countenance a stiff and formal expression which his conversation by no means tended to remove, for he had but little to say [which] was natural with one who had mingled but little in general society."[3]

From the first, Jackson viewed cadet regulations as unbending rules of conduct. Discipline must be maintained above all else. The new major never seemed to realize that he was teaching young boys, not soldiers. He treated the teenagers as adults. (His own youth at Jackson's Mill may have had much to do with that attitude.) If a cadet knowingly violated school regulations, he could expect no mercy. Duty and obedience to orders were as sacred to Jackson as passages in the Bible. He was personally responsible for the dismissal from the institute of several young men who broke the rules. One of them was within two weeks of graduation when he was expelled after an argument with Major Jackson in class.[4]

Because of poor eyesight, Jackson would not read by the artificial light of candles or lanterns. He memorized his lectures the afternoon before the next morning's classes. Then he presented the material in a polite but unchanging tone with the high-pitched drawl he always had.

Daily marks on recitations formed a large part of the final grade. The power to memorize was the key to passing Jackson's courses. Original thinking had no place in his section room. The major himself was simply incapable of giving parallel examples or drawing the same conclusion with different words.

Humor rarely surfaced in his classes. The closest thing to a joke came when Jackson once asked the class why a telegram could not be sent from Lexington to Staunton, thirty miles away. Cadets offered all of the scientific theories they knew, all to no avail. A frustrated student finally suggested that possibly no telegraph line existed between the two towns.

"Yes, sir!" an excited Jackson responded. "This is right!"[5]

Weaker students fell further behind in Jackson's rigid classes. The major's aloof attitude and constant enforcement of rules struck many cadets as dictatorship. Even his walk irritated students. One cadet remembered Jackson's "curious way of holding his head very straight, whilst his chin would appear as if it were trying to get up to the top of his head."[6]

Such first impressions by frightened or uncaring students failed to uncover what one termed the "grand, gloomy & peculiarly *good* man" behind the steel exterior.[7]

Jackson became the butt of jokes and pranks. Cadets scrawled phrases or pictures on the blackboard before he entered the section room. Some whispered and giggled during class. Once, as Jackson was walking beneath the arch of the barracks building, someone dropped a brick from an upstairs window. The brick barely missed the professor, who continued walking as if nothing unusual had occurred.

His favorite course was artillery tactics, which he taught in the afternoon on the parade ground. Four small howitzers were used for instruction. Jackson "loved the guns" with almost motherly affection, a cadet noted. He also let nothing interfere with daily drill. One afternoon a thunderstorm struck. Driving rain swept across the parade field and sent cadets scurrying for cover. They looked out in amazement and watched as Major Jackson continued the drill in the rain by himself until the class period ended at 4 P.M.[8]

A sense of duty led Jackson to remain at his academic post. Painfully aware of his limitations, he continually made efforts to improve his performance. At one point he even attempted to write his own textbook in order to make his disliked courses at least more understandable. Jackson was never a sterling teacher, but his labors slowly gained sympathy rather than cynicism from faculty and cadets.

Colonel Smith recognized Jackson's weaknesses as a teacher, yet the superintendent thought the major "a brave man, a conscientious man, and a good man" who tried hard to succeed.[9] Cadet Randolph Barton came to hold Jackson "in high estimation," despite the fact that "no one recalls a smile, a humorous speech, anything from him . . . He was simply a silent, unobtrusive man doing his duty in an unentertaining way."[10]

Making the adjustment from army routine to civilian society was likewise an uphill struggle for Jackson.

"I am very much pleased with my situation," he said in his first letter from Virginia to Laura. "Lexington is the most beautiful place that I remember of having ever seen in connexion with the surrounding country."[11]

The seat of Rockbridge County then had a population of eleven hundred whites and six hundred slaves.[12] The very wealthy were few in number; so were the very poor. Families were large, with an average of six people to a home.[13] Lexington was established enough to be prosperous and small enough for everyone to know when a stranger was in town.

Daniel Harvey Hill became
Jackson's friend in Mexico, was a mathematics
professor at Washington College
in Lexington, and served under Jackson
in the Civil War.

VMI was not the only institution of higher education there. Literally next door to the military school was Washington College, a widely respected liberal arts college founded in the 1700s. Two campuses gave Lexington a distinct atmosphere of learning, culture, and social maturity.

It took Jackson a good while to become part of such an environment. Feelings of uncertainty made him hesitant. No wife or church membership paved his way. Yet three people stepped forward to become his first friends in Lexington.

Harvey Hill, a Mexican War compatriot, taught mathematics at Washington College. Always devout and often crabby, Hill and Jackson from the first had one thing in common: They both suffered from dyspepsia. Hill's wife, Isabella, was a minister's daughter

and openly friendly, especially to those like Jackson who needed friendship. John Blair Lyle, a bachelor in his late forties, owned a local bookshop. Lyle was a generous and congenial man with an ear for music and a heart for the Presbyterian church. His bookshop had long been a community center where gentlemen met to browse and talk. Jackson's pursuit of knowledge made him a regular patron—and hence an acquaintance to many local residents.

Townspeople, like VMI cadets and faculty, were slow to warm to the new professor. He was polite but stiff. A good listener, Jackson tended to stare seriously at a person and say nothing. Invitations to social events were made at first out of courtesy and later out of reluctance. Jackson gave the impression of attending receptions and dinners only from a sense of duty.

He was too uncomfortable around strangers, too given to standing at ramrod attention, and too lacking in conversational skills. Idle talking was beyond him. He took a man at his word. Occasionally he met an individual who sprinkled his sentences with "you know" expressions. Jackson would interrupt the person each time to admit that he did not know the point being made.[14]

Such behavior brought him a quick reputation as an oddball. Stories floated around town of his strange habits. Several revolved around Jackson's concerns over his health. A dinner invitation did not alter his diet. Jackson would have his meager evening meal at home and consume only water at the banquet. Once, at a dinner, he shocked his hostess by commenting: "The moment a grain of black pepper touches my tongue, I lose all strength in my right leg."[15]

A college student who attended a function solely to meet the Mexican War hero was stunned at what he saw. "There was little animation, no grace, no enthusiasm. All was stiffness and awkwardness. He sat perfectly erect, his back touching the back of the chair nowhere; the large hands were spread out, one on each knee, while the large feet, sticking out at the exact right angle to the leg occupied an unwarranted space. . . . The figure recalled to my boyish mind what I had once seen —a rude Egyptian-carved figure intended to represent one of the Pharoahs."[16]

Faint memories of his "sainted mother" led Jackson to believe that "all ladies are angels." He was exceedingly courteous to every female, regardless of age or circumstance. At a party, Jackson felt an obligation to give first attention to the young girl who appeared most unattractive or neglected. "This became so well known," one Lexingtonian noted, "that to be singled out by Jackson was the mark of a wallflower in other people's eyes."[17]

In time, however, community respect took the place of community ridicule. As one resident declared: "It was only when we came to know him with the intimacy of hourly converse that we found that much that passed under the name of eccentricity was the result of the deepest underlying principle, and compelled a respect which we dared not withhold."[18]

What helped the emergence of a genuinely good man was the most important event in Jackson's life: He finally found a religious home.

On Sundays, Jackson had been attending morning worship at various churches in Lexington. His three closest friends provided the sparks that lit the long-smoldering faith inside him. Harvey Hill was a lifelong and active Presbyterian. Isabella Hill's father was a Presbyterian minister who instilled in all of his children an abiding love of God. John Lyle led the local Presbyterian choir and rarely missed a service. At the urging of the three, Jackson

Jackson found his true faith at the Lexington Presbyterian Church. There he served as a Sunday school teacher, deacon, and supervisor of a Sunday afternoon class for all slaves in the Lexington area.

went to see Reverend Dr. William Spottswood White.

One of the most learned clergymen in Virginia, the fifty-one-year-old White held degrees from three colleges, had been chaplain at the University of Virginia, and had served on the Washington College Board of Visitors. For the past three years White had been pastor of the Lexington Presbyterian Church, the largest of the many Presbyterian churches in the Shenandoah Valley.[19] White was of medium height, but feeble health caused him to walk with a limp. He was known far and wide as "a devout and earnest man of God, whose kindness and affability made him" an inspiration "to the young and to strangers."[20]

The professor and the minister had several deep conversations. Jackson's childlike intensity almost overwhelmed White. Patiently he carried Jackson through the creed of the church. Jackson declared that "the simplicity of the Presbyterian form of worshipping and the preaching of well-educated ministry" impressed him most favorably.[21]

William Spottswood White, Jackson's pastor in Lexington, became the general's mentor, guide, and spiritual adviser. Yet Jackson could never stay awake during Dr. White's sermons.

White's guidance was sufficient. On November 22, 1851, Jackson officially joined the Presbyterian Church. He did so by vowing never to "violate the known will of God."[22] He kept his word.

Presbyterian doctrine of that day did not emphasize national issues and missionary efforts. Personal behavior and individual salvation were the foundations for eternal life. Jackson accepted such teachings eagerly. His life now consisted of only two goals: to love God fully, and to have God love him. The faith of this grown man became that of a child. As he joyfully wrote his sister: "No earthly calamity can shake my hope in the future so long as God is my friend."[23]

His favorite passage from the Bible became "And we know that all things work together for good to them that love God, to them who are the called according to *his* purpose."[24]

To be a good Presbyterian meant for Jackson adopting a new code of conduct. Henceforth, he would never dance, drink, gamble, curse, or use tobacco. He readily adopted tithing, the practice of contributing a tenth of one's income to the church. Daily prayer and Bible-reading became foundations of his life.

The Bible instructed Christians to "keep holy the Sabbath-day." So be it. Jackson would not read a newspaper or discuss nonreligious topics on Sunday. Church services, prayer, and private meditation filled his Sabbath. He even refused to mail a letter after Thursday, lest it still be in transit on the Lord's day and thus disrespectful.

Lexington Presbyterian Church became his home, his new haven from the cares of the world. He attended every service from baptisms to burials. Jackson believed that Dr. White (as well as all other clergy) had direct contact with God. Therefore, Dr. White was Jackson's superior officer.[25] Jackson reported to him several times each week for theological discussions. A suggestion from White became an order in Jackson's mind. When White once expressed the idea that Jackson might want to learn to pray in public, the new convert went through a long and painful period of overcoming his shyness to perform publicly in the name of the Lord.[26]

Prayer became Jackson's vehicle on the road to salvation. He once confessed: "I have so fixed the habit [of praying]

in my own mind that I never raise a glass of water to my lips without a moment's asking of God's blessing. I never send a letter without putting a word of prayer under the seal. . . . I never change my classes in the section room without a minute's petition on the cadets who go out and those who come in."[27]

One imperfection in his Christian practices Jackson could not overcome. He slept through every sermon. He might hear Dr. White's opening words; after that, a churchgoer remarked, "all was lost."[28] When asleep in church, Jackson still sat upright in those two ninety-degree angles. Only his head slumped forward.

Jackson's conversion was fulfilled in Lexington. His journey down the path of life was now void of doubt. While he often preached in letters to his sister, he never tried to force his beliefs on other people. Faith was private, just as it was rewarding.

At the end of his first year at VMI, Jackson felt pleasure. He sent an unusually cheerful letter to Laura. "I have for months back admired Lexington, but now for the first time, have I truly and fully appreciated it. Of all places which have come under my observation in the U. States, this little village is the most beautiful."[29]

CHAPTER VI

SEARCH FOR HAPPINESS

JACKSON FELT MORE comfortable when the 1852–53 school year began. He had gained some teaching experience; his list of friends in Lexington was slowly expanding; his faith was now firmly on a Presbyterian course. The major began paying more attention to young ladies, and they were showing real interest in the tall, twenty-eight-year-old professor with large and piercing blue eyes.

Bashfulness prevented Jackson from courting eligible women with enthusiasm. Although polite in every way, his attempts at conversation were too often "child-like and simple."[1] He began spending much time at the home of the Washington College president, the Reverend Dr. George Junkin. It was not the Presbyterian clergyman who appealed to Jackson as much as it was one of his daughters, Elinor.

She was a year younger than Jackson, with chestnut hair, bright eyes, and a ready smile. "Ellie" was the most devout of the Junkin children. She and Jackson first met when the two started teaching Sunday school together.

One evening Jackson was visiting his friends Harvey and Isabella Hill. Instead of talking about faith and academics, as he usually did, Jackson kept bringing up the subject of Ellie Junkin. "I don't know what has changed me," he said to Hill. "I used

Jackson was twenty-eight when he met Elinor Junkin and fell in love for the first time. Fourteen months after their marriage, "Ellie" died in childbirth.

to think her plain, but her face now seems to me all sweetness."

Hill roared with laughter. "You are in love!" he replied. "That's what is the matter!"[2]

Jackson pondered the situation until he was sure that Hill was correct. Then he began courting Ellie in the proper fashion of the day. A major roadblock quickly developed: Ellie's sister Margaret.

"Maggie" Junkin was several years older than Jackson. Redheaded, well-versed in literature, the elder Junkin girl was shy around everyone but Ellie. The two girls were so close that they shared the same room, dressed alike, thought alike. Maggie took an instant dislike to Jackson because he was threatening to take Ellie away.

Ellie accepted Jackson's proposal of marriage, then broke the engagement. Jackson was crushed. Harvey Hill noted: "I don't think I saw anyone suffer as much as he did" for several weeks. Jackson moaned that he probably would "become a missionary and die in a foreign land."[3]

The couple got back together and, on August 4, 1853, were married at the Junkin home. Maggie was grief-stricken; Ellie could not hold back tears at the thought of leaving her sister. Jackson came up with what he thought was a good solution: He took both sisters on the honeymoon.[4] The trio visited New York, Niagara Falls, Montreal, and Quebec before returning to Lexington. Housing in town was scarce, so Jackson lived with his in-laws. The Junkin

The Junkin residence on the Washington College campus was Jackson's home for three years. His room was the wing on the extreme right in this postwar photograph.

family, including Maggie, accepted him as a son and brother.

Jackson had never been so happy. Now he had the things he had wanted since childhood: a home and a family. Best of all, he had "an intellectual, pure, and lovely lady" as his wife.[5] She was his "great source of happiness," he told Laura.[6]

In this 1855 photograph of "the major," the sadness and emptiness following the death of his first wife is visible in Jackson's eyes.

Ellie removed much of Jackson's shyness and dislike of crowds. With Ellie at his side, Jackson came to find pleasure in Lexington social circles. He was always a frugal man who invested money with care—a practice he surely developed as a result of his father's careless ways. Now Jackson received invitations to serve as a partner or on the board of directors of a number of local businesses. Jackson's rigid eating habits gave way to a more normal diet. His health improved noticeably.

The cold, stern professor became less aloof, more approachable. Ellie was there to start his day on a cheery note. There were no more long and lonely evenings, because she was there as well. Jackson did not merely love Ellie; he adored her.

Fourteen months after their wedding, she was dead.

When Ellie became pregnant early in 1854, Jackson looked forward impatiently to having a child of his own. Childbirth in the nineteenth century was a dangerous ordeal. It was not unusual for a mother to lose a third of her children at birth, or to die herself in the delivery process.[7] Yet all seemed well as Ellie's final weeks of pregnancy passed.

On October 22, double tragedy struck. Ellie died after giving birth to a stillborn baby. In a flash, Jackson lost everything he had loved. Grief was crushing. "I do not see the purpose in this, the most bitter, trying affliction of my life," he told a friend.[8] To an equally brokenhearted Maggie, Jackson said: "I cannot realize that Ellie is gone; that my wife will no more cheer the rugged and dark way of life. The thought rushes in upon me that is insupportable—insupportable!"[9]

Ellie and the child were placed in the same coffin and buried in the town cemetery. For a long time thereafter, Jackson visited the grave every day. Several times that autumn he was heard to exclaim: "Ah, if it might only please God to let me go now!"[10]

The one thing that brought Jackson safely through the disaster was faith. Late in the year he reassured his sister: "Religion is all that I desire it to be. I am reconciled for my loss and have joy and hope for a future reunion where the weary are at rest."[11]

Jackson thereafter sought even harder to do the Lord's work. He devoted more time to the boys' Sunday school class he taught; often he went from door to door in Lexington to beg funds for the Bible Society; he was there whenever Dr. White needed a volunteer. Jackson was always trying to strengthen his faith by strengthening the faith of others.

This sort of crusade led to the most extraordinary religious project he ever undertook. In Jackson's eyes, all humans were God's children and entitled to Christian teachings as a way toward salvation. That included those who were in bondage. Jackson's views on slavery were simple. The Almighty had ordained that some people must be slaves. No man had the right to question God's will. What the good Christian should do is treat slaves as kindly as they would hope blacks would treat them if the situation were reversed.

Such is the "Golden Rule." Jackson put it to work by organizing a Sunday school class for slaves in the Lexington area. Many obstacles stood in his path, including opposition from some whites and a Virginia law at the time prohibiting whites to teach slaves to read and write. Nevertheless, in the autumn of 1855, Jackson began the Sunday afternoon school.

Dr. White was impressed at the way Jackson "threw himself into this work with all of his characteristic energy and wisdom."[12] Local hostility faded as enrollment climbed to one hundred slaves of all ages. Volunteers came forward to help with prayers, singing, and Bible instruction.

Every class began with Jackson standing in front of his black pupils and clapping his hands as they sang his favorite hymn: "Amazing grace, how sweet the sound/That saved a wretch like me . . ."

Even after Jackson left for war, the black class remained on his mind. "How is the colored Sunday school progressing?" he would ask Dr. White. When told that all was well, Jackson "never failed to respond with a strong expression of gratitude."[13]

A second and ill-fated love affair developed during this time. Jackson and Maggie Junkin shared the heaviest sadness over the death of Ellie. Their common grief drew them closer together. In time, and possibly to their surprise, the two fell in love. Yet an insurmountable religious barricade stood in their way. By Presbyterian doctrine, once Jackson had married Ellie, her family became his family. His sister-in-law, in the eyes of the church, became his sister. Marriage between brother and sister was out of the question.[14]

Life had dealt Jackson another cruel blow. He needed to get away—to go somewhere to think deeply about his future. Thus, when the school year ended in June 1856, Jackson fulfilled a longtime desire by departing on a tour of Europe.

He visited England, Scotland, Belgium, France, Germany, and Italy. Battlefields and military museums held no appeal for Jackson. He was more interested in God's wonders embodied in art, sculpture, and the architecture of cathedrals and other grand buildings. As he traveled he thought about his life. The trip, he informed Maggie, was "full of enjoyment and profit."[15]

Jackson returned to Lexington with a clear decision: He must marry again and seek anew the happiness that kept drifting away. No search was necessary. Jackson knew whose hand in marriage he wanted.

Three years earlier he had become acquainted with Isabella Hill's younger sister,

Margaret Junkin, Ellie's older sister, became one of Jackson's closest friends. They may have fallen in love, but church law forbade a man from marrying his sister-in-law.

In 1857, Mary Anna Jackson became Jackson's second wife and was unquestionably the person he loved most in the course of his life.

Mary Anna Morrison. The sibling lived at Cottage Home, North Carolina. Her father, the Reverend Robert Hall Morrison, was a Presbyterian clergyman and first president of Davidson College. Anna was small in stature but possessed of large brown eyes, a pleasing personality, and an abiding faith.

Jackson sent her a letter and made a quick visit to the Morrison home at Christmastide. The two began a steady correspondence. Although seven years apart in age, Anna and Jackson were open, honest, and devout. Love blossomed by mail.

At one point Jackson wrote: "In my daily walks I think much of you . . . as a gift from our Heavenly Father."[16] A few weeks later he confessed: "When in prayer for you last Sabbath, the tears came to my eyes, and I realized an unusual degree of emotional tenderness."[17]

In the late afternoon heat of July 17, 1857, Jackson and Anna were married at Cottage Home. A northern honeymoon followed because Jackson was eager to show his bride the places he liked: New York, West Point, Saratoga, and Niagara Falls. Like her husband, Anna enjoyed sight-seeing, walking, and other outdoor activities.

Like her husband, too, Anna had delicate health. She became ill during the honeymoon. A physician recommended that she undergo water treatments. Jackson took her to his favorite resort, Rockbridge Alum Springs, for three weeks of therapy. The couple then proceeded to Lexington improved in health and deeply in love.

In their first year of marriage, the couple lived in a hotel and in a boardinghouse while searching for a home. The person who insured that Anna was fully introduced into Lexington society was Maggie. She, too, had just been married (to widower John T. L. Preston, a wealthy landowner and VMI professor). Maggie was anxious that her "brother's" wife be comfortable in new surroundings. However, illness soon began to hamper both Jackson and Anna.

Perhaps Anna's ongoing ill health triggered a similar condition in Jackson. Yet his major ailments were real: an eye disorder (uveitis), severe pain in the facial muscles (neuralgia), and an ear infection that left his hearing permanently impaired. In spite of sicknesses, the Jacksons took active roles in the Presbyterian Church. Anna helped Jackson with the black Sunday school class. She never saw him look more earnest "than when telling those poor people the story of the cross."[18]

Their life together was mutual joy. Anna found her husband "rather more studious than I would like him to be." Yet, she added, "he was the most tender, affectionate and demonstrative man at home that I ever saw. His heart was as soft as a woman's; he was full of love and gentleness."[19]

Jackson's feelings for his wife were total devotion, with doses of playful pranks and affectionate language added. His favorite addresses for Anna were "My Sunshine" and "Esposita" (little wife).[20]

Ten months after their wedding, a Lexington merchant noted in his register that Major Jackson had purchased a "$3.25 crib." Anna gave birth to a daughter. Mother

The Jackson home on East Washington Street in Lexington.
It later became the town hospital and is now the most popular museum
dedicated to Jackson.

and child appeared to be fine. The baby was named Mary Graham in honor of Anna's mother. Two weeks later, the same merchant recorded the sale of "1 fine cloth coffin" to Jackson. Mary Graham had died of a common illness known as jaundice.[21]

Jackson faced this death with the same submission as he had many others in earlier times. God had a reason for inflicting this loss. Jackson accepted divine judgment with obedience. The death of his second child had another, noticeable effect on Jackson: He became even more attentive to and affectionate with all children.

In the autumn of 1858, the Jacksons found a home. It was a two-story structure with a full basement only a block off Main Street. The Presbyterian Church was two blocks away. Jackson could easily walk to the VMI campus. Real happiness came again to the couple. They had a home with every door on "golden hinges," Jackson exclaimed, "a place for everything and everything in its place."[22]

Six slaves had become part of the household. Four blacks were wedding gifts from Dr. Morrison, Anna's father. The other two, Albert and Amy, were elderly slaves who each had begged Jackson to purchase them after the deaths of their masters. Jackson looked on them as more than servants; they were treated as members of the family.[23]

Once everyone settled into the house (which needed many repairs), a set routine went into place. Jackson was ever a soldier with a passion for organization. Home life was no exception.

He rose promptly at 6 A.M. and knelt for private prayer. Next came a cold bath, regardless of the season. A brisk half-hour walk followed. Jackson also had some gymnastic equipment that he used when the weather was bad. At precisely 7 A.M., family prayers took place. Jackson, Anna, and the servants all made their petitions to God. Breakfast followed. Jackson said grace "with both hands uplifted" and with "childlike simplicity and earnestness."[24] He left home at the same time each morning for his 8 A.M. class.

Life in his section room had changed for the better. Jackson's reputation had grown steadily and had stopped the pranks that marked his first years as a professor. He now wore a full beard and mustache but the same ill-fitting blue uniform coat. A cadet stated in wonder: "In the section room he would sit perfectly erect and motionless, holding his pencil in one hand and his class book in the other, listening with grave attention . . . He was ready at any moment to refer to any page or line in any of the books and then to repeat with perfect accuracy the most difficult passages . . ."[25]

Another cadet of the late 1850s stated: "Listening to his terse, well-rounded sentences, always instructive and full of meaning . . . I felt that he possessed power which, in stirring times, would make him a leader among his fellows."[26]

Morning classes ended at 11 A.M. Jackson returned home and spent at least an hour in Bible-reading. Lunch, the largest meal of the day, came at 1 P.M. A half hour's conversation with Anna followed the meal. If an artillery class was not scheduled in the afternoon, Jackson worked in his backyard garden, rode out to the two-acre farm he owned on the edge of town, or performed repairs on the house. He and Anna would usually take a late-afternoon walk or chat in the parlor.

Following a light supper, Jackson returned to the parlor and stared at the wall for perhaps an hour while reviewing in his mind the next day's class assignments. Anna noted that her husband would sit "as silent and as dumb as the sphinx" until he had the material firmly memorized. Then he would turn to her "with a bright and cheerful face."[27] The remainder of the evening belonged to her. Bedtime was 10 P.M. without fail.

Ill health continued to plague the couple. September 1859, found Jackson refreshed from a summer at the spas. "Under the blessing of Providence," he wrote Laura, "my health has much improved."[28]

By then, his prominence in Lexington had likewise risen. Jackson was now one of the town's most respected citizens. The

*In October 1859, John Brown sought
to start a slave insurrection at
Harpers Ferry, Virginia. Jackson was
a witness at Brown's execution
for murder and treason.*

major had stock in three banking institutions and sat on the board of directors of one. He was a partner in a local tannery. He owned a home and a farm. Many regarded him as, next to Dr. White, the bedrock of Lexington Presbyterian Church. The years when he was considered a bumbling, eccentric professor were past.

October 1859, brought a dark cloud from the north. A militant abolitionist named John Brown and eighteen followers seized the federal arsenal at Harpers Ferry in the northern end of the Shenandoah Valley, barely one hundred and fifty miles from Lexington. Brown's intention was to arm thousands of slaves and lead them as an army through the South on a fiery trail to freedom. The issue of slavery had become a divisive point at a national level.

The Brown band killed three men before a company of U.S. Marines arrived at Harpers Ferry from Washington. The soldiers, under the command of Army Colonel Robert E. Lee, stormed the engine house where Brown and his group were barricaded. The invasion ended in a matter of minutes. Half of the raiders were killed, the other half captured. Brown was speedily convicted of murder, treason, and insurrection. He was sentenced to die in December.

Jackson was never a political activist, but he kept abreast of the times through newspapers. Like most of his neighbors, he was a Democrat who considered the independent rights of the separate states a foundation of the federal union. Throughout the 1850s questions of slavery had inflamed larger issues involving the rights of individual states to determine their own courses of action. The Northern states fell into clear opposition with those in the South. Neither abolitionists nor Southern extremists would bend. Such inflexibility is dangerous in a democracy.

The news of Brown's raid created turmoil throughout Virginia.

The arsenal at VMI contained thirty thousand muskets and five hundred barrels of gunpowder.[29] Such stores were an inviting target for any radical group. VMI cadets expected to be called to duty at any moment. Next door, at Washington College, a sophomore declared that "the military fever broke out among the student body . . . like measles."[30]

One person far above the noisy commotion was Major Jackson. The course of the nation, he believed, would be what God in His wisdom thought it should be. Worrying about it showed a weakness of faith.

The execution of John Brown was to take place at Charles Town, the county seat of the Harpers Ferry area. Fear existed of other abolitionists in the North making an armed attempt to free Brown. Preservation of the peace became uppermost in the minds of Virginia officials. The state's militia system was too old for the crisis at hand. Governor Henry A. Wise therefore called on the VMI corps of cadets to serve as gallows guard. They would surround the scaffold and prevent any rush to block Brown's hanging.

Eighty-five cadets, two howitzers, and three faculty members traveled by road and railroad to Charles Town. Major Jackson was in charge of the artillery detachment. At 11:30 A.M. on December 2, John Brown plunged through the scaffold trap door to his death. Jackson, standing at attention only a few feet away, had a clear view of everything. Later that day he described the execution of Brown in a long letter to Anna. Jackson wrote in part: "He behaved with unflinching firmness. . . . Brown had his hands tied behind him, & ascended the scaffold with apparent cheerfulness. . . . The sheriff placed the rope around his neck, threw a white cap over his head . . . In this condition he stood on the trap door . . .

for about 10 minutes . . . The rope was cut by a single blow, & Brown fell through about 25 inches . . . With the fall his arms below the elbow flew up, hands clenched, & his arms gradually fell by spasmodic motions—there was very little motion of his person for several minutes, after which the wind blew his body to & fro."

Jackson confessed to praying for Brown's soul. "I hope that he was prepared to die, but I am very doubtful—he wouldn't have a minister with him."[31]

Brown's death only deepened the national crisis. Tensions between North and South rose as the months of 1860 passed. The sense of compromise that held America together was fading. Men no longer talked; they shouted. And the more they shouted, the heavier the atmosphere for shooting became.

The major grew anxious. "What do you think of the state of the country?" he asked Aunt Ann Neale on his thirty-eighth birthday. "Viewing things at Washington from human appearances, I think we have great reason for alarm, but my trust is in God; and I cannot think that he will permit the madness of men to interfere so materially with the Christian labors of this country . . ."[32]

The end of a long and fatiguing school year found both Jackson and Anna desiring treatment for their worrisome health problems. The couple traveled to a resort in Brattleboro, Vermont. When it proved unhelpful, they transferred to the "Round House Water Cure" spa at Northampton, Massachusetts. There, through the waters and an understanding doctor, came marked improvement in physical conditions.

Not completely so in mind, however. While in New England the Jacksons encountered hostility because they were Southerners. The major held his resentment in check, his wife said. He "heard and saw enough to awaken his fears that it might portend civil war; but he had no dispute with those who differed from him, treating all politely, and [making] some pleasant acquaintances."[33]

The new school year at VMI began with much thought on the upcoming 1860 presidential election. Andrew Jackson's Democratic Party had fallen apart. It had not one but three candidates on the national ballot. Its opposition, the new Republican Party, had nominated an unknown Illinois attorney named Abraham Lincoln. Not all Republicans were abolitionists, but Southerners believed all abolitionists to be Republicans. "If the 'Black Republicans' are victorious," a VMI faculty member asserted, "God save the Union." Southern homes would become targets of Northerners determined to eliminate slavery and destroy Southern society.[34]

Voters went to the polls in November. Lincoln got more votes than any of the others and won election as president of the United States. South Carolina promptly left the Union. Six other Southern states did the same over the next two months. "One nation, under God" no longer existed.

Jackson never changed his thinking in the 1860-61 political upheaval. Firm allegiance to the Union ran deep in his soul. On the other hand, he believed that his native Virginia had certain rights guaranteed by the Constitution. Federal coercion, especially in the form of an invasion by troops, was illegal. To his nephew and namesake, Jackson wrote: "I am in favor of making a thorough trial for peace, and if we fail in this, and the state is invaded, to defend it with a terrific resistance."[35]

He spoke with equal intensity to his pastor. "If the general government should persist in the measures now threatened, there must be war. It is painful to discover with what concern they speak of war . . . They seem not to know what its horrors are. I have had an opportunity of knowing enough on the subject to make me fear war as the sum of all evils."[36]

Secessionists (or "fire-eaters," as they were called) had endured enough talk and threats. Action was needed. In February 1861, those Southern states out of the Union met in Montgomery, Alabama. They drafted a constitution, established a congress, elected Mississippi Senator Jefferson Davis as president, and announced the existence of the Confederate States of America.

In Lexington, unrest mounted between those who clung to the old Union and those who supported the Confederacy. On April 13, a major fracas occurred. A cadet got into a fight with a local citizen. The face-off became a free-for-all involving several people. The whole VMI cadet corps rushed into town. Some of the cadets carried their muskets.[37] Faculty members managed to intercept the students and ordered them into the institute's auditorium.

Superintendent Smith reprimanded the cadets for their conduct. Law and order must always be upheld, the colonel said loudly. At that point, Jackson entered the room. Cadets began shouting, "Jackson! Jackson!" "Old Jack!"

The professor shook his head and refused to speak. Colonel Smith told him: "I have driven in the nail, but it needs clinching. Speak with them."[38]

Jackson moved onto the stage. He stared at the corps for a moment. Suddenly he looked taller, and stronger. His eyes flashed as he slowly spoke. "Military men make short speeches, and as for myself I am no hand at speaking anyhow. The time for war has not yet come, but it will come and that soon, and when it does come, my advice is to draw the sword and throw away the scabbard![39]

Cadets bounded to their feet with cheers and applause. "Hurrah for Old Jack!" "He is the right stripe!"[40] A proven fighter had spoken to young men. A leader was there to guide them if the hour came.

The hour had already come. When Federal authorities refused to abandon Fort Sumter in the middle of the harbor of Charleston, South Carolina, Confederate batteries on April 12 began a thirty-four-hour bombardment that forced the Sumter garrison to surrender. Union president Lincoln responded by calling for seventy-five thousand volunteer soldiers to put down an insurrection "too powerful to be suppressed by the ordinary course of judicial proceedings."[41]

Lincoln's call for troops to make war against the South ended Virginia's neutrality. The "Old Dominion" and three other Southern states then seceded from the Union and cast their lot with the Confederacy. Virginia had existed for 180 years before the Constitution created a "United States of America." That government was only seventy years old and weak in many respects. To a Virginian, patriotism meant loyalty to his state. On the other hand, to a Northerner, patriotism meant an unbroken Union. Citizens of North and South were going to war against each other to uphold conflicting American principles.

Secession divided Virginia more sharply than anywhere else in the fractured country. Friends ceased to be friends; family ties broke apart. The extreme western counties of Virginia had much more in common with their Ohio neighbors than they did with fellow citizens in faraway areas like Richmond and the tidewater. Fifty-five of those counties (including the area of Jackson's Mill and Weston) refused to accept secession. They moved toward the creation of their own state of West Virginia.[42]

The breakup of the Union also cost Jackson the last immediate family member he had. Laura Jackson Arnold was as strong-willed as her brother. All of her ties save those to Jackson were with her western Virginia region. With the explosion of civil war, Laura became first a strong Unionist and then a defiant activist. She broke off all communication with her brother. Jackson maintained his customary silence and kept the deep hurt of losing a sister to himself. A lifetime of shared love disappeared in the smoke of disunion.[43]

A rush to war followed. In Virginia, as elsewhere, young men flocked to enlist in units being organized. Colonel Smith felt it his duty to offer the services of the VMI corps. Governor John Letcher, a native of Lexington, desperately needed drillmasters for the thousands of recruits gathering in Richmond. He ordered the corps to proceed at once to the capital. Major Jackson received his first war order. As the senior officer on duty, he would lead the marching column.

Departure time was Sunday, April 21, 1861, at 12:30 P.M. The corps was in line, fully equipped, and impatient to leave an hour beforehand. Jackson had eaten a late breakfast at home. He then knelt with Anna and committed his family and himself to the protecting love of his Heavenly Father. "His voice was so choked with emotion," Anna recalled, "that he could scarcely utter the words."[44] After a warm embrace, Jackson rode to the institute and took his place at the head of the line.

He refused to leave until the appointed hour. Then Jackson rose in his saddle and shouted a clear command. The column wound down a hill and out of Lexington. Jackson would never see his adopted hometown again.

❋ CHAPTER VII ❋
"STONEWALL" AT MANASSAS

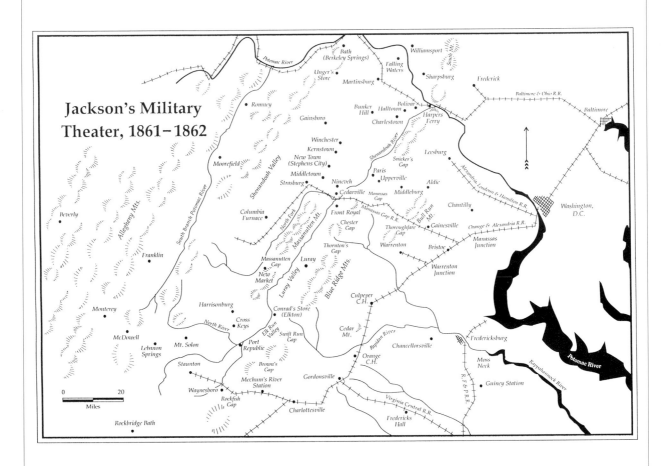

Jackson's Military Theater, 1861–1862

THOMAS JACKSON DID not enter the Civil War merely to defend Virginia. His was a higher mission: to wage a religious crusade. Jackson believed that God had placed a curse on America for reasons man could not know. From his reading of the Old Testament, he was convinced that the bloodshed of battle was the only way to wash away the curse and regain God's blessings.

Victory would come to the most faithful side. The Southern Confederacy existed because the Heavenly Father deemed it so. Jackson was a soldier of the South; hence, he would be a soldier of the cross.

Once in Richmond, the VMI cadets eagerly went to army camps and began teaching recruits (most of whom were older than the VMI boys) what they had to learn to become soldiers. Jackson found himself with no command and no orders. Governor Letcher soon appointed him a colonel of state volunteers. When Jackson's name came before the Virginia Convention for confirmation, a delegate asked: "Who is this Major Jackson?"

The representative from Rockbridge County promptly answered: "He is one who, if you order him to hold a post, will never leave it alive to be occupied by the enemy."[1]

On the following day, Colonel Jackson received his first orders. He was to take command of the arsenal, training grounds, and defenses at Harpers Ferry. Since he was a native of northwestern Virginia, his appointment might help strengthen Southern feelings around that remote outpost of the Confederacy.

Everything about the assignment was unpleasant. Harpers Ferry sat in the hollow of a "Y" formed by the juncture of the Shenandoah and Potomac Rivers. One of the largest arsenals in the Confederacy was there. Two of the North's major supply lines, the Baltimore and Ohio Railroad and the Chesapeake and Ohio Canal, passed by the village. Harpers Ferry was extremely important to both sides in this war, but the place could not be defended.

Mountains loomed on every side of the town. Cannons posted on the hillsides or mountaintops could fire point-blank into the streets. The highest and most commanding

The village of Harpers Ferry stood on high ground and was surrounded by higher ground. On the left is the Potomac River; on the right is the Shenandoah River. The wooden railroad trestle across the Potomac was destroyed nine times during the Civil War. This 1861 drawing shows Southern soldiers on duty. Above them is the first national flag of the Confederacy, the "Stars and Bars."

of the ranges, Maryland Heights, was neutral territory and could not be legally used by the South.

Jackson nevertheless moved quickly to bring some order to all the chaos inside the little town. He had the undamaged arms machinery transferred from the arsenal to Richmond. Protective earthworks soon encircled the town limits. Campsites were laid out in orderly fashion. Yet Jackson's most complicated task was what to do with hundreds of enthusiastic young boys flocking to the Ferry to defend their homeland. This growing mob needed to be organized and drilled, disciplined and made aware of obedience to orders. Eager lads must learn to camp and cook, to fire a musket and use a bayonet.

Today those youths were recruits; tomorrow they would be soldiers because somewhere shortly down the road, they must be fighters.

The holiday atmosphere under Virginia militia that had been occupying Harpers Ferry gave way to strict military routine under Jackson. Seemingly everywhere was Colonel Jackson, clad in the plain blue VMI faculty uniform and behaving with the meekness of a college professor. A newspaper correspondent looked at Jackson and wrote: "The Old Dominion must be sadly deficient in military men, if this is the best she can do."[2]

Looks were deceiving. Under Jackson's eye, recruits stopped talking and

A group of Confederate recruits such as Jackson would have seen when he arrived at Harpers Ferry.

Jackson secured his favorite mount, "Little Sorrel," while in command at Harpers Ferry. This photograph of the horse was made after the war.

listened. They marched and shoveled until they were too tired to think. Soon they reacted to orders without hesitation, and did basic things without being told. Jackson taught them that it was natural to make mistakes while learning. It was neglect of duty and failure to obey that would not be tolerated. As the weeks passed, young recruits came to look—and to feel—like soldiers.

Some four thousand Confederates at Harpers Ferry slowly gained pride in themselves. This transformation came from the efforts of one man who hardly looked inspiring. He "never spoke unless spoken to; never seemed to sleep," a young recruit observed. "He walked along, the projecting visor of his blue cap concealing his features

. . . and high boots covering the largest feet ever seen . . ."[3]

In those first war weeks at Harpers Ferry, Jackson acquired his most beloved military possession: his favorite horse. His men had seized an eastbound livestock train. Jackson needed a new mount. After selecting a large stallion, he noticed a small but well-rounded horse. That would make a fine present for Anna, he thought. Jackson bought that animal as well. When he rode the horse to insure that it was tame enough for his wife, Jackson discovered that it had a smooth pace, even temper, and great powers of endurance. He kept the horse for himself. At first it was called "Fancy." It shortly became "Little Sorrel" and proved to be thoroughly devoted to its master.

By mid-May, over five thousand Confederate volunteers were at Harpers Ferry, and more were expected. The number was too great to be under a mere colonel. The Confederate government sent one of its highest ranking officers, General Joseph E. Johnston, to take charge. Johnston looked on Jackson as his second-in-command and put him at the head of Virginia's First Brigade.

Jackson's new command consisted of four regiments totaling twenty-six hundred men. The regiments were the 2nd, 4th, 5th, and 27th, plus the four guns of the Rockbridge Artillery from Lexington. (The 33rd Virginia was added to the brigade a couple of weeks later.) All of the units had one thing in common: They were raised in the Shenandoah Valley area. Jackson had been drilling these regiments the hardest

Confederate general Joseph E. Johnston was one of Jackson's fellow Virginians and the only officer to command the major army in both the Eastern and the Western military theaters.

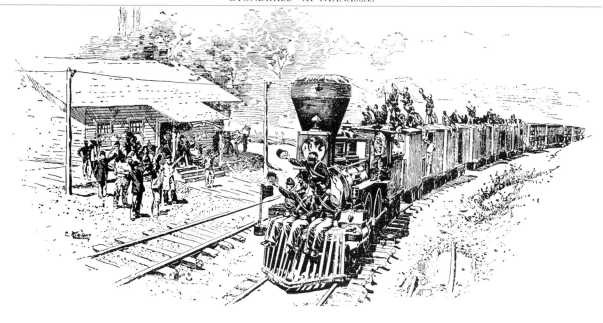

*Jackson's troops rode trains like this from the Shenandoah Valley
to their first battle at Manassas.*

because he considered them to be the best among all the forces at Harpers Ferry.

He knew the unit officers, and they knew him. A strong bond began to develop between commander and soldiers from the day Jackson assumed command. The men affectionately called him "Old Jack." He in turn informed Anna: "I am very thankful to our Heavenly Father for having given me such a fine brigade."[4]

The colonel was fair and careful, yet demanding where discipline was concerned. He always sought to look out for the welfare of his soldiers.[5] This was difficult to do in the face of poor supplies. A soldier at the Ferry wrote his father: "I cannot eat any thing hardly that is brought to us by the Quartermaster for we have Beef here now in our tents that has been lying here for

several days without any salt on it and you may depend upon it: dont smell like ripe peaches."[6]

For the first time in his life, Jackson became truly homesick. He sent at least a note to his wife whenever time permitted. On one occasion he confessed that her "sweet, little sunny face is what I want to see most of all."[7]

Johnston's complaints that overwhelming numbers of the enemy stood in his front led Confederate authorities to give him permission to abandon Harpers Ferry. The Confederates fell back to Winchester. Because every road in the area converged on Winchester, it was the key to the immediate region as well as to the lower (northern) end of the Shenandoah Valley. A Union force under aged General Robert Patterson made a cautious pursuit of Johnston. Meanwhile, Jackson fidgeted at much movement and no action. He told Anna: "I trust through the blessing of God, we will soon be given an opportunity of driving the invaders from this region."[8]

On July 2, the Federals came too close. Jackson moved out with the 5th Virginia and a couple of the Rockbridge Artillery guns. A sharp fight occurred at Falling Waters that produced about seventy-five casualties in all. Federals backed away. The

General Irvin McDowell commanded the Union forces in the opening major battle of the war at Manassas.

affair was only a skirmish, a brief engagement between two small detachments. However, it demonstrated anew Jackson's calmness under fire. It was clear evidence that he deserved the promotion that came shortly. The former artillery professor was now an infantry brigadier-general.

Two weeks later came the call to full battle. A hastily organized force of thirty-three thousand untested Federals marched from Washington. Their objective, thirty miles inside Virginia, was a railroad junction called Manassas. Confederate General P. G. T. Beauregard had twenty-two thousand equally green troops at Manassas. He needed reinforcements to present a more solid line of defense. Johnston received orders to join Beauregard with his Shenandoah Valley soldiers as quickly as possible.

Thanks to a perfect screening movement by Johnston's cavalry chief, Colonel J. E. B. Stuart, Confederates left Winchester without Federals knowing it. Johnston marched his eleven thousand men over the mountains into the piedmont region to a station on the Manassas Gap Railroad. From there excited volunteers occupied every space on trains that bore them to Manassas and the linkup with Beauregard's forces. Federal and Confederate numbers were about equal when, on a sultry Sunday, July 21, the Union host under General Irvin McDowell attacked.

Two things about the day bothered Jackson. It was the Sabbath, a day he normally reserved for the Lord. It was also

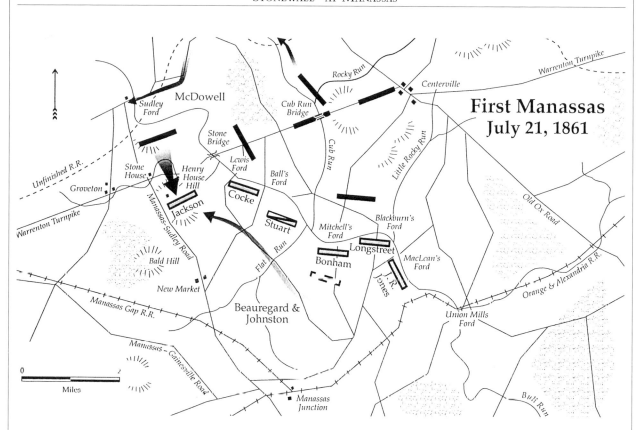

**First Manassas
July 21, 1861**

his wife's thirtieth birthday. He would have enjoyed thoughts of her if circumstances had permitted.

Beauregard's front extended along the southern bank of a sizable stream called Bull Run. Jackson and his men were on the far right of the line when the Federal assault came against the Confederate left flank. A frantic shifting of Southern troops began. Those on one end of the line had to march under fire to the other end of their position.

Jackson's Virginians were among the lead elements of that transfer. They double-timed five miles to the new position. One of Jackson's men said the march consisted of "running that distance like panting dogs with flopping tongues . . . thirsting for water almost unto death, and worn and weary indescribably."[9]

Around 11 A.M., Jackson's brigade reached Henry House Hill. It was the anchor or end of the Confederate left and the highest elevation in the area. Evidence of fighting was everywhere: dead soldiers, discarded equipment, the ground chewed by cannon fire, gun smoke drifting across the fields as disorganized soldiers were abandoning the area. Injured men were limping or being borne to the rear. Their ghastly wounds and cries of pain caused one of Jackson's youths to wish he was "a thousand miles away and in the trundle bed at [my] mother's home."[10]

Jackson's quick eye for detail told him that whoever controlled the top of Henry House Hill controlled that entire sector of the battlefield. He ignored the bursting shells and deafening roar of battle. Carefully he placed his five regiments just behind the brow of the hill out of sight of the enemy but in support of cannons Jackson placed on the hilltop.

For almost three hours, inexperienced volunteers lay on the reverse slope and endured shell fire as the two sides waged a vicious artillery duel. Occasionally an enemy shell whistled over the hilltop and exploded among the helpless men. "I tell you," a college student in the 4th Virginia confessed, "I said all the prayers I knew, even 'Now I lay me down to sleep.'"[11]

The Confederates grimly held their positions because their teacher stood so firm. "Steady, men, steady! All's well!" Jackson repeated quietly as he rode back and forth along the line.[12] Beneath his calmness, a former VMI cadet stated, they "saw the warrior and forgot the eccentric man."[13]

Few of the volunteers were aware in all the confusion that Jackson had been wounded. In battle he acquired an odd

At Manassas, General Barnard Bee of South Carolina was trying to rally his disorganized regiments when he shouted the cry that gave Jackson the immortal nickname "Stonewall."

habit of thrusting his left arm toward the sky with the palm facing outward. He made that action in the heat of the artillery duel. He jerked his hand down. Blood was pouring. A bullet or piece of shrapnel had broken his middle finger. Jackson wrapped a handkerchief around the hand and turned his attention back to the battle.[14]

Slowly but steadily, Union forces drove Confederates up the side of Henry House Hill. A Southern brigadier, General Barnard E. Bee, was desperately trying to rally his broken lines when he saw Jackson amid the battle smoke. Bee rode quickly to his old West Point friend. "General!" he shouted. "They are driving us!"

Jackson looked at the approaching Federal waves with stern determination. He answered: "Sir, we will give them the bayonet."

Bee was thinking only that Jackson was offering a firm place on which the troops could form. He galloped into the midst of his retreating men. Pointing his sword toward the crest of the hill, he yelled: "Look, men! There is Jackson standing like a stone wall! Let us

This painting, Jackson at First Manassas, *is more inspirational than accurate. During the battle, Jackson was mounted on his horse. The general never wore as fanciful a hat as is shown.*

determine to die here, and we will conquer! Follow me!"[15]

A few moments later, Bee fell mortally wounded. He never knew that he had just given to Jackson what became the most famous nickname in American military history.

Union soldiers were only yards away from the top of Henry House Hill—and victory—when Jackson gave the signal. His men stood up, fired a volley of musketry into the faces of the enemy, and charged down the hill with a unique scream known thereafter as the "Rebel Yell."[16]

Close, intense fighting raged up and down the side of the hill. Men fired their muskets, used the weapons as clubs, fought with their fists, and grappled in every known way as both sides struggled for control of the ground. At one point, Jackson rode into a ravine and ordered a group of men into action. "Now if you see any Yankees coming out of those pines up there," he shouted in his high-pitched voice, "give them . . . pepper!"

The soldiers hooted with laughter. As they charged forward, one looked at Jackson and yelled: "That fellow is not much at cussin,' but something in a fight!"[17]

Around 4:30 that hot day, the arrival of fresh Confederate troops from the Shenandoah Valley and the exhaustion of

Federals who had been engaged for hours brought the battle to an end. Hard-fought victory had come to the South. For Jackson, that was not enough. He pleaded for permission to head after the retreating enemy. "Give me ten thousand men and I will take Washington tomorrow!" he insisted.[18] Confederate officials were satisfied with the outcome of the battle. Many Southerners even expected the Civil War to end after this engagement.

That night Jackson's personal physician, Dr. Hunter McGuire, placed the broken finger in a splint. No antibiotics or manageable painkillers existed in that day. Hence, and for several weeks thereafter, discomfort from the injured finger hampered Jackson in many of his activities.

Battle evaluations followed the contest at Manassas. Confederate losses were 1,982 men; Union casualties were 2,896 soldiers, almost half of whom were captured. Jackson's brigade had one of the heaviest losses: five hundred men killed, wounded, and missing. On the other hand, a member of Jackson's staff wrote home, "Our brigade is almost immortalized; but for us the day would have been lost."[19]

As for the new "Stonewall," praise came from the highest level. Beauregard called him an "able, fearless soldier" and added: "His prompt timely arrival before the plateau of the Henry house, and his judicious disposition of his troops, contributed much to the success of the day."[20]

Jackson in typical fashion saw divine assistance as the reason for Southern victory. "Whilst great credit is due to other parts of our gallant army," he wrote Anna, "God made my brigade more instrumental than any other in repulsing the main attack."[21]

Back in Lexington, townspeople gathered daily at the post office for news of the battle. The mail arrived, and Dr. White recognized Jackson's familiar scrawl on an envelope. "Now we shall know all the facts!" he shouted.

A hush settled over the crowd. White opened the letter, which Jackson had written the night after the fighting. "My dear pastor, in my tent last night, after a fatiguing day's service, I remembered that I had failed to send you my contribution for our colored Sunday school. Enclosed you will find a check for that object, which please acknowledge at your earliest convenience, and oblige yours faithfully, T. J. Jackson."[22]

Not one word about the battle! No hint from the hero of the Confederacy's first major victory! His obligation to his black friends occupied Jackson's thoughts.

Inactivity marked the weeks after battle at Manassas. Confederate forces edged closer to Washington. Routine camp life filled the days around Fairfax Courthouse. Jackson was not idle. He fervently believed that "the patriotic volunteer, fighting for country and his rights, makes the most reliable soldier on earth."[23] However, the volunteer needed constant training to be a "reliable soldier."

Drill, drill, and more drill was the order of the day in Jackson's brigade. Idleness led to laziness, he maintained, and laziness led to poor performance in the

*President Jefferson Davis was also commander in chief
of Confederate military forces.*

field. "Every officer and soldier who is able to do duty," he declared, "ought to be busily engaged in . . . hard drilling, in order that, through the blessing of God, we may be victorious in the battles which in His all-wise providence may await us."[24]

With sickness ever-present and a constant threat to life, the general moved his camp often for the health of the men. Jackson never stopped the search for better clothing, more supplies, newer weapons. One of the keys to his greatness as a commander was his attention to the little things that soldiers want and need.

One thing Jackson's men rarely got was a furlough. A leave of absence was granted only in case of extreme emergency. Duty required a soldier to be ready for action at all times. Jackson himself set the example. Not once in his Civil War career did he take a furlough of any kind.

Such dedication did not stop him from being lonely. Clergymen visited his tent often to pray and discuss theology with the general. However, Jackson missed Anna. He wrote her warm letters and expressed his love constantly. When no further military activity seemed likely for the year, Jackson invited Anna (then living with her parents in North Carolina) to visit him in camp. Jackson's men, especially his staff officers, treated her royally while a proud husband beamed with pleasure.

By then, details of Jackson's gallantry at Manassas had circulated widely. Friends and strangers sent presents of food, sweets, and clothing. The attention greatly embarrassed Jackson. Any thanksgiving should be to the Heavenly Father. "What I need," he confided to Anna, "is a more grateful heart to the 'Giver of every good and perfect gift.'"[25]

Autumn brought a reorganization of the Confederate army in Virginia. The War Department consolidated all forces into a single Department of Northern Virginia, with General Joseph E. Johnston in command. Inside the department were to be three military districts. Each would have its own general. One of the divisions was the Shenandoah Valley.

It had been defenseless since July. Citizens there had begged loudly for some high-ranking and proven officer to take charge of military affairs. The person should be a man they knew and who knew them.

Meanwhile, Jackson's repeated urging for advance and attack had become irritating in government circles. Several Confederate officials—notably President Jefferson Davis—looked on him as a fanatic or "loose cannon." A command in isolated western Virginia, over the mountains from the main theater of war, might be the best place for the professor-soldier. His ties with Lexington and the Valley, plus his roots in the northwestern mountains, made Jackson a logical choice.

In October, he received promotion to major-general and assignment to command of the Valley District. Some doubts existed in the army that Jackson was capable of such high responsibility. One official stated: "I fear the Government is exchanging our best Brigade Commander for a second or third class Major General."[26]

A sad note for Jackson existed in the new assignment. He was to go alone. That meant saying good-bye to his beloved First Brigade—the now-famous "Stonewall Brigade." Jackson did not know, on November 4, when he rode in front of the assembled ranks, that the five Valley regiments would soon rejoin him. Seated on Little Sorrel, he praised the soldiers for "hard marches, the exposures and privations" they had endured. He reminded the men that they began service as the First Brigade and that they would always be the First Brigade in his heart.

His voice began to break with emotion. Several soldiers were weeping. Finally Jackson shouted: "May God bless you all! Farewell!"[27]

With tears in his eyes, the general rode from the field and headed toward new duty.

CHAPTER VIII

✺ INDEPENDENT COMMANDER ✺

J ACKSON'S ORDERS WERE to defend the Shenandoah Valley against Union threats from any direction. Whatever thoughts the new departmental commander may have had for an attack at some point vanished when he reached Winchester, his new headquarters, and reviewed the situation. At least six thousand Federals were at various posts as close as twenty miles to the north. Another four thousand enemy soldiers occupied Romney, forty-three miles to the west.

To defend against such numbers, Jackson had pieces of three widely scattered

militia brigades "to a greater or less degree in service," a handful of disorganized cavalry, and some cannon without cannoneers.[1] The Southern "army" he had inherited numbered less than seventeen hundred old men, young boys, and green recruits.

"Alta Vista," the Winchester home of Colonel Lewis Moore, became Jackson's major headquarters. The main entrance to the home is at the left facing a side street.

Jackson established his first Winchester headquarters at the Taylor Hotel, downtown. This photograph was taken in the 1920s, after electricity and paved streets had come into use.

General Joseph Johnston's main Confederate army was eighty miles to the east.

Much needed to be done. Jackson wasted no time in getting started. Winchester was the key to the lower (northern) end of the Valley. It was a commercial center of over four thousand residents. Nine roads in the area passed through it. So vital to military operations was Winchester in the Civil War that it changed hands an incredible seventy-two times.[2]

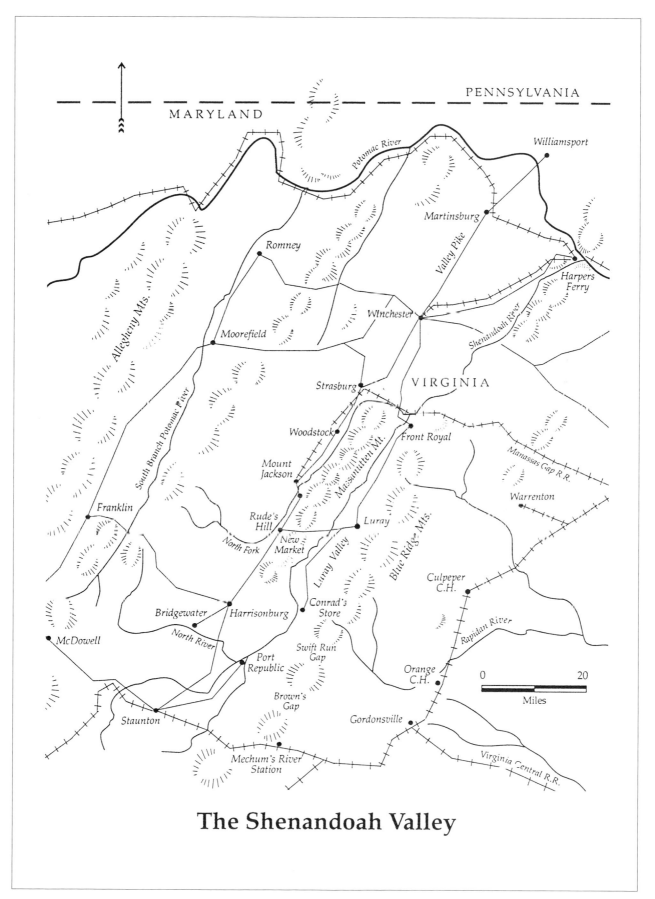

The Shenandoah Valley

For his headquarters, Jackson first used the Taylor Hotel. He then switched to a private home to get away from the crowded downtown. Shortly after his arrival in Winchester, Jackson acquired a body servant. Jim Lewis was a Lexington slave whose owner leased him to Jackson. The elderly Lewis became devoted to the general. He prepared meals and proudly watched over him like a mother hen. Lewis became a beloved figure around headquarters. A member of Jackson's staff exclaimed after the war: "Faithful, brave, big-hearted Jim, God bless him!"[3]

Jackson's initial and most pressing task was to get more troops. He was aware that Federals could move against him in force from the west and north at any time. At his insistence, the Stonewall Brigade returned to his command. Jackson's call for all state militia in the Valley produced thirteen hundred eager but untrained volunteers.

They quickly found themselves undergoing the shock of hours of daily drill. Discipline was constant and tight. Soldiers were not allowed outside the town; visitors were not permitted inside. Under the general's watchful eye, Winchester became both a training camp and a fortress. However, Jackson was not one to sit and wait.

To be victorious, a general must control the war by making things happen. The best defense was offense. Winter was near, and with it would be sickness and camp grumbling among the men. Anna noted of her husband: "He remembered the saying of Napoleon, that 'an active winter's campaign is less liable to produce disease than a sedentary life by camp-fires in winter quarters.'"[4] So within a month after arriving at Winchester, Jackson asked the War Department for permission to launch an offensive.

His first request was for General William W. Loring's three brigades totaling five thousand men to be ordered to Winchester from the mountains far to the southwest. With these reinforcements, Jackson proposed to move across the mountains and seize Romney. It was a road hub, railroad station, and key to control of the South Branch of the Potomac River. Union forces there were a danger to Jackson's position at Winchester.

In addition, a strike at Romney would reassure citizens in Jackson's home area of northwestern Virginia that the Confederacy cared for their safety and loyalty. Jackson admitted in his request that the campaign would be "an arduous undertaking." Yet he was convinced of success "through the blessing of *God* who has thus far so wonderfully prospered our cause."[5]

The War Department gave approval, and Jackson began full-scale preparation for the advance. He waited impatiently for Loring's large force to arrive. Jackson kept his men busy that December by trying to destroy dams on the Chesapeake and Ohio Canal. With the Baltimore and Ohio Railroad broken and unusable, the one-hundred-and-eighty-five-mile canal was a valuable commercial artery for the North.

Confederates remained hidden from

Federal view during the daylight hours and worked by night. Waist-deep in the icy waters, they hacked at the reinforced earthen dams with axes, picks, and crowbars. Occasionally Federals would spot the dam-breakers and open fire with artillery. One of Jackson's recruits, under enemy shelling for the first time, confessed: "I laid so close to the ground that it seemed to me I flattened out a little [while] yearning for a leave of absence."[6]

It was in returning to Winchester from one of those expeditions that Jackson for the first time lost his dignity. A staff officer wrote:

"After riding along some distance, the General spied a tree hanging heavy with persimmons, a peculiar fruit of which he was very fond. Dismounting, he was in a short time seated aloft among the branches, in the midst of abundance. He ate in silence and when satisfied started to descend, but found that it was not so easy as the ascent had been. Attempting to swing himself from a limb to the main fork of the tree, he got so completely entangled that he could move neither up nor down and was compelled to call for help."

Staff officers came to his rescue.[7]

Early in December, the War Department assigned General Richard B. Garnett to command Jackson's old unit, the Stonewall Brigade. Garnett was older than Jackson and a member of Virginia's tidewater aristocracy. Jackson took an instant dislike to Garnett and might have protested more loudly except for a wonderful Christmas gift: Anna arrived from North Carolina. Knowing that he would likely be in Winchester until springtime, the general asked his wife to join him. She needed no urging. They settled in comfortably at the general's headquarters. Anna had no trouble endearing herself to soldiers and citizens alike.

Loring's troops drifted into Winchester during Christmas week. Jackson was already

General William Loring lost an arm in the Mexican War. He served under Jackson in the 1862 Romney Campaign and complained continually of Jackson's "utter disregard for human suffering." Jackson later filed court-martial charges against the Florida officer.

*This wartime sketch by William L. Shepherd
could easily represent the hardships of Confederate
soliders on the Romney march.*

upset at having Garnett under his charge. William Loring gave him even worse concern. A native of North Carolina and a lifelong soldier, Loring had lost an arm at the Battle of Chapultepec. He had much military experience, but officers found him to be a weak leader who always suggested reasons for delay. Down in the ranks, Loring was regarded as "an officer who knew nothing."[8]

January 1, 1862, was a spring-like day. As the lead elements of his force of eighty-five hundred men and twenty-six guns marched from Winchester, Jackson made a quick visit to the Reverend James R. Graham. He asked his friend and local Presbyterian minister if he and his family would allow Anna to stay with them while he was gone. The Grahams agreed at once. When Jackson

told Anna good-bye, he broke his usual privacy by embracing and kissing her in public. Then he mounted Little Sorrel and galloped to join his soldiers.

The Romney campaign lasted three and a half weeks. For Jackson, it was a disaster.

Overnight the weather changed. Temperatures plunged; snow and sleet, driven by frigid winds, whipped the struggling columns day and night. Up to ten inches of snow covered the ground at times. Roadways frozen to hardness grew treacherous from ice and snow. Wagon trains with food and supplies regularly fell behind. Hunger accompanied the cold. A number of men broke arms and legs from losing their balance. A Virginia artilleryman was almost moved to tears when he saw many of the horses "bruised by their falls—all were covered with dried sweat and from one horse's knees there were icicles of blood which reached nearly to the ground."[9]

Soldiers had to sleep on hard earth without tents, a blanket being their only covering from the falling snow. The camp the next morning had the appearance of a large cemetery carpeted in white. Then, a Lexington soldier wrote, "these mounds were burst asunder and live men popped out of them, as if a resurrection were in progress."[10]

Horrible weather only increased Jackson's frustrations. The march had all the aspects of Napoléon's pitiful retreat from Moscow. Jackson was unable to get any of his unit commanders to do anything right or on time. Loring's men were constantly complaining and tardy. One of Loring's brigade commanders deliberately headed his men in the wrong direction—back toward the wagons carrying food.[11] Midway through the campaign, Jackson officially requested that Garnett be removed as head of the Stonewall Brigade. Jackson also sent two colonels home on "furlough" rather than endure their failing performances.[12]

The general's frustrations even extended to sternness toward the soldiers in the ranks. He displayed little sympathy to his men on this march. A staff officer felt that Jackson "classed all who were weak and weary, who fainted by the wayside, as men wanting in patriotism. If a man's face was as white as cotton," Jackson "looked upon him merely as an inefficient soldier and rode off impatiently."[13]

Federals abandoned Romney before Jackson got there. On January 14, Confederates occupied the town and seized sixty thousand dollars' worth of military stores. Skirmishes along the way had cost Jackson only four killed and twenty-eight wounded, but fully a third of his army was on the sick list. Loring's command seemed incapable of further action.

Jackson decided to leave Loring and his men at Romney for the rest of the winter while the main body of Confederates returned to protect Winchester. In his official report, Jackson made no mention of the lost opportunities and disappointments that he had met. He cited only the successes achieved "through the blessing of God."[14]

Back in Winchester, the general accepted the invitation of the Grahams to live at the Presbyterian manse. The Jacksons ate with the Grahams and took an active part in family devotionals. Anna later wrote: "We spent as happy a winter as ever falls to the lot of mortals on this earth."[15]

That was not exactly true, for late in January the Romney campaign blew up in Jackson's face. General Loring was most unhappy at being left in what he considered an exposed position at Romney. He sent influential Colonel William B. Taliaferro, armed with a petition signed by eleven officers, to Richmond to appeal directly to the President.

Jefferson Davis listened, believed the slanted stories of hardship he heard, and ordered Secretary of War Judah Benjamin to have Jackson recall Loring's command to

Winchester. Jackson promptly did as told—then submitted his resignation from the army. "With such interference in my command" from uninformed civilians hundreds of miles from the scene, Jackson stated, "I cannot expect to be of much service in the field." He would return to teaching duties at VMI.[16]

Jackson's resignation created an instant uproar throughout Virginia. His soldiers and the residents of Winchester raised loud shouts of anger at the mistreatment of their beloved general. Governor John Letcher gave Benjamin a verbal lashing. Confederate congressmen and minister-friends appealed to Jackson to consider how badly Virginia needed all of her sons.

After a stormy week of communiqués and conferences, Jackson withdrew his resignation. Davis controlled his anger; Benjamin was relieved to get away from a hornet's nest of criticism levied against him. Loring was transferred elsewhere, but not before Jackson filed court-martial charges against him for gross neglect of duty.[17]

Federals meanwhile reoccupied Romney and laid such waste to the nearby country that Jackson himself protested in disgust.[18] On that note the Romney campaign came to an end. Jackson had lost every major gain he had made on the expedition. "For the only time in the war," one writer declared, "his competence was questioned. His future in the army had been placed in doubt. His first independent command was a dismal failure."[19]

A different opinion prevailed in his small army. Daily drill resumed to sharpen the men even more as soldiers. Elevation of morale came with improvement and pride in oneself. Affection for Jackson was widespread. "He is beloved by all," a private wrote home. "Whenever Gen. Jackson comes in sight of his old brigade they yell out as if they had gained a victory."[20]

Inside the Graham home, Jackson was a different person. He gave to Anna "every attention & tenderness," the Reverend Graham noted. Anna was not the only object of Jackson's affection, the minister added. "His fondness for children was remarkable." Jackson loved to play with the three oldest Graham children. They looked on him as a second father. Often he got on his hands and knees and made horse-like sounds while the squealing youngsters sat on his back like riders.[21]

Nathaniel P. Banks was a powerful Massachusetts political leader when Lincoln appointed him an army general. Banks's patriotism was high; his military knowledge proved feeble.

*An artist's imagination of how the Battle of Kernstown looked.
Confederates are attacking from the right.*

During those winter months, Anna became pregnant for a second time.

March brought a renewal of military operations. With Loring's troops gone, Jackson had no more than thirty-six hundred men. His responsibilities were heavy. He had to protect the left flank of the main Confederate army in central Virginia, guard the Shenandoah Valley against all Union invaders, and expect no reinforcements in the process. Now Federal columns totaling at least thirty-eight thousand soldiers were inching southward toward Winchester. Jackson gave no thought to retiring to safety across the mountains. "If the Valley is lost," he declared, "Virginia is lost."[22]

Jackson could not attack against such overwhelming numbers of Federals. What he proposed to do became the key to the great campaign that was to follow. He informed authorities in Richmond: "If we cannot be successful in defeating the enemy should he advance, a kind Providence may enable us to inflict a terrible wound and effect a safe retreat in the event of having to fall back."[23]

Anna bade her husband a tearful farewell and started home to North Carolina. Jackson had grown fond of Winchester, not only because of its people but also because of its high military value. He did not want to give up the town without a fight. On March 11, as his army moved southward out of town, Jackson summoned his brigade commanders. He had a plan. The Confederates would march a short distance from Winchester; then, after dark, Jackson's force would return and attack the unsuspecting Federals who were in Winchester.

The plan failed when brigade leaders misunderstood Jackson and led their men too far south to turn around and make a night assault. Jackson was furious. Through tight lips he snarled: "That is the last council of war I will ever hold!"[24] He kept his word by making a habit never to tell anyone of his intentions.

Slowly Jackson retired forty-two miles up the Valley to Mount Jackson. Union forces under General Nathaniel P. Banks occupied Winchester. Although he was the fourth-ranking Union general at the time, Banks was no soldier; he was a prominent Massachusetts politician. Lincoln appointed several political leaders to the rank of general to give them a chance to make a reputation in what was thought to be a short war. The politicians so honored would then feel indebted to Lincoln for the opportunity. Banks tried hard to be a good general. The talent was just not there.

With Winchester in Federal control, Banks dispatched part of General James Shields's division eighteen miles to Strasburg to watch for Confederates in general and Jackson in particular. Jackson used the week at Mount Jackson to make his men forget the nightmare of the Romney campaign. He fed them well, drilled them well, and made them feel discipline and pride. His soldiers cheered him on sight. "Old Jack" (their favorite name for him) still wore the faded blue coat of a VMI professor and a flat, round-topped cap (kepi) that seemed to flop over his eyes. Little Sorrel bore no resemblance to a great war horse. Yet it was the lack of airs— the plainness of the man and his mount—that helped promote an affectionate closeness with the soldiers.

Sleet was falling on March 21 when Shields's regiments began falling back to Winchester. Jackson concluded that Shields was retiring for one reason: All Federals in the Valley were going to unite with General George B. McClellan's Army of the Potomac for a multifront offensive on the Confederate capital, Richmond. To allow the union of two strong Union forces would give the North an unbeatable military concentration.

Jackson could not let that happen. He quickly started his men marching northward on the Valley Turnpike. "Press on! Press on!" Jackson urged as he rode back and forth along the ranks. Confederates marched forty-one miles in two days. Fully a third of Jackson's soldiers fell out along the roadside from exhaustion.[25] Yet time was vital.

On the afternoon of March 23, Jackson and barely twenty-five hundred troops approached the hamlet of Kernstown. Winchester was four miles away. Jackson sent his cavalry chief, Turner Ashby, to determine what Federal resistance lay ahead. Colonel Ashby, small and dark, was a splendid horseman on his white stallion. Brave to a fault, Ashby unfortunately led by direction rather than by discipline. He and his men were always patriotic but oftentimes disorganized. On this day, Ashby sent back word that only four Union regiments—about Jackson's strength—were in Kernstown. They were preparing to march northward.

The pious Jackson now faced a

dilemma. Here was a great opportunity for battle. Yet it was Sunday, a holy day that Jackson deeply respected. He quickly concluded that fighting a crusade for the Lord—as he believed he was doing—was sufficient justification to wage war on the Sabbath. "I felt it my duty," he later told Anna. "Necessity and mercy both called for the battle."[26]

Weary Southerners deployed for combat on the left side of the turnpike. At Jackson's signal, the men surged forward. They struck the enemy line, which buckled and then became strong again. Something was wrong. Jackson soon realized that the intelligence on the enemy's numbers was wrong. A full Union division—not four but twelve regiments—stood in battle line.

Jackson did everything he could to gain victory. He was "intense and magnetic, directing and energizing his soldiers," a cannoneer declared.[27] A member of the Stonewall Brigade recalled that the general "showed great courage in the battle, exposing himself constantly on the front lines."[28]

Three hours of intense fighting raged across a low, wooded ridge. Jackson admitted a few days later: "I do not recollect ever having heard such a roar of musketry."[29] Confederates began running out of ammunition as they hammered at the Union lines. A smaller force attacking a larger force rarely succeeds. Under darkness, Jackson's little band retraced its steps southward up the Valley.

Kernstown had been a defeat for Jackson (the only one he would ever suffer).

Jackson was guilty of several mistakes. He had accepted Ashby's report on Union strength at Kernstown without verifying it. In giving battle, he had sent weary troops into action without making any inspection of the ground or enemy dispositions. Little overall control seemed to exist after fighting began. Once Jackson learned of the enemy's superior numbers, he continued to attack.

Confederates lost 455 men killed and wounded, plus 263 other soldiers captured. These numbers were a fourth of his strength in the battle. Union losses were 568 of 10,000 soldiers engaged.[30] On the other hand, Jackson's assaults convinced Union authorities in Washington that they were dealing with a dangerous foe in the Shenandoah. Banks received orders to remain in the Valley in case Jackson struck again.

Southerners marched gloomily all the way to Conrad's Store, seventeen miles east of Harrisonburg in the center of the Valley. That point was at the base of Swift Run Gap through the Blue Ridge Mountains. From there, Jackson could attack the flank of any Union forces marching up the Valley Turnpike; he could wage a defensive battle on good ground, or he could withdraw across the mountains. Some of Banks's forces advanced to Harrisonburg, then fell back forty-five miles to Strasburg to shorten the lines of communication with headquarters in Winchester. As far as Banks was concerned, Jackson was now little more than a nuisance.

That low estimation was satisfactory to Jackson. He spent April filling his ranks

Jedediah Hotchkiss was a transplanted New York, schoolmaster by trade, and a skilled mapmaker by hobby. His knowledge of terrain was a valuable asset to Jackson.

as best he could. The new Confederate conscription act, which ordered men into the army, increased Jackson's force to six thousand soldiers.

The general tended to overlook what had been done well because that was part of duty. What had not been done well were the things that had to be corrected. There had been too much straggling on the road to Kernstown. So drill and more drill filled the time until the men became more durable and more the fighting force Jackson wanted.[31]

Improving the army was not easy. Winter snows had turned into spring rains. The countryside was a gigantic swamp. "Our encampment is worse than any barnyard," a Virginia officer observed, "for in places there seems no bottom."[32]

The way to eliminate lax discipline was to find better field commanders. Jackson removed Garnett from command. His successor, General Charles S. Winder, was the hard taskmaster that Jackson liked.

Reorganization also took place on Jackson's staff. Thirty-four-year-old Jedediah

Hotchkiss became chief topographer, or mapmaker. Jedediah Hotchkiss had moved to Virginia from New York. He was a schoolmaster by profession, but drawing maps was his great hobby. The long-bearded Hotchkiss, a few years younger than Jackson, taught the general every nook and cranny of the great valley that was about to become a battle arena. To head the staff, Jackson selected the older Reverend Robert Lewis Dabney. This proved a bad choice. Dabney was a preacher and theology professor totally untutored in military subjects. Yet ministers were capable of anything, Jackson reasoned. Dabney's presence could stimulate greater faith among the troops. The army, Jackson told Anna, might become "an army of the living God as well as of its country."[33]

Dabney protested that he did not deserve a major's rank and senior position on the staff. He freely confessed ignorance of military matters.

"You can learn," Jackson answered.

The minister began to yield to the request. He asked when the general wished him to begin such duties.

Jackson replied: "Rest today and study the Articles of War, then begin tomorrow."[34]

Meanwhile, not one but three Union armies were moving to destroy Jackson. A force of fifteen thousand Federals under General John C. Fremont were two ranges over in the Allegheny Mountains to the west. Another forty thousand enemy soldiers were to the east of Jackson at Fredericksburg. Banks's divisions were to the north in the Strasburg-Winchester region. But inside the

Union ranks, no one had any idea exactly where Jackson was or what he intended to do.

Ashby's cavalry dashed hither and yon in the Union army's front, thus screening Jackson's true whereabouts. In mid-April, Banks confidently informed the War Department: "Ashby still here. We have a sleepless eye on him and are straining every nerve to advance as quickly as possible."[35]

Billy Yanks inside the army did not share such optimism. "Here we are," a Massachusetts officer lamented, "following a mirage into the desert."[36]

A master plan began to take shape in Jackson's mind. What he first hoped to do was keep Fremont and Banks west of the Blue Ridge and isolated from each other. At the same time, Jackson did not want General Irvin McDowell's Union army at Fredericksburg leaving to reinforce McClellan advancing on Richmond. If Jackson could somehow pin down Fremont, Banks, and McDowell, and attack and defeat each, one by one, that would enable all other Confederate forces in Virginia to concentrate against McClellan's one hundred and twenty thousand soldiers.

Deception, rapid marches, and unexpected attacks might accomplish the goals, Jackson thought. As for the overwhelming numbers of the enemy, he would let God handle that problem.

General Robert E. Lee was then President Davis's chief military adviser. Like Jackson, Lee was a gambler. He not only approved Jackson's proposal; Lee sent him eight thousand additional troops under the eccentric but dependable General Richard S. Ewell. Another twenty-eight hundred Confederates, under General Edward Johnson and stationed in the mountain passes west of Staunton, were also added to Jackson's command.

That gave Jackson a total of seventeen thousand soldiers. Nearby, to the west, north, and east of him, were poised almost seventy thousand Federals. Being greatly outnumbered did not bother Jackson. That problem was always present. So was his determination to forge ahead with what forces he had. The Valley commander certainly agreed with Lee, who encouraged Jackson to attack, and added: "The blow, wherever struck, must, to be successful, be sudden and heavy."[37]

Jackson ordered Ewell's division into the Conrad's Store encampment. Ewell was to keep an eye on Banks. "Old Jack" then marched away to the south. On April 28, Banks reassured Washington authorities: "The enemy is in no condition for offensive movements." Two days later, as Jackson led his men southward in a steady rain, the Union commander announced triumphantly that "there is nothing more to be done by us in the valley."[38]

✳ CHAPTER IX ✳

VICTORY IN THE VALLEY

For three days, Confederate soldiers trudged through rain and deep mud. All they knew was that they were heading toward Mechum's River Station on the Virginia Central Railroad. The sun came out just as they arrived at the depot.

Jackson's men boarded trains they thought were heading east toward the defenses of Richmond. Instead, the locomotives puffed west—back into the Shenandoah Valley. Jackson had used deception to trick the enemy into thinking he had abandoned the Valley for good.

On May 4, Staunton residents near panic at being deserted were startled when trains loaded with Jackson's soldiers wheezed to a stop in the middle of town. Jackson promptly sealed off Staunton to mask his presence. His plan was working. As the Southern troops arrived at Staunton, Union General Banks was informing authorities that Jackson's "greatly demoralized and broken" forces were fleeing to the safety of Richmond.[1]

Confederates rested for a day before Jackson led them on another tiring march. This one was thirty-five miles westward over rugged mountains to the village of McDowell. There the lead elements of Fremont's Union army—six thousand Midwestern soldiers under General Robert H. Milroy—were moving toward Staunton and the all-important Virginia Central Railroad.

On the afternoon of May 8, Jackson's soldiers opened fire from a commanding hilltop. Federals made several assaults up steep slopes in an effort to break Jackson's line. They failed; and at sundown, after a spirited fight, Milroy's troops withdrew beyond McDowell. They had inflicted twice as many casualties on Jackson as they had suffered, but Jackson held the field. The next day, Jackson's first report to Richmond was a humble, one-sentence declaration: "God blessed our arms with victory at McDowell yesterday."[2]

Jackson then ordered his engineers to chop down trees and build roadblocks to close all mountain passes in the area. This would prevent Fremont from moving east, and it would protect Jackson's western flank against further Union threats. That accomplished, the stern and determined Jackson was now ready to clear the Shenandoah Valley itself of all Federal intruders.

One person made happy by such a move was Confederate General "Baldy Dick" Ewell. Jackson's second-in-command was a character in a war full of characters. Of average height, Ewell was mostly bald, had bulging eyes, and barked commands in a high-pitched voice. He had no control over a hot temper, yet he was a solid soldier always ready for battle.

Ewell and his division had been

General Richard Ewell ("Old Bald Head," to his men) served as Jackson's second-in-command for most of the Valley Campaign. Ewell grumbled about Jackson's secrecy and hard marches, but he came to have both respect and affection for "Stonewall."

sitting at Conrad's Store for three weeks. They had no idea where "that old fool" (as Ewell called Jackson) was or what Ewell was supposed to do. The nervous general poured out his frustrations over Jackson's secrecy to a niece: "I have been keeping one eye on Banks, one on Jackson, all the time jogged up from Richmond, until I am sick and wore down. . . . Now I ought to be en route to Gordonsville, at this place, and going to Jackson, all at the same time."[3]

Understanding terrain had always been difficult for Jackson. Recognizing this weakness, the general constantly consulted with his mapmaker, Jedidiah Hotchkiss.

The Shenandoah Valley Turnpike Jackson knew ran down the middle of the Valley floor from Winchester to Staunton. Parallel to it in the east, and stretching forty miles from Harrisonburg to Strasburg, lay a thickly wooded ridge called Massanutten Mountain. It was high enough to conceal the Blue Ridge Mountains farther to the east. A narrow road ran parallel to the Turnpike and snaked through the narrow valley formed by the Massanutten and Blue Ridge ranges. At only one point in that forty-mile stretch could the Massanutten be crossed: the pass at New Market.

Put simply, the middle of the Shenandoah Valley resembled a huge "H." The left upright was the Valley Turnpike between Harrisonburg and Strasburg; the right upright was the road to the east of

*Jackson's famed "foot cavalry" on the march. In the background,
soldiers are taking apples from a nearby orchard.*

*A postwar photograph of the key road running east from New Market and
crossing through the pass of the Massanutten Mountains.*

the Massanutten between Conrad's Store and Front Royal; the crossbar was the winding lane that zigzagged from New Market in the Valley to Luray in the hidden section behind the Massanutten.

Jackson's strategy was to march rapidly northward down the Valley, sneak through New Market Pass, unite with Ewell's division coming from Conrad's Store, and then continue north concealed behind the Massanutten. Hard marching would take him to Front Royal and Strasburg, less than twenty miles from Winchester. By defeating Union forces at those two advance posts, Jackson would have a clear route to the Federal supply base at Winchester. His seventeen thousand troops also gave him a two-to-one advantage in numbers over Banks.

That march in the third week of May was something no veteran under Jackson ever forgot. The general laid out every detail. The marching day began at 3:30 A.M. Troops moved four abreast. They carried their gun and equipment any way that was comfortable. The pace was a fast "route step"—walk as you please so long as you keep up with the column. Ten minutes of rest followed every fifty minutes of walking. The marching day lasted seventeen hours.[4]

Confederates swept through Harrisonburg and continued northward at such a rate that the infantrymen thereafter called themselves "foot cavalry"—implying that they could walk at least as swiftly as cavalrymen could ride. They were on their way to becoming "the fastest and hardest hitting force the country had ever seen."[5]

On one occasion, while the army was enjoying a brief rest, the Reverend Dabney preached at a field service. His biblical text appropriately was Matthew 11:28: "Come unto me, all ye that labour and are heavy laden, and I will give you rest."[6]

A dramatic moment broke the silence of the march. One of Ewell's privates wrote: "Hearing loud cheering to the rear, which came nearer and nearer, we soon saw that it was Stonewall himself, mounted on that old sorrel." Clad in a dusty uniform, perspiration glistening in his beard, head uncovered, Jackson galloped swiftly past the line. "We took up the shout," the private continued, "and gave a hearty greeting to the great captain, who had come to lead us to victory, and the mountains echoed and re-echoed with the great acclaim."[7]

Fortunately, Union soldiers did not hear the cheers.

Mile after mile, soldiers tramped through dust and mud. Men fell from ranks in a small but steady stream. Leg cramps, stomach cramps, and exhaustion from heat took a heavy toll. Yet the hard march accomplished its purpose.

On May 23, the enemy discovered Jackson's whereabouts in painful fashion. The Confederate 1st Maryland crashed like a tidal wave into the Union 1st Maryland garrison at Front Royal. Townspeople rushed into the streets to greet the Confederates. Nineteen-year-old Lucy Buck was struck by her first glimpse of the liberating Southerners. She saw "a grey figure upon horseback seemingly in command . . . *Seeing* was *believing,* and I

*This peaceful scene of Union soldiers on parade at Front Royal became chaos
when on May 23, 1862, Jackson unleashed a surprise attack.*

could only sink to my knees with my face in my hands and sob for joy."[8]

Union losses at Front Royal were 904 men, including 750 captured in the surprise attack. Jackson lost thirty-five men.

The next day, increasingly weary Confederates managed to get astride the Valley Turnpike. On the previous day, Banks had refused to believe danger existed, by shouting, "By God, sir, I will not retreat!"[9] Now he and sixty-five hundred Federals made a dash from Strasburg to Winchester. Confederates struck sharply at their flanks, but many of Jackson's men fell out of ranks to rest or to loot abandoned food-wagons.

On through the night, an iron-willed Jackson drove his soldiers. Most were in a

daze from fatigue. One wrote: "Moving at a snail's pace and falling asleep at the halts and being suddenly wakened up when the motion was resumed, we fairly staggered on, worn almost to exhaustion by the weariness of such a march."[10]

Around 2 A.M. on May 25, a colonel appealed to Jackson. "My men are falling by the roadside from fatigue and loss of sleep. Unless they are rested, I shall be able to present but a thin line tomorrow."

Jackson quietly replied: "Colonel, I yield to no man in sympathy for the gallant men under my command; but I am obliged to sweat them tonight, that I may save their blood tomorrow." Jackson reconsidered for a moment, then granted the men two hours to rest. He stood watch himself, a lone sentry for his pursuing army.[11]

At 4 A.M. ("early dawn," Jackson called it), troops resumed marching in the darkness. It was the Sabbath day, but rest and meditation were out of the question. Barely pausing from the advance, Jackson's soldiers made a full-scale attack. They clambered over the Union defenses. Federal soldiers broke in fright and raced through the streets of Winchester. "Order forward the whole line!" Jackson shouted. "The battle's won!" Then, while a staff officer stared in disbelief, the usually calm general waved his cap in the air and cheered loudly.[12]

Jackson galloped into the downtown and was greeted as a conquering hero. He later confided to Anna: "I do not remember ever having seen such rejoicing as was manifested by the people of Winchester as our army passed through the town . . . The people seemed nearly frantic with joy . . . Our entrance into Winchester was one of the most stirring scenes of my life."[13]

Midmorning found Banks's entire command fleeing in near-panic for the safety of the Potomac River. Jackson's men gave loud choruses of the "Rebel Yell" and pursued for several miles before being ordered to return to Winchester.

Three days of fighting from Front Royal to Winchester had cost Jackson four hundred men. His army had seized 3,030 soldiers, 9,300 small arms, and such a wealth of food, military stores, and medical supplies that Confederates gleefully referred to their Union opponent afterward as "Commissary

Banks." Jackson himself was being hailed as the "Liberator of Winchester" and the "Champion of the Valley."[14] He paid no attention to such praise.

The day after the battle, Jackson issued an order congratulating his men. "The hardships of forced marches are often more painful to the brave soldier than the dangers of battle," he stated. However, the "severe exertions" which the men suffered are "now given in the victory of yesterday." The events of the past three days were proof that "the hand of a Protecting Providence" had led them from success to success.[15]

President Lincoln now entered the Valley Campaign. He wired McClellan near Richmond: "In consequence of Gen. Banks' critical position, I have been compelled to suspend Gen. McDowell's movement [from Fredericksburg] to join you. The enemy are making a desperate push upon Harper's Ferry, and we are trying to throw Fremont's force & part of McDowell's in their rear."[16] Jackson's plan was working perfectly to that point.

The War Department started reinforcements to the hapless Banks. If General James Shields's thirty thousand Federals moving west from Fredericksburg joined forces around Strasburg with Fremont's seventeen thousand soldiers heading east through the mountains, Jackson's little army would be trapped between two Union hosts coming from opposite directions.

Lincoln watched the Federal strategy get underway. He predicted that the outcome would be "a question of legs."[17]

Close coordination and solid execution were necessary, but the side that moved with greatest dispatch would win.

Both Fremont and Shields failed to see the need for speed. Jackson, on the other hand, got his men on the road and made them earn anew their nickname of "foot cavalry." In less than a day, some Confederate units marched as much as thirty-five miles in an effort to escape the Union trap.

Meanwhile, as Ewell led his division past Strasburg, he spotted what was the advance of Fremont's army to the west.

Ewell ordered General Richard Taylor's Louisiana brigade to make a lunge toward the Union flank. Fremont's men scattered at the approach of the Louisianians. It was a "walk-over," Taylor wrote scornfully. "Sheep would have made as much resistance as we met."[18] Jackson's force reunited and marched past the two supposedly converging Union forces. That defeat coupled with Shields's slow advance from the east assured the Confederates' escape. One Confederate later boasted that Jackson's men "slipped through the jaws of the closing vise like a greased rat."[19]

Lead officers in Fremont's Union army arrive in the Valley too late to trap the retreating Jackson. The Confederate wagon train can be seen moving left to right on the Valley Turnpike.

While this move was taking place, major events developed elsewhere in Virginia. General Joseph E. Johnston took advantage of McDowell not joining McClellan. On May 31, Johnston attacked a portion of the Union army east of Richmond at Seven Pines. Confused fighting raged for two days. In the middle of it, Johnston fell seriously wounded. President Jefferson Davis wasted no time in naming General Robert E. Lee to command the Army of Northern Virginia.

This appointment pleased Jackson, who urged his tired troops to maintain a steady pace as they continued up the Valley. Ashby and his cavalry burned bridges and conducted raids here and there to keep the Federals slowed down and off balance. Horrible weather persisted. For hours the men trudged through rain and mud. Straggling and sickness thinned the ranks. Captain James Edmondson of the 27th Virginia in the Stonewall Brigade noted that his regiment a month earlier had 418 able-bodied men but was now down to 150 staggering soldiers. "I never saw a brigade so completely broken down and unfitted for service," Edmondson wrote.[20]

The marches were terrible ordeals, but they put Jackson's men well ahead of their pursuers while they gave the general time to consider a place and time for attack. Jackson left the Valley Turnpike at Harrisonburg, turned east, and made for the Port Republic area at the base of the Blue Ridge Mountains. There was where he would make his stand.

Fremont made a cautious chase on the Turnpike while Shields advanced up the Luray Valley Road. Ashby's bridge-burners kept the two Union forces from uniting. Yet on June 6, in a skirmish on the outskirts of Harrisonburg, Jackson lost his chief of cavalry. The dashing Ashby had known his finest hours in the past few days. He was killed while leading an attack on foot against advancing Federals. "As a partisan officer I never knew his superior," Jackson reported. "His daring was proverbial. His powers of endurance incredible."[21]

Jackson had no time to mourn. The enemy was where he wanted him: divided by the South Fork River and advancing. On June 8, Ewell's portion of the Confederate army easily beat back Fremont's weak assaults at Cross Keys. Jackson, three miles away at Port Republic, barely escaped capture that Sunday.

The general was preparing to attend morning worship services when a Union raiding party of one hundred and fifty cavalry and four cannons came out of nowhere into Port Republic. Jackson dashed through the town with bullets whizzing around him and successfully reached high ground on the other side of the river. Confederates soon routed the Union party in what became Jackson's most narrow escape in the Civil War.[22]

Jackson on the hilltop watched the Union horsemen flee Port Republic. Slowly he raised both hands heavenward. Soldiers in the town below saw their pious general silhouetted against the blue sky and burst into loud cheers.[23]

The next day was Jackson's turn to do battle. In early morning he attacked Shields's

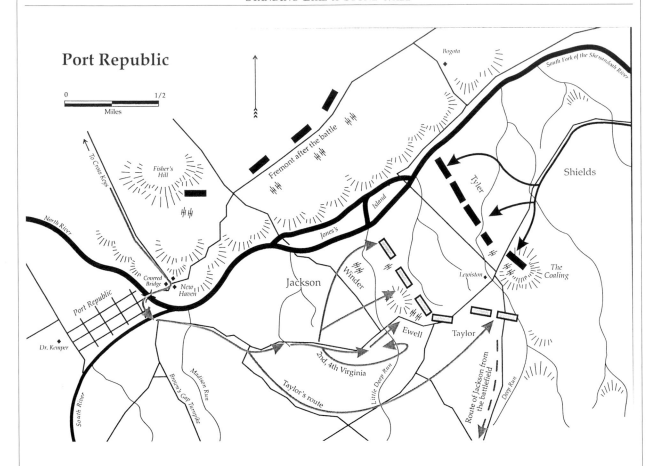

lines north of Port Republic. Jackson was reckless in his tactical execution. Unwilling to wait until he had all of his troops at hand, he threw his units into action in piecemeal fashion. Personal weariness may have been the excuse.

Spearheading his assault was Jackson's old command, the Stonewall Brigade. It was thrown back with heavy losses. For the next two hours, the hardest fighting in the campaign took place. Union artillery on a mountain spur to Jackson's right sent deadly salvos into the Confederate flank, while Federal infantry in the center grimly poured musketry into the attacking lines. Taylor's Louisiana brigade, arriving from Cross Keys, assailed the artillery position.

Just as it appeared that Taylor's assaults would fail, other regiments from Ewell's division reached the field and added their weight to Taylor's drive.

Federals slowly abandoned the field. At the moment of victory, one of Jackson's men saw the general sitting on Little Sorrel. Jackson's head was bowed; his right hand pointed upward. Again the time for thanksgiving was at hand.[24] Confederate losses were eight hundred men killed and wounded. Shields's casualties, including those captured later in the day on the retreat, exceeded one thousand soldiers.[25]

By nightfall, both Fremont and Shields were retiring in beaten fashion toward Winchester. One of the most remarkable campaigns in military history had ended. Among the first men to recognize what Jackson had done was "Baldy Dick" Ewell. At the beginning of the campaign, Jackson's subordinate had fretted and fumed and called the general insane. "I take it all back!" Ewell now exclaimed. "I will never prejudge another man. Old Jackson's no fool. He has a method in his madness!"[26]

With never more than seventeen thousand poorly equipped soldiers, Jackson had completely scattered sixty-five thousand Federals sent to destroy him. His men had marched 676 miles in 48 days, fought four battles as well as a dozen skirmishes and delaying actions. Confederates had inflicted five thousand casualties at a loss of barely half that number. Immense quantities of arms and supplies had been seized.

Union General Irvin McDowell saw Jackson's genius. He remarked to a fellow officer midway through the campaign: "If the enemy can succeed so readily in disconcerting all our plans by alarming us first at one point, then at another, he will paralyze a large force with a very small one."[27] Even a New York newspaper openly praised Jackson. "He handles his army like a whip, making it crack in out of the way corners where you scarcely thought the lash would reach."[28]

Not only had Jackson routed the enemy from the Shenandoah Valley. The Civil War, which appeared to be close to Union victory in the early spring, had been turned upside down in Virginia by late spring. This all happened because of one man.

Jackson demonstrated in the Valley his two principles for success in battle. "Always mystify, mislead, and surprise the enemy, if possible; and when you strike and overcome him, never let up in the pursuit so long as your men have strength to follow; for an army routed, if hotly pursued, becomes panic-stricken." Second, "never fight against heavy odds, if by any possible maneuvering you can hurl your own force on . . . the weakest part of the enemy and crush it. Such tactics will win every time, and a small army may thus destroy a large one in detail, and repeated victory will make it invincible."[29]

As in all of his military activities, Jackson steadfastly refused to take any credit for achievements. He told his wife in a short note: "God has been our shield, and to His name be all the glory."[30]

The only praise Jackson might have accepted he never heard. It came from one of his young cannoneers, who wrote home: "It is such a comfort and a great cause for thanksgiving to have such a Christian as Jackson as our general. No wonder the blessing of God attends his army in such a signal way."[31]

In the days that followed, deep weariness in Jackson became more evident. The long campaign in the Shenandoah with its hard marches, foul weather, heavy fighting, strong emotions, pressing responsibilities, and little time for rest had sapped the general's strength. Fatigue and his strong personality caused a number of conflicts with subordinates in the campaign. Jackson had removed Garnett and a Georgia colonel from command; he had argued with Generals Ashby, Winder, and Arnold Elzey; a quarrel with Major Harman led the quartermaster to offer his resignation (which Jackson refused to accept).

As tired as he was, Jackson after Port Republic began thinking of a new attack against the Union invaders. Two possibilities existed. One was to drive northward again and perhaps invade not only Maryland but Pennsylvania as well. This option did not appeal to him unless he was strengthened with large reinforcements.

The other choice for Jackson was to slip across the Blue Ridge Mountains and move rapidly to Richmond. There he would join with General Lee and assist in a counteroffensive against McClellan's forces. That massive Army of the Potomac was the biggest threat in Virginia. It must somehow be checked.

Meanwhile, Jackson gave his men a few days' rest in the fertile farmland around Port Republic. On Sunday, June 14, the general called his men to a day of worship and thanksgiving. Field services were held in every encampment, with Jackson attending as many of the meetings as he could. "How I do wish for peace," he wrote Anna at this time. Later he asked her almost prayerfully: "Wouldn't you like to get home again?"[32]

By mid-June, Lee made the decision to summon Jackson's forces to Richmond. Union General McDowell's forty thousand men were poised at Fredericksburg to join McClellan. To offset such an action, Jackson had to travel twice the distance to reach the capital before McDowell got there.

It could be done. Combining the forces of Lee and Jackson would require elements for which Jackson was now famous: secrecy and hard marches. Having Jackson at Richmond would fulfill two of Lee's greatest talents: concentration and inner lines of defense.

The psychological impact of Jackson's presence was another factor in Lee's thinking. "Jackson now ranked as the hope of the Confederacy," one writer asserted. "No other star burned so brightly in the firmament, no other general dared so much. . . . Everywhere in the South, and in many parts of the North, the name 'Stonewall' was magic."[33]

On June 17, Jackson put his army in motion. Brigade commanders got no instructions as to where they were going. Secrecy covered everything, which prompted one hot-tempered general to exclaim: "I believe [Jackson] hasn't more sense than my horse!" When that officer received orders to backtrack to the spot where he had begun his march, he exploded. "Didn't I tell you he was a fool?" he shouted to an aide.[34]

All the soldiers knew was that they were heading east across the Blue Ridge. "Never take counsel of your fears," Jackson always warned.[35] Under "Old Jack's" leadership, pride and confidence drowned out the fears. The men knew, too, that hard marching was the path to victory.

A joke circulated through the ranks

The general, receiving cheers from his men as
"Little Sorrel" gallops past the column. Jackson always removed his hat to
acknowledge such affection from the soldiers.

as the men struggled up the mountainside. Two soldiers were enjoying a brief rest when one wearily said: "I wish all the Yankees was in Hell!"

"And faith," his companion answered, "I don't wish anything of the sort."

The first man said: "The divvel you don't, and why don't you?"

"Because," came the reply, "Old Jack would have us standing picket at the gate before night and in there before morning—and it's too hot where we is to suit me!"[36]

Chapter X

Exhaustion and Disappointments

Secrecy marked Jackson's every military movement and gave a new and different meaning to the name "Stonewall." When told to get their men on the road for a march, division and brigade commanders could never learn where they were to go. Jackson would answer their queries by telling them to follow the troops in front of them.

"He mystified and deceived the enemy by concealment from his own generals and his own staff," an aide noted. "We were led to believe things that were very far from his purpose." Jackson liked it that way. He once observed: "If I can keep my movements secret from my own people, I will have little difficulty in concealing them from the enemy."[1]

Becoming more weary with each passing day, Jackson wrapped himself in even greater secretiveness. He informed only his chief of staff, Major Robert L. Dabney, where he was headed. Then he slipped away from his army and headed for Charlottesville accompanied only by three aides. As Jackson passed through Charlottesville, an old man recognized him and shouted: "General, where are you going?"

"Can you keep a secret?" Jackson asked.

"Yes," the man replied eagerly.

"Ah, so can I," Jackson said as he ended the conversation.[2]

All that night and half of the next day Jackson traveled fifty-two miles to Richmond. Mud-splattered and bone-tired, he arrived in midafternoon on June 23 at army headquarters just outside the capital. Along with other high-ranking generals—James Longstreet, A. P. Hill, and D. Harvey Hill—Jackson entered the office of the new commanding general, Robert E. Lee. Jackson was impressed the moment he saw the man now leading the Army of Northern Virginia.

Robert E. Lee was seventeen years older than Jackson. Three decades of distinguished service in the U.S. Army had made Lee by 1861 one of the most respected American officers on duty. Lee had declined an offer to command all Union forces at the beginning of the Civil War. His Virginia roots were too deep. His fate, and that of his native state, were intertwined as one.

Gray hair and beard made Lee appear older than he was. Lee the gentleman was always evident in his calm manner and courteous behavior. He seemed almost out of place in the uniform of an army commander. His dark brown eyes, an English visitor noted, were "remarkably direct and honest as they meet you fully and firmly."[3]

Jackson's respect for Lee was obvious and exceeded his feeling for any other officer in the field. A Confederate who knew them both asserted that Jackson came

George B. McClellan, first commander of the Union Army of the Potomac,
was in the same West Point class as Jackson. McClellan thought his Confederate opponent
"a man of vigor and nerve, as well as a soldier."

to regard Lee "with mingled love and admiration. To excite such feelings in a man like Jackson, it was necessary that Lee should be not only a soldier of the first order of genius, but also a good and pious man. It was in these lights that Jackson regarded his commander, and from first to last his confidence in and admiration for him never wavered."[4]

To his generals that afternoon, Lee outlined a bold and risky maneuver. McClellan's army was just east of Richmond on the peninsula formed by the eastward flowing Pamunkey and James Rivers. The average width of the peninsula was sixteen miles. A third stream would also play an important role. The Chickahominy River ran diagonally across the peninsula and cut straight through the Union army. Some seventy thousand of McClellan's troops were south of the Chickahominy. North of the river, which was heavily swollen by recent rains, was General Fitz John Porter's Union corps of thirty thousand soldiers.

Thanks to a daring reconnaissance (scouting mission) by twelve hundred horsemen under General "Jeb" Stuart, Lee knew that Porter's right or northern flank was "up in the air." It was neither anchored on some strong terrain feature nor curved back to form a strong defensive front.

Lee's plan was to shift the bulk of his army—forty-five thousand men—to Porter's front. Jackson and his eighteen thousand "foot cavalry" were to march in from the west. Lee could then launch an attack on two fronts. While Jackson turned Porter's flank and struck from the rear, Lee would assail Porter's front. Lee and Jackson together should be able to drive southward. They would not only cut off McClellan from his supply base on the Pamunkey River; the two Confederate wings could topple one Federal unit against the other until McClellan's invaders were driven into the James River.

Fun-loving, daring, and dependable "Jeb" Stuart commanded the cavalry in Lee's army. Stuart and Jackson became good friends despite the fact that they were completely unalike in personality.

The grand assault was set for June 26, three days after the conference. Lee was taking an enormous gamble by transferring most of his army to the Union right flank. If McClellan should learn of the movement, only a fourth of Lee's small force stood between the Army of the Potomac and Richmond. Further, the Southern general with the farthest distance to travel for the attack—Jackson—would make the first strike. Yet as outnumbered as he was, Lee had to take chances. Otherwise, the law of averages or simple odds would work against him.

Jackson was the key to the success of the entire strategy. After a four-hour meeting at Lee's headquarters, Jackson remounted Little Sorrel and started back on another all-night ride to join his army.[5] He found his forces both scattered and behind schedule. Lax discipline by subordinate officers had created disorder. His forces were strung out in the rain for fifteen miles.

Over the next two days, Jackson led his men on a grueling forty-mile march in hot and muggy weather. The general got only eight hours' sleep during those three

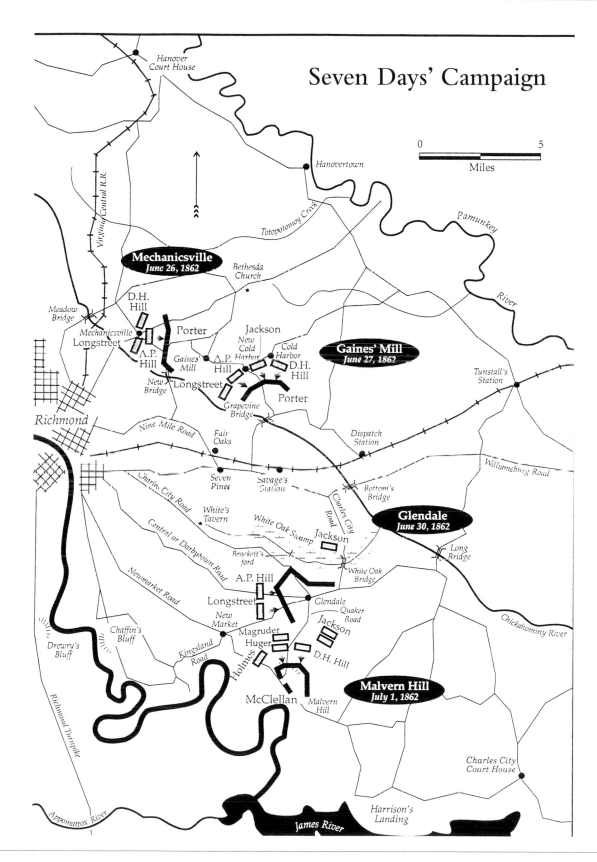

Seven Days' Campaign

0   5
Miles

Hanover
Court House

Hanovertown

Pamunkey

Totopotomoy Creek

River

Virginia Central R.R.

Mechanicsville
June 26, 1862

Bethesda
Church

Meadow
Bridge

D.H.
Hill

Mechanicsville

Porter

Jackson
New
Cold
Harbor

Cold
Harbor

Gaines' Mill
June 27, 1862

Tunstall's
Station

Longstreet

A.P.
Hill

Gaines'
Mill

A.P.
Hill

D.H.
Hill

New
Bridge

Longstreet

Porter

Richmond

Grapevine
Bridge

Nine Mile Road

Fair
Oaks

Dispatch
Station

Williamsburg Road

Seven
Pines

Savage's
Station

Bottom's
Bridge

Charles City Road

White's
Tavern

White Oak Swamp

Jackson

Glendale
June 30, 1862

Long
Bridge

Central or Darbytown Road

Brackett's
ford

White Oak
Bridge

Newmarket Road

A.P. Hill

Longstreet

Glendale

Quaker
Road

Chickahominy River

Chaffin's
Bluff

New
Market

Jackson

Drewry's
Bluff

Kingsland
Road

Magruder

Huger

D.H. Hill

Holmes

Malvern Hill
July 1, 1862

Richmond Turnpike

McClellan

Malvern
Hill

Charles City
Court House

Appomattox River

James River

Harrison's
Landing

days of activity. He was still hours late when the Seven Days' battles began on June 26 at Mechanicsville.

For the Confederates, everything went wrong from the start. The fault lay mainly with the hero of the hour, Jackson.

When the Valley soldiers failed to reach the attack point, three divisions of Lee's army attacked the Union position on their own. The fighting at Beaver Dam Creek was a frightful, botched affair from start to end. Confederate losses were fifteen hundred men to three hundred and sixty casualties for the Federals.

Jackson was less than three miles away during the battle but never reached the field. Lee's instructions for Jackson's march contained so many unfamiliar road names, and so many possible options, that Jackson's weary mind reacted with bewilderment.[6] No local guide was there to help. In addition, aide Henry Kyd Douglas of his staff declared, Jackson "knew nothing about the country—with which every other [Confederate] General of high rank was doubtless familiar."[7]

The mere presence of Jackson on the peninsula did threaten Porter's flank enough for the Union general to withdraw his men under darkness to an even stronger point at Boatswain's Swamp and Gaines' Mill. While Porter was making his five-mile retreat, Lee's chief of cavalry rode into Jackson's bivouac for a brief conference. Jeb Stuart and Jackson had several similarities. Both were tall, well-built, and possessed of deep faith, high patriotism, and a combative spirit.

Their differences were more pronounced. Stuart was a dashing cavalier who enjoyed gaiety, jokes, and colorful uniforms. Jackson disliked all of those things. Stuart's adjutant, Captain William Blackford, was struck by the contrast in appearance between the two men. Stuart, clad in bright uniform and shining boots, rode a great stallion. Jackson "was mounted upon a [horse] of very sorry appearance, though substantial in build, and was dressed in a threadbare, faded, semi-military suit, with a disreputable old Virginia Military Institute cap drawn down over his eyes."[8]

McClellan had now abandoned thoughts of capturing Richmond. That night of June 26, both he and Lee were thinking the same thing: whether the Federal army might be defeated. McClellan determined to establish a new base at the other end of the peninsula on the James River.

Federal units began what McClellan called "a strategic withdrawal." Lee mistakenly assumed that McClellan would fight to control the land north of the Chickahominy. Fitz John Porter's second gallant stand on June 27 pointed to such a conclusion.

Lee opened attacks on Porter at Gaines' Mill. Again Jackson was late. Even though he met with Lee early in the morning, the two generals seemed to misunderstand the intentions of the other. Lee still wanted Jackson to make a sweeping movement and turn Porter's flank—this time at Gaines' Mill. Jackson took Lee's orders to mean that he was to march toward the important road junction of Cold Harbor, far in the rear of the Union forces, and be ready to attack if Porter retreated in that direction.

An artist's impression of General Robert E. Lee (left) conferring with Jackson on the Virginia peninsula.

"Old Jack's" failures throughout this campaign stemmed from a number of factors. His tardiness during the first two days of action gave him no time to make any careful preparations. He was in strange country he had never before seen. The vigilant Turner Ashby was dead. Jackson's terrain guide and mapmaker, Jed Hotchkiss, was in Staunton on detached duty. No decent maps were available. Jackson's men were worn out from marching and could not increase the pace to meet Lee's schedule. Blazing heat, and wilting humidity from the river bottoms beat down everyone. Lee's directives were few and not always clear.

A guide sent to lead Jackson to the action at Gaines' Mill mistakenly led the Confederates away from the battle. This meant a useless three-mile march and more time lost. When Major Dabney of the staff asked Jackson if the latest delay might be fatal, the general answered in an even tone: "No, let us trust that the providence of our God will so overrule it, that no mischief shall result."[9]

Despite Jackson's trust in God, his nerves were on edge and his temper grew increasingly short. Groping blindly on a steaming peninsula was unpleasant. Not knowing the whereabouts of either friend or foe was agonizing. But there was more. Unknown to everyone, Jackson was reaching the limit of his endurance. He was slowly going into a stupor caused by complete fatigue.

On into the afternoon Jackson's forces slowly gravitated toward the roar of combat. They finally came onto the field at Gaines' Mill. Brigades rushed into battle position where they were needed. Word swept down the battered Confederate line. "A deafening shout burst from our men," one of Longstreet's privates asserted. "Thousands of throats took it up and rent the very air . . . Stonewall Jackson here!"[10]

Jackson was covered with dust, his kepi pulled down over his eyes, his body slumped in the saddle from fatigue. Lee rode swiftly to him. "Ah, General," the commander said, "I am very glad to see you. I had hoped to be with you before."

If Jackson was aware of the veiled criticism, he made no sign. He merely gave a quick jerk of his head as he surveyed the field of battle.

Lee continued: "The fire is heavy. Do you think your men can stand it?"

Jackson was silent for a moment, then answered: "They can stand almost anything! They can stand that!"[11]

It was 7 P.M. and the sun was setting when the largest assault of the Civil War to that point occurred. The entire Confederate line—over fifty thousand soldiers—surged forward with a roar of gunfire and cheers. They charged through swamps and dense underbrush; they scrambled up wet hillsides and slammed into the Union lines.

A Virginia soldier from the Valley later wrote: "If you can form an idea of a hundred or more cannon and one hundred thousand or more small arms, and sometimes thousands of men—yelling at the top of their voices—than you can begin to understand the raging terror and the roaring, lumbering noise of this battle that was going on."[12]

Billy Yanks waged a determined stand, but weight of numbers from this desperate, all-or-nothing attack by Lee finally broke the Federal lines.

Jackson had watched the action intently. One of his colonels studied the general with equal interest. "His teeth were clinched," the colonel observed, "his lips clamped closer than ever, and the blaze of his eye alone betrayed excitement. Straight in the saddle, straighter than usual . . . he sat, his head raised up, catching every sound."

Suddenly Jackson jerked and raised his right arm. The colonel thought he was being summoned and rode over to Jackson. Instead, he found the general with his arm raised and head bowed—in silent prayer for the victory.[13]

Union soldiers retired across the Chickahominy, burning bridges behind them. Gaines' Mill would be the costliest engagement of the Seven Days' campaign. Total losses on both sides were more than 15,200 men, including 2,300 killed outright in battle.

Lee not only had won a hard-fought victory, he now controlled all the land north of the Chickahominy. The Union army was in full retreat toward the James River. Lee's hope now was to smash McClellan's army as it withdrew across the peninsula.

Yet this was Lee's first experience at commanding an army in battle. His orders were few; and when they did come, they seemed too complicated for his division leaders to execute. Cooperation, missing at Mechaincsville and Gaines' Mill, would be lacking for the remainder of the campaign. It would cost the Confederates dearly.

Jackson spent June 28 cleaning up the battlefield and rebuilding bridges across the Chickahominy. A staff officer watched burial details move out onto the Gaines' Mill battleground. "They buried friend & foe alike in the same trench," he wrote. "They would dig large ditches, wide, and tumble these dead men in without ceremony or decency even. It was shocking to one unaccustomed to the cruelties of war."[14]

Work was still in progress on the bridges the following day when another mix-up took place. General John B. Magruder, Jackson's former battery commander in the Mexican War, commanded a division in Lee's army.

Magruder received a directive to attack Savage Station, an advance Federal base on the York River Railroad. Magruder was led to believe that Jackson was to lend assistance in the assault. However, Jackson's orders from Lee were to guard the Chickahominy crossings and block any Union movements from the north or east. That left Magruder alone. His weak and halfhearted attacks at Savage Station produced casualties and little else.

The battle order on June 30 called for Jackson to march due south and menace the rear elements of the retreating Union army. Meanwhile, Generals Longstreet and Powell Hill were to sweep west and then circle in on the Union right flank. Longstreet and Hill were both under the impression that Jackson would make a supporting attack. Jackson had no orders to that effect.

One of the crude wooden bridges that Jackson used in crossing the Chickahominy River.

*Some of the wounded soldiers Jackson met
when his forces swept through Savage Station during
the Seven Days' campaign.*

Early in the morning, Jackson reached Savage Station. Federals had abandoned the depot, leaving behind twenty-five hundred wounded and sick soldiers as well as tons of military supplies. When an officer grumbled about how expensive it was going to be for the Confederates to house all of those prisoners, Jackson quietly replied: "It is cheaper to feed them than to fight them."[15]

While his men cleaned up the Savage Station area, Jackson sent a quick note to Anna. "I had a wet bed last night, as the rain fell in torrents. I got up about midnight, and haven't seen much rest since. I hope that our God will soon bless us with an honorable peace & permit us to be together again . . ."[16]

The march resumed down a narrow, twisting road. Around noon, Jackson arrived at White Oak Swamp. What was normally a shallow stream was now a vast quagmire of waterlogged underbrush and slime. Federals had burned the one bridge across the bog.

Jackson's advance came to a full stop. While the general sought to locate a ford or usable road that would take his forces to the other side, Union cannons hidden in thick woods opened a direct fire into the Southern ranks. Jackson personally rode with the head of his cavalry, Colonel Thomas T. Munford, through the swamp in search of a crossing. Enemy musketry quickly drove him back to the woods on the north side. Another movement had been thwarted.

At that point, Jackson lost the last ounce of strength. His iron endurance could take no more. Exertions in the Valley, the exhausting round-trip ride to confer with

Lee at Richmond, the rush to get his men a third of the way across the state—these factors became the foundation.

The Seven Days' campaign then brought long hours of duty and marches, battles and anxieties, worries and contemplations, frustrations and failures. All of this caught up with Jackson at White Oak Swamp. Further, he was ill—the only time in the Civil War that he confessed to being sick. He was suffering from what he called "fever and debility."[17]

Around 3:00 that afternoon, Jackson sat down on a log. He remained motionless and silent as officers reported. After a while, he walked to a large oak, eased to the ground, and propped against the trunk, then instantly slipped into a deep sleep. Hours passed; cannons barked, musketry crackled, men shouted. Jackson slept through it all. A staff officer in the Stonewall Brigade rode to the headquarters area. Everyone was standing around idly. "It looked to me," the officer said, "as if on our side we were waiting for Jackson to wake up."[18]

How worn out the general was became evident to his staff when they sat together at sundown for supper. Jackson's head dropped to his chest. He fell asleep again, this time with a biscuit clinched between his teeth. A few minutes later, he reawakened. Jackson stared blankly at his aides and then exclaimed: "Now, gentlemen, let us at once to bed, and rise with the dawn, and see if tomorrow we cannot *do something!*"[19]

July 1 was the last day of the Seven Days' battles. Lee had suffered high casualties. Among those lost were nine of his thirty-eight brigade commanders. Still, the Confederate commander searched for one great blow that would cripple if not destroy the Army of the Potomac.

The final engagement was the most disastrous for the Southern army. Lee found McClellan drawn up on Malvern Hill. This broad height rose only fifty yards above the countryside, but it gave those atop the hill an open field of fire. Union cannons bristled from one end to the other. Rows of blue-clad infantry stood poised in support of the guns. Behind Malvern Hill, Union

naval vessels anchored in the James had large-caliber pieces to lend assistance to McClellan's army.

Lee had so much difficulty in getting his army into battle position that the attack did not come until late afternoon. When Confederate artillery moved up to provide support fire, Federal cannons destroyed them. Fifty Union guns at a time would focus on each Southern battery. More than once, Jackson dismounted and helped roll cannons into place—only to see the gun blown apart by enemy fire.

At other times, aide John Gittings

The June 30, 1862, action at White Oak Swamp.
Union artillery in the foreground is bombarding Jackson's troops
on the plain in the distance.

*General Robert E. Lee, commander of
the Confederate Army of Northern Virginia and widely considered
to be among America's greatest soldiers.*

noticed, the Valley warrior "sat erect on his horse, in the hurricane of canister and grape [shot]; his face was aflame with passion." Gittings added: "Before he was entirely obscured from our view, the soldiers would turn, at brief intervals, to look back on him."[20]

Lee's infantry attacks withered under concentrated fire. On no other battlefield in the Civil War did Union artillery so dominate the action as occurred at Malvern Hill. Jackson's brother-in-law, General Harvey Hill, watched his ranks torn apart by shells. "It was not war, it was murder," he snarled.[21] Lee lost five thousand men in the one-sided contest.

At one point, he almost lost Jackson as well. The general was behind the lines, writing a memo while seated against a tree beside the road. A Union shell exploded in the road, killed several marching soldiers, and showered Jackson with dirt. The general calmly shook the paper clean and continued writing.[22]

That night, faithful servant Jim Lewis prepared as large a supper as he could. Lewis then made a bed for Jackson in a nearby farmyard. The general stretched out and quickly fell asleep. Around 1 A.M., Generals Ewell and Harvey Hill came to give reports. No one dared awaken Jackson. So generals and aides all squatted around the sleeping form like a circle of frogs.

Jackson partially awoke. He listened as the generals warned of a possible attack by McClellan the next day. Half-asleep, Jackson answered: "Oh, no, there will be no enemy there in the morning."[23]

Through the dawn mist of July 2, Confederates were surprised to see Malvern Hill deserted. McClellan had pulled his army back to the banks of the James River. The campaign, now over, had cost Lee twenty thousand men to McClellan's sixteen thousand losses.

The battles had been indecisive. Even were one to assess it as a Confederate defeat, Lee's boldness had both shattered McClellan's grand strategy and saved Richmond—at least for the moment. In addition, Lee's overall success had come at a time when Confederate defeats in the west at Shiloh and New Orleans had brought morale to a new low. Now the Southern nation had a rekindled spirit.

Jackson arose on July 2 and, true to character, wanted to press forward for a resumption of battle with the enemy. Heavy rain was falling, the roads were mud lanes, and the exact location of the Union army was unknown. Two days passed before Lee gave orders to advance slowly toward the James.

A day's march through deep mud netted but three miles. By then, Jackson's temper had grown short, his conversation testy. That night he told his staff: "Jim will have breakfast for you punctually at dawn. I expect you to be up, to eat immediately, and be in the saddle with me. We must burn no more daylight."

Jackson was awake at first light the next morning. Jim Lewis had a hot breakfast waiting. Only a sleepy Major Dabney joined the general. Jackson angrily shouted: "Jim, put the food in the chest, lock it, have the chest in the wagon and the wagon moving in two minutes! Do you hear?"

Without eating, the general mounted Little Sorrel and galloped away. Old Jim commented: "My stars, but the General is just mad this time—most like lightening struck him!"[24]

McClellan's army was too strongly entrenched to be attacked. Lee drew back to the old Confederate encampments around Richmond. Jackson and his men at last got some much-needed rest. The two armies would stare defiantly at each other for the next several weeks. As they did so, a new danger threatened Virginia.

Northern authorities had created a new field force to operate against Richmond. Known as the Army of Virginia, it consisted of the scattered divisions of Banks, McDowell, and Fremont that had pressured Jackson in the Shenandoah Valley. The commander of the army was General John Pope, a swaggering braggart. When Pope reportedly dated one of his early directives "Headquarters in the Saddle," Southern soldiers hooted that they could whip any Yankee general who put his headquarters where his hindquarters ought to be.[25]

Pope moved his army into north-central Virginia. From the Confederate viewpoint, he could not be allowed to drive uncontested through the heart of the state. Lee had to gamble again.

On July 13, Lee divided his even smaller force. While the main army continued to watch McClellan, Jackson with his and Ewell's divisions were ordered to the rail junction of Gordonsville in the central piedmont. There Jackson was "to observe the enemy's movements closely [and] to avail himself of any opportunity to attack that might arise."[26]

Jackson promptly left Richmond with eighteen thousand men on eighteen trains, fifteen cars each. His job was to stop fifty-one thousand Federals from seizing the middle third of Virginia. Once again Jackson was leading an independent command; once again he was going up against heavy odds.

He had no concerns. Subjected to cheers wherever he went, Jackson told Anna: "People are very kind to me. How God, our God, does shower blessings upon me, an unworthy servant."[27]

✵ CHAPTER XI ✵

A SECOND VISIT TO MANASSAS

JACKSON WAS ALWAYS tone-deaf where music was concerned. This was evident when, on the way to Gordonsville, he stopped for the night at a private home. The general was in a good mood and chatted easily with the family. A young girl began playing the piano and singing for him. Jackson listened intently.

She finished a song. Jackson showed his pleasure by saying: "Miss, won't you play a piece of music they called 'Dixie'? I heard it a few days ago and it was, I thought, very beautiful."

The girl stared red-faced and silent, then managed to reply: "Why, General, I just sang it."[1]

Jackson headed west with a new chief of staff. The Reverend Dabney had resigned from the army because of health problems. At the head of Jackson's staff was twenty-two-year-old Alexander "Sandie" Pendleton. He had entered Washington College at the age of thirteen. Pendleton wrote clear, precise orders and possessed a photographic memory for details. Whenever someone would request information on some minute point, Jackson was inclined to answer: "Ask Sandie Pendleton. If he does not know, no one does."[2]

The rest of Jackson's "military family" was now established. John A. Harman, a former stagecoach owner, was quartermaster. He was a good man in spite of his rough nature and penchant for swearing. "Soldiers used to say," one officer wrote, "that Harman could start a mule train a mile long by his strong language at the back end."[3]

Wells J. Hawks, the commissary officer, was a transplanted son of Massachusetts, former mayor of Charles Town, and veteran Virginia legislator. Hawks had a genius for having food available for soldiers when it existed nearby. Dr. Hunter McGuire was the medical director and looked much younger than his mid-twenties. McGuire had organized the medical service in the Valley, made improvements in the use of ambulance wagons, and developed the first system of mobile field hospitals in the Confederacy.

Jed Hotchkiss would continue to the end as Jackson's mapmaker. Among the volunteer aides were Henry Kyd Douglas, theological student James Power Smith, and Jackson's young brother-in-law, Joseph G. Morrison. All told, the men surrounding Jackson made for one of the most talented staffs in the Civil War.

A continuing problem Jackson now had was that his fame so often interfered with his efforts at secrecy. One of Jeb Stuart's aides was a giant Prussian named Heros Von Borcke. He noted at this time: "The great Stonewall gave but little thought to the comforts of life, but he was so much

*Jackson's men were poorly clothed and
poorly equipped, but they prided themselves on long marches,
hard fighting, and complete faith in their general.*

the pet of the people that all the planters and farmers in whose neighborhood he erected his simple tent, vied with each other in supplying him abundantly with the delicacies of the table."[4]

Jackson arrived at the rail junction of Gordonsville on July 19 and officially pronounced the village "Headquarters, Valley District." Until that moment, his soldiers had not known their destination. A disgusted brigadier general wrote his wife: "I feel like a wandering Jew. Jackson is never satisfied unless he is marching or fighting so that I have no hope of seeing you until the war is over."[5]

Lee's instructions to Jackson were twofold: to guard the Virginia Central Railroad and to attack any Federals who advanced too close to the line. Jackson posted strong guards all along the rail tracks. The Virginia Central's value to Richmond was life itself. It was the one line into the Shenandoah Valley, from which came the food necessary for the capital's survival.

The line, if captured, could be a boulevard for Federals moving on Richmond.

As always, discipline became the first order of business in Jackson's camps. Many courts-martial went into session to deal with the large number of accumulated cases involving disobedience of orders, Jackson soon confessed to having every one of his general officers serving as a judge on at least one tribunal.[6]

Hours of daily drill kept the men occupied. Maintaining clean camps, Jackson believed, was a key to good health. Policing encampments was a regular duty. "Home" for Jackson in Gordonsville was the front yard of the Barbour residence. Mrs. Barbour's son-in-law was the Reverend Daniel B. Ewing, whom Jackson had met a month earlier on the way to Richmond. Although the general lived in his headquarters tent, he spent many pleasant hours with the Presbyterian cleric and his family. The hospitality of the Ewings, their deep faith, plus the presence of loving children in the manse, reminded Jackson of the happy weeks with the Grahams in Winchester.

In mid-July, General John Pope's new

Confederate general A. P. Hill was an aggressive and bold fighter, but his pride, sensitivity, and failure to move promptly brought a long and bitter feud with Jackson.

Union army moved south in the direction of Culpeper and Gordonsville. Lee reacted by sending Jackson needed reinforcements: the battle-hardened Light Division, under proud and strong-minded A. P. Hill. Lee knew that Hill and Jackson were not cordial. The two Virginians had known one another since West Point days but had never been friends. Of late, Hill thought Jackson too unreliable and overly pious; Jackson considered Hill lacking in both discipline and genuine faith.

Lee was concerned that Jackson's lone-wolf ways might anger the easily riled Hill. The army commander tried to calm the atmosphere. Hill "is a good officer with whom you can consult," Lee wrote Jackson. Then, in pointed reference to Jackson's insistence on secrecy, Lee added: "By advising well your division commanders as to your movements, much trouble will be saved you in arranging details, as they can act more intelligently."[7]

The advice fell on deaf ears.

Only days after Hill's arrival, Jackson's spirits rose with a message from Lee: "I would rather you should have easy fighting and heavy victories. I now leave the matter to your reflection and good judgment."[8] Jackson quickly put his forces in motion. Pope's army was strung out for twenty miles across the piedmont. The head of his column was advancing south from Culpeper, only a day's march from Jackson.

Confederates headed north with their old enthusiasm as Jackson's "foot cavalry." As usual, the men had no idea where they were going. Jackson paid no attention to grumblings of uncertainty. If the enemy force moving toward him was only part of Pope's huge army, Jackson hoped— "through the blessing of Providence"—to destroy it and then turn his attention to what remained of Pope's Army of Virginia.[9]

Jackson's unbreakable faith in secrecy backfired. He was leading 22,500 men and fifteen batteries of artillery in a column that stretched seven miles. Only Jackson knew where they were all going. He had hoped to keep Federals unaware of his movements. Yet on the night of August 7–8, Jackson changed the order of march for the following day without telling any of his division commanders.

August 8 was chaos. Units were bumping into one another when they were moving at all. Major traffic jams developed on the one-lane country roads. One division barely covered a mile the whole day. The heat of August in Virginia is always brutal. Add the wool clothing of the soldiers, the forced marches, and thick dust enveloping everything, and the situation was—in a word—horrible.[10]

Soldiers fainted from the heat; many died from the exertions. On the Union side, General George H. Gordon wrote of that day: "If we were not conforming to Pope's order to live on the country, we were doing the next thing to it—we were dying on it."[11]

Worse, in Jackson's view, the enemy now knew of his presence. He spent much of that night praying for guidance. His servant, Jim Lewis, was prompted to comment: "The General is a great man for praying at all times. But when I see him get up a great many times in the night to pray, then I know there is going to be something to pay."[12]

Early on August 9, Jackson told Lee in a note that "the expedition will, in consequence of my tardy movements, be productive of but little good."[13] Then he started his men forward at a brisk pace.

Boastful John Pope led a new Union army into central Virginia and quickly encountered Jackson's army, first at Cedar Mountain and next at Second Manassas.

*A depiction of the battle at Cedar Mountain. The central figures seem to be
a Federal soldier leading a captured Confederate to the rear.*

When a staff officer rode up beside Powell Hill and asked the division commander where the army was heading, Hill sarcastically replied: "I suppose we will go the top of the hill in front of us. That is all I know."[14]

About noon, eight miles from Culpeper, Jackson's lead elements met Federals in strength. The site was rolling farm country dominated by a rectangular hill known as Cedar Mountain. Dense woods, grain fields, and pasture land were intermixed. In other words, that section of the Virginia piedmont offered good positions for both defense and offense.

As at Port Republic, Jackson was overeager to get at the enemy. Not only did he fail to make a careful survey of the battle terrain, he also ordered his advance brigades to move into battle while the largest of the three divisions (Hill's) was still miles away from the scene of action.

Intense fighting exploded across the countryside as nine thousand Federals under Jackson's old Valley foe, General Nathaniel Banks, assailed about the same number of Confederates. The temperature soared to ninety-eight degrees, making this one of the hottest battles of the entire Civil War.

Banks attacked at all points of Jackson's line. The Confederates held, in spite of anxious moments through the afternoon. Near 5 P.M., as Jackson still fought with barely half of his command,

Federals executed a turning movement and swept around the Confederate flank. This unexpected attack, Jackson confessed, "fell with great vigour upon our extreme left, and by the force of superior numbers, bearing down all opposition, turned it and poured a destructive fire into its rear."[15]

Southern regiments began breaking apart and falling back. The lead units of Hill's division double-timed onto the field, but it would be a while before all of Hill's brigades reached the battle. Jackson's command was facing disaster.

At that point, the general galloped into the center of the most intense fighting. A tree knocked off his cap and gave the odd sight of Jackson bareheaded in battle. Paying no attention to bullets whizzing everywhere, his face flushed by the fever of the crisis, Jackson was going to try to turn back the wave of oncoming Federals by the single power of his being.

He moved Little Sorrel left and right among his fleeing soldiers. Jackson tried to draw his sword from the scabbard, but he had so rarely used the blade that it had rusted in its holder. The general unhooked the scabbard from his belt. Waving it (with the sword inside) over his head while clutching a Confederate battle flag in his other hand, he shouted encouragement above the roar of combat. Soldiers remembered him yelling a number of things: "Jackson is with you!" "Rally, brave men and press forward! Your general will lead you!" "Jackson will lead you! Follow me!"[16]

Retreating Confederates halted. Inspired by their general, men turned back toward the battle. A staff officer wrote of that moment: "Jackson usually is an indifferent and slouchy looking man but then, with the 'Light of Battle' shedding its radiance over him, his whole person had changed. . . . The men would have followed him into the jaws of death itself. . . . Even the old sorrel horse seemed endowed with the style and form of an Arabian [steed]."[17]

General William B. Taliaferro, one of Jackson's brigadiers, rushed up and urged the general to retire to a point of safety. This was no place for the army commander to be. Jackson muttered, "Good, good!" and started back. Powell Hill's full division was now entering the fray. Jackson rode to one of Hill's brigade leaders. "Press forward, General, press forward!" he exclaimed.[18]

Broken brigades rallied; fresh brigades reinforced the line. The Union attack slowly ground to a halt and then began receding. Jackson was not content. The sun was setting when he led his army in a pursuit of Banks's defeated forces. Darkness, musketry from Federal squads hidden in woods, plus a sudden bombardment from Union artillery caused Jackson to halt the chase. A night attack against unknown numbers in unexpected places was too risky even for Jackson the gambler.

The next day was a nightmare on the Cedar Mountain battlefield. From a cloudless sky the sun baked the earth. Scores of wounded soldiers North and South lay unattended in the heat, their miseries too horrible to describe. Jackson dispatched surgeons to care for as many of the helpless as possible. Burial details put the dead in long, shallow ditches. Confederates gathered up arms and other discarded equipment on the field. To the War Department, Jackson sent a brief message that began: "On the evening of the 9th instant, God blessed our arms with another victory."[19]

Such success had not come cheaply. Jackson's losses were 223 killed and 1,060 wounded. Union casualties were 314 killed, 1,445 wounded, and 622 captured.[20]

Jackson's performance at Cedar Mountain, coming on the heels of the peninsular disappoints, had not been good. His secretiveness and lack of communication with subordinates produced widespread confusion from the start of the campaign. The battle was three separate and disconnected fights on left, center, and right because of Jackson's negligence in consolidating his lines.

On the other hand, Jackson had personally been the factor that blocked defeat when his lines were collapsing. He gained control of the battle as well as himself. Displaying the personal leadership his men expected and loved, he led them to another smashing triumph. Cedar Mountain brought the conqueror of the Valley back into clear focus. One North Carolina soldier was convinced that Old Jack was "the greatest man now living."[21]

Military operations changed dramatically in the space of a few days. McClellan's army began abandoning the Richmond front. The Union general was under orders to return to the Washington area and reinforce Pope's drive into central Virginia. (McClellan did not move promptly enough to be of any major help to a rival general whom he disliked.) Lee knew that Pope was too strong for Jackson. McClellan's departure from the peninsula freed Lee to join his lieutenant at Gordonsville. The Army of Northern Virginia began a rapid reassembly to the west.

Jackson and General James Longstreet each commanded half of Lee's forces. The peevish Longstreet harbored resentment if not jealousy over Jackson. Stonewall paid no attention to Longstreet's feelings. How well a general performed in battle was Jackson's sole concern. A similar concern existed with Lee's best division commander, Powell Hill. Relations between Jackson and Hill were growing more strained.

Personal opinions became unimportant when Lee revealed his plans to his lieutenants. Pope had committed a tactical blunder. The Federal commander had placed his army in the triangle of land formed by the juncture of the Rappahannock and Rapidan Rivers. If Lee could move his forces swiftly, the protective position taken by Pope could be his death trap.

Jackson took the lead. His men set a customary fast pace. Yet a snag here, a hindrance there, an obstacle someplace else, kept delaying the Confederates. Pope finally saw what was taking place and beat a hasty retreat.

Lee continued the pursuit. Jackson ordered his men to be on the road before sunup the next morning. Hill's division would be in front. As Jackson rode forward to start the march in the predawn hours of

August 21, he discovered all of Hill's troops still in camp. Jackson raged in anger and ordered one of Hill's brigades to begin marching at once. Hill took offense at being bypassed. The rift between the two men deepened.

Meanwhile, Lee faced a growing dilemma. The farther north he pursued Pope, the closer Pope got not only to Washington but to possible reinforcements from McClellan's army landing near Fredericksburg. Somehow, Lee thought, there must be a way to get at least part of his force between Pope and Washington. Doing that would enable the Confederates to surround Pope and isolate him long enough for Lee to move in for the kill. As Lee pondered what to do, the key player in his thoughts became Jackson.

On Sunday afternoon, August 24, Lee held a council of war in the middle of an open field. Only Lee, Longstreet, Jackson, and Stuart were in attendance. Lee proposed a daring gamble. He would divide his smaller army again in the face of the enemy.

This time, Jackson, with twenty-three thousand men and Stuart's cavalry, would make a great sweeping march to get behind Pope while Longstreet's thirty thousand troops created loud demonstrations along the Rappahannock line to conceal the movement. If Jackson could get around Pope's right flank, he could drive across the rear of the Union position and cut its supply and communication lines with Washington.

Should Pope turn and start after Jackson, that would take the Federal army away from Fredericksburg and reinforcements.

Further, while Jackson held Pope's attention, Lee with Longstreet would move into position to deliver a crushing blow on Pope's blind side.

Lee was taking a dangerous risk. Success or failure was going to depend on how well Jackson moved and what he was able to accomplish if he got deep in Federal-held territory. Secrecy and speed must be the key ingredients. As Lee knew, no one used those elements to greater advantages than his obedient and silent general.

Another officer aware of all of these possibilities was Union General McClellan. In mid-August he had warned Pope: "I don't like Jackson's movements. He will suddenly appear when least expected."[22]

Dawn, August 25, found Jackson's twenty-three thousand ragged, weather-beaten soldiers marching away from Lee's army. Every man knew that he was part of some big and exciting movement, but no one was sure of what Old Jack had in mind. He kept everything to himself. Just before mounting his horse, he had scribbled a note to Anna: "I only have time to tell you how much I love my little pet dove."[23]

The march proceeded north by west. Behind the long column could be heard artillery fire as Lee's cannon kept Pope occupied. On through the day local guides led Jackson's men through a variety of shortcuts. "We did not always follow roads," a Johnny Reb noted, "but went through corn fields and bypaths. Occasionally we marched right through someone's yard."[24]

Jackson rode up and down his line. "Close up, men, close up," he repeatedly

Second Manassas

Map labels: Washington, D.C.; Alexandria, Loudoun & Hamilton R.R.; Manassas Gap R.R.; Salem; Chantilly; Manassas Gap; Front Royal; Thoroughfare Gap; Centreville; Groveton; Fairfax C.H.; Alexandria; Gainesville; Orange & Alexandria R.R.; Warrenton; Bristoe; Manassas Junction; North Fork; Massanutten Mt.; South Fork; Blue Ridge Mts.; Jackson; Warrenton Junction; Pope; McClellan; Potomac River; Brandy Station; Conrad's Store; Culpeper C.H.; Acquia Creek; Cedar Mt.; Falmouth; Rapidan River; Chancellorsville; Fredericksburg; Rappahannock River; Orange C.H.; Gordonsville; R.F. & P.; Guiney Station; Mechum's River Station

Scale: 0 — 15 Miles

urged.[25] He was acutely aware that twenty-three thousand soldiers trying to get around Pope's army without being seen was slim indeed; and if Pope learned of his whereabouts, Jackson's band might well be destroyed. However, Jeb Stuart's cavalrymen were screening the movement. Jackson had complete confidence that the cavalry chief he most admired would keep him protected and informed.

Late in the afternoon, as the long, weary column neared the end of the day's march, Jackson dismounted from Little Sorrel. He climbed atop a huge boulder by the side of the road and gazed steadily at the ill-clad soldiers filing past. To the men, Jackson resembled some giant god about to make history. Soldiers began to cheer. A staff officer stopped them; such noise might alert the Federals to their presence. Somehow the Southerners had to display their love. So as they marched by him, they removed their hats and smiled in heartfelt affection.

Jackson was moved almost to tears. Turning to an aide, he remarked: "Who could not conquer, with such troops as these?"[26]

The "foot cavalry" marched twenty-five miles that day. Bloodstains in the dirt marked the trail where barefooted soldiers had trod. Many went to bed on the ground without supper. There was little grumbling. Before sunrise the next morning, they were on the move again. Jackson knew that he would have to push his men hard that day. This was the day to complete the encirclement of the Union army.

An artist's conception of how much the soldiers loved Jackson. The black man in the lower right of the picture was probably a servant with his master in the army.

The ranks were tired, hungry, and silent. Thick dust covered the long line. Soon the head of the column approached Thoroughfare Gap in Bull Run Mountains. To Jackson's relief, the pass was undefended. As Confederates descended to the floor of the Virginia piedmont, Stuart and his cavalry rode into view. Stuart brought good news: The way ahead was clear. Jackson was twenty miles in the rear of Pope's army and moving straight toward the Orange and Alexandria Railroad, the major Union artery for Pope's army.

In midafternoon, after a twenty-nine-mile march, Confederates seized Bristoe Station and cut the telegraph line. Southerners were famished and weary, but much work remained to be done. Jackson's men wrecked two trains that chugged into Bristoe. They also destroyed a bridge that knocked the railroad out of commission.

The alarm was now sounded. Pope was a general who had a talent for ignoring what he did not wish to hear. He had firmly believed that Jackson's movement from the start was a retreat to the Shenandoah Valley. Now Pope could not deny Jackson's presence in his rear. The Union general put his army into motion. He was abandoning the Rappahannock line and coming after Jackson.

*Thoroughfare Gap in the Blue Ridge Mountains became a vital point in
a number of movements by the opposing armies. Here a Manassas Gap Railroad train
curls through the rugged country.*

Stonewall expected that; for as long as he stood astride the railroad, Pope had no choice but to come to him. Jackson now moved again. His troops were bone-tired as Jackson led them on a new march in the dead of night. A Virginia soldier observed with scientific reasoning: "I had read that walking was an excellent form of exercise because it brought into play every muscle of the body, and having walked nearly sixty miles in two days, I was convinced that the reason assigned was valid, for the muscles of my arms and neck were almost as sore as those of my legs."[27]

Hollow-eyed, with faces drained of expression, men shuffled through the darkness. Each soldier could only keep his eyes fixed on the feet of the soldier in front of him. Hair, beard, and clothing had a layer of gray dust, giving the appearance of a long line of ghosts moving over the land. Then, as the sun rose following seven more miles of marching, Jackson's men beheld a sight that resembled paradise.

Ahead of them was Manassas Junction. Everywhere one looked were mountains of food and other supplies. Waiting to be taken were fifty thousand pounds of bacon, one thousand barrels of corned beef, two thousand pounds of salt pork, and two thousand barrels of flour. Canned oysters and other delicacies existed by the box load. Tons of goods were stacked in piles, in warehouses, and on two trains each a half-mile long.[28]

Jackson loosened his strong ties of discipline and gave the men several hours to take what they wanted. However, he ordered all captured whiskey poured on the ground. Many of Stuart's troopers managed to fill their canteens with liquor and, said one, "were as happy as a lamb with two mammies."[29]

It was near midnight when Jackson departed Manassas Junction. "Having appropriated all we could," he reported, "& unwilling that [the supplies] should again fall into the hands of the enemy," he ordered the depot torched.[30] The night sky was red from flames of tons of burning supplies as Jackson led his men a half-dozen miles to the place where he would await Pope— and Lee.

The site was a mile west of the battlefield. There Jackson had gained his nickname a year earlier. A low ridge extended along the northern side of the turnpike up which the Union army would be marching. From that position, Jackson had a long sweep of the road without being seen. He could assail Pope's flank or conduct a strong defense. Further, Jackson's right flank would extend toward Thoroughfare Gap and the road Longstreet's half of the army would be using for the linkup with Jackson.

Once his men were packed in the

Jackson's men feasting on captured Union stores at Manassas Junction. To hungry and ill-equipped soldiers, the August 27, 1862, event resembled gift-time on Christmas morning.

woods, Jackson began an impatient wait. He was "cross as a bear," an aide stated. "The expression of his face was one of suppressed energy and reminded you of an explosive missile, an unleashing spark applied to which would blow you sky high." [31]

Late that afternoon of August 28, a compact line of blue-clad soldiers came into focus on the turnpike. Jackson moved his troops to the edge of the woods. Then, to the amazement if not the horror of Confederates, Jackson came out of the woods alone and rode leisurely back and forth as he scanned the line of moving Federals. Some of the Billy Yanks saw the lone, dingy horseman but paid no attention. Probably a farmer watching them out of curiosity, they thought.[32]

Back into the woods Jackson slowly rode. To a small group of officers he said calmly: "Bring out your men, gentlemen."[33] Suddenly the afternoon silence was shattered by the fire of three Southern batteries and by Rebel Yells from hundreds of Confederate soldiers charging down the incline.

The fighting at Groveton (as the battle was called) lasted only two and a half hours, but a division commander termed it "one of the most terrific conflicts that can be conceived of."[34] Neither side gave ground. "It was a standup combat, clogged and unflinching in a field almost bare," General Taliaferro of Jackson's command stated of the opposing sides. "In the dying daylight . . . they stood, and although they could not advance, they would not retire. There was some discipline in this, but there was much more of true valor."[35]

Casualties mounted at a staggering rate. Union losses were eleven hundred of twenty-eight hundred engaged; Jackson's losses were twelve hundred of forty-five hundred in the battle.[36] The veteran Stonewall Brigade lost two of every five men. Two Georgia regiments each suffered seventy percent casualties. Worse for Jackson, two of his three division commanders fell wounded. One of them, the brave "Dick" Ewell, suffered a shattered knee that cost him his leg and kept him out of action for almost a year.

Pope now understood Jackson's exact location, but he remained convinced that the Confederate general was trying to get away from the Federals. An angry Pope concentrated his army when he came to see that Jackson was making a stand. Some fifty thousand Federals were massed in front of barely a third of that many Southerners. A confident Pope informed Washington that he shortly would have Jackson's army in his grip. "I do not see how it is to escape without heavy loss," he concluded.[37]

The Union commander had a right to feel upbeat. Casualties and sickness had reduced Jackson's three divisions to no more than eighteen thousand men. The 27th Virginia (which had begun the war with one thousand members) numbered twenty-five soldiers.

Friday, August 29, was a day of intense combat and bloodshed. Jackson was on wooded high ground, part of his line running along an unfinished railroad cut that offered near-ideal protection. Pope hammered the line, first with artillery and next with repeated infantry attacks. Wave after wave of gallant Union soldiers advanced up the ridge under heavy fire. They struck the woodland with point-blank musketry.

A South Carolina officer described the Union assaults: "They closed in upon us from front and right and left, pressing up with an energy never before witnessed by us. . . . Line after line of theirs was hurled upon our single one . . . The firing was incessant. They seemed determined not to abandon the undertaking; we were resolved never to yield."[38]

On through the afternoon the struggle raged. Jackson watched carefully as his lines took a pounding. His words of encouragement reminded the soldiers that they were serving under the South's most famous general. Jackson's spirits rose when the lead elements of Longstreet's corps streamed through Thoroughfare Gap and began forming on Jackson's far right. Yet Longstreet chose to delay his attack until he was sure Pope was giving total attention to Jackson.

Thus, Stonewall had to earn his title anew, and without help. Fighting became hand-to-hand in places as men used bayonets and swung muskets like bats. On Jackson's left, a Louisiana brigade ran out of ammunition and threw rocks at the charging Yankees.

Six times the Federals attacked Jackson's position. The lines bent but never quite broke. "Hour after hour, minute after minute," a member of Jackson's staff wrote, the men prayed "that the great red sun, blazing and motionless overhead, would go down."[39] Slowly the sun dipped over the western horizon and the fighting came to a close for the day.

Battle losses were in the thousands as the two opposing armies stared at one another less than a quarter-mile apart. Jackson had gained a major victory, even though new combat would come with the dawn. His medical director, Surgeon McGuire, commented that night: "General, we have won the battle by the hardest kind of fighting."

A softness came over Jackson's face. "No, no," he replied, "we have won it by the blessing of Almighty God."[40]

Agonizing screams of the wounded and dying filled the night. Tense waiting

At Second Manassas, part of Jackson's line ran out of ammunition and began hurling stones at the attacking Federals.

marked the morning of August 30. Federals marched and countermarched in view of the entrenched Confederates. Jackson conferred with Lee and Longstreet for reassurance that the full Army of Northern Virginia was ready for Pope.

He carefully inspected his lines and gave words of courage to his men. Then Jackson dismounted and rested against a large tree. Morning became afternoon. Near 3 P.M., a single Union cannon pierced the silence. "That's the signal for a general attack!" Jackson shouted as he bolted toward his horse.[41]

A terrific volley of musketry came from the Union lines. After that, long columns of Federals surged toward Jackson's position. Everything was a repetition of the previous day.

A member of the Stonewall Brigade wrote: "It was a continuous roar from right to left. . . . The enemy would form in the woods and come up the slope in three lines as regular as if on drill, and we would pour volley after volley into them as they came; but they would still advance until within a few yards of us, when they would break and fall back to the woods, where they would rally and come again. They charged in this manner three times . . ."[42]

The roar of artillery and musket fire was constant; men yelled and screamed amid thick gun smoke that settled over the land; hand-to-hand combat spread the length of Jackson's line as Pope's full army pressed with all its might. Jackson could not continue alone. He called on Longstreet for help.

Lee's other corps commander opened a devastating cannon fire into the unprotected flank of the Union army. As it recoiled in pain and confusion, Longstreet motioned his infantry into action. Jackson's weary troops saw what was coming. They gained a second breath and joined in the charge. Confederates swept the field as the Battle of Second Manassas became a scene of slaughter. A Northern correspondent noted that the Southerners "came on like demons emerging from the earth."[43]

For a mile and a half, Lee's army drove the battered Union forces. Pope's men did not give way to panic, but they were disorganized, shell-shocked, and thoroughly whipped. Darkness brought an end to the pursuit and to the battle. A rear guard action at Chantilly the following day was a stalemate that ended the campaign.

Second Manassas (often called Second Bull Run in the North) had been the bloodiest battle of the Civil War to date. More than three thousand dead and fifteen thousand wounded lay in a small area of only eight square miles. Jackson's casualties were frightful: 805 killed, 3,547 wounded, 35 missing.[44] Dead soldiers littered the fields and woods. One of Jackson's artillerymen noted the day after the battle: "I could have walked a quarter of a mile in almost a straight line on their dead bodies without putting a foot on the ground."[45]

Jackson's gallant stand a second time at Manassas had surely saved Lee's army. He had now become a ghost-like figure who popped up anywhere and spread terror among the Federals. Citizens as far north as

The soundly defeated Union army crossing Bull Run
as it slowly made its way back to Washington.

Harrisburg, Pennsylvania, feared that Jackson would "drop into their midst like a fallen angel, and devour them."[46] Many Northerners regarded him as "a species of demon," and a Union general warned his wife back in Pennsylvania: "Escape if you can, for he is a cold blooded rascal."[47]

On the night of August 30, when the only gunfire came in the distance, Jackson rode across the battlefield. He saw a young wounded Confederate struggling to get back to the railroad embankment. The general quickly dismounted, touched the soldier, and asked his unit.

"I belong to the Fourth Virginia, your old brigade, General," he said with pain in his voice. "I have been wounded four times but never before as bad as this. I hope I will soon be able to follow you again."

Jackson placed his hand on the youth's forehead. In a voice husky with emotion, he said: "You are worthy of the old brigade, and I hope with God's blessing you will soon be well enough to return to it."

The general summoned Dr. McGuire and entrusted the soldier to his personal care. The young soldier tried to thank Jackson, but tears choked his voice. He looked thankfully at the general. Old Jack nodded his head with understanding.[48]

✸ CHAPTER XII ✸
THE BLOODIEST DAY

FROM THE MOMENT the Civil War began, Jackson had urged at every opportunity that the Confederates take the war into the North. Invade the land of the invaders. Let Union citizens know the fears and destruction of war in their yards.

Jackson got his wish early in September 1862. A number of factors influenced Lee's decision to wage an offensive in the North.

Artist Adelbert Volck of Baltimore, Maryland, did this sketch of Jackson in the 1862 Maryland Campaign when the general was lost in thought. "I was about done with it," Volck said, "when Genl. Jackson looked around at me with a pleasant smile and turned away."

The Confederate army could not remain long in northern Virginia because the region had been stripped of food and forage. Washington was the most heavily defended city in North America. Attacking it was out of the question. To retire southward would be to give up all that had been gained in the past three months. Nor could the Southern army just sit and wait. As Lee wrote President Davis: "Although weaker than our opponents in men and military equipments, [we] must endeavor to harass, if we cannot destroy" the Union forces.[1]

On the positive side, Maryland was thought to be full of Southern sympathizers. Hundreds of its sons were already in Confederate service. Others might come forward if Lee's army could liberate the state from Union control. Should Maryland be secured for the South, Washington would be geographically surrounded by Confederate territory. A war-weary North might then ask for peace.

Most importantly, another crushing victory by Lee—this time inside the North itself—might be the event that would bring England and/or France into the struggle on the South's side. Foreign recognition and manpower had been the factors that had brought freedom to the American rebels in the 1770s. That same assistance might bring freedom to the American rebels of the 1860s.

Lee ordered his army to gather at

*Confederate soldiers removing shoes and trousers as they wade across
the Potomac River into Maryland.*

Leesburg for the Potomac River crossing.
The town was only thirty-five miles upriver
from Washington. An invasion from that
point would cause Union forces to abandon
Virginia in order to defend their capital.

An eager Jackson led his men toward
Leesburg at a brisk pace. The soldiers were
lean and accustomed to hard marching, but
they were also tired and hungry. Shaggy hair
hung down unwashed faces. Bits of rope
served as belts for tattered trousers. Dirt
crusted skin and clothing. Perhaps as many
as half of the troops were barefooted.

As for food, a Virginia private
commented: "For six days not a morsel of
bread or meat had gone in our stomachs.
Our menu consisted of apples and corn. We
toasted, we burned, we stewed, we boiled,
we roasted these two together, and singly,

until there was not a man whose form had
not caved in, and who had not a bad attack
of diarrhea."[2]

Jackson was sympathetic. Yet time
was important; the march had to be forced.
He made that point clear to his command.
General A. P. Hill seemed to ignore it.

On the morning of September 4, Hill
was half an hour late getting started. Jackson
then watched with mounting anger as Hill,
riding well ahead of his column, gave no
attention to the stream of stragglers falling
out along the way. When Hill's men failed
to halt for a scheduled rest break, Jackson
himself rode up and stopped the column.

An angry Hill galloped to the scene
and demanded to know who had halted his
line. A heated exchange followed, after
which Hill unbuckled his sword. If you are

going to give orders to my men without going through me, Hill told Jackson, you might as well command the division. With that, Hill held out his sword in surrender.

The commander ignored the offer. "Put up your sword and consider yourself under arrest for neglect of duty," Jackson snapped.

Hill was sent to march in humiliation at the rear of his troops. Thus, the best division commander in Lee's army was without a command as that army launched an invasion.[3]

Lee's army was thinned by casualties, sickness, and soldiers who had taken unauthorized leave ("French furlough") rather than become invaders like the detested Yankees. The Confederate force barely numbered forty thousand troops. At the Potomac, men who owned shoes tied them together by the laces and hung them around their necks. Soldiers rolled trousers up to their knees, then entered the water.

"I never expect as long as I live to witness so inspiring a spectacle," a captain wrote. "As I . . . looked back at the long dark line stretching across the broad shallow river I felt I was beholding what must be the turning point in our struggle."[4]

Maryland citizens crowded the roadside to greet the Southern army. Everyone wanted to see the legendary "Stonewall" Jackson. To his embarrassment, people offered food, the hospitality of their homes, and a variety of presents. Little Sorrel had been missing for several days (the horse was later returned). Jackson needed a better mount than the one he was riding. The general reluctantly accepted the gift of a strong gray mare.

The next morning, when Jackson spurred the horse, it bucked and threw its rider to the ground. Jackson was so stunned and sore that he spent the rest of the day riding in an old wagon.[5]

The other two highest ranking generals were also hurting. Lee had suffered a fall caused by his horse. The commander broke one hand and badly sprained the other—injuries that certainly limited his concentration on military matters. General James Longstreet was hobbling from an infected blister on his heel.

Lee halted the army at Frederick, the principal city in western Maryland. It was time to take stock of the situation. Where the Union army was would influence whether the advance would continue to the ultimate target of Harrisburg, Pennsylvania.

On Sunday night, September 7, Jackson and two aides rode into town to attend church services. Jackson thought the minister "a gifted one, and the building beautiful. . . . My heart was in sympathy with the surroundings."

That may have been so, but Jackson went to sleep during the sermon and did not hear the minister, a strong Union man, ask God's blessings on the president of the United States.[6]

The following day, Lee made a major decision. McClellan had taken command of Pope's forces along with his own army and was moving northwest in pursuit of Lee. A second disappointment had come to Lee:

The people of western Maryland were not giving much support to the Confederate army. Lee was in hostile territory, with the enemy army closing in on him.

A change in plans took place. The northern drive would continue by a different route. Lee's army would cross South Mountain, the Maryland extension of Virginia's Blue Ridge chain. From Hagerstown or some point in the valley beyond, Lee would establish supply lines to the Shenandoah Valley and Richmond. Yet a major snag existed. A twelve-thousand-man Federal garrison was at Harpers Ferry, blocking Lee's planned line of communication with Virginia. Lee had expected the garrison to withdraw when the Confederates crossed the Potomac. It did not. Harpers Ferry must be secured.

The logical man to carry out the assignment was Jackson. He was familiar with the strengths and weaknesses of the Ferry; a large number of his soldiers came from that region. Jackson, Lee knew, would move quickly. That was essential; because until Harpers Ferry was in Southern hands, Lee could not resume the invasion.

Jackson approved the plan that became Confederate strategy. Each of his three divisions would depart Lee's army on separate routes. They would approach the Ferry from north, east, and west. This would prevent the garrison from escaping and also block reinforcements coming to its aid. Artillerist Jackson would place cannons on the heights overlooking Harpers Ferry from three sides and blast the place into submission.

Lee was repeating a dangerous gamble: He was dividing his army in the face of the enemy, this time inside enemy territory. While Jackson went southwest, Longstreet would move due west over the mountains to Hagerstown. Harvey Hill's division would take position in the mountain passes and act as a rear guard. Lee believed that as long as secrecy of movements prevailed, the shifting of the army could be successful and the army reunited before McClellan posed a real threat.

All of these plans were carefully spelled out in Special Orders No. 191, copies of which went to every Confederate division commander. On September 10, the movements got underway. Jackson gave his men strict orders for the advance. A South Carolina officer stated: "We were to march three miles an hour and no more, except in great emergencies; we were to rest ten minutes in every hour; the sick and those unable to march were to be transported in the ambulances. . . . No good Samaritan could be expected along this new war-path."[7]

Two days after Confederates left Frederick, the Union army arrived and occupied the abandoned campsites. A Federal soldier stumbled upon a copy of Special Orders No. 191 lying on the ground. General McClellan suddenly was privy to the greatest security leak in American military history. The Union commander knew not only that Lee's army was divided into five parts, he knew where the parts were and when they expected to reunite.

Unfortunately for the Union cause,

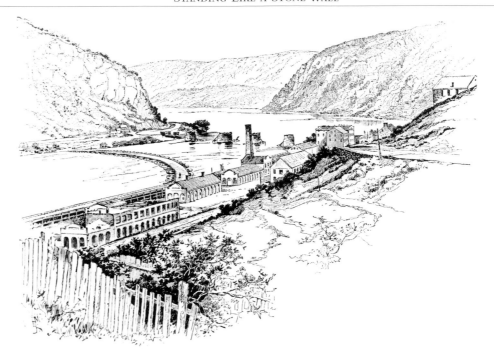

By September 1862, Harpers Ferry was a shell of what it once had been.
Notice the empty pilings where the railroad bridge had stood.

McClellan failed to take advantage of his unbelievably good fortune. His movement toward Lee was cautious to the point of being snail-like. At times the Federal general seemed to feel that the Confederate order had been purposefully planted in order to lead him into a trap.[8]

Meanwhile, Jackson's three wings slowly converged on their target. Lee's schedule began to go awry because it was too tight in the beginning. Jackson's column had the longer distance to cover: over seventy miles. For a while, his soldiers set a steady pace. Weariness soon enveloped the ranks. Jackson was a day late in reaching Harpers Ferry. Public praise was one of the problems.

He was becoming the living symbol of the Confederate cause. When Jackson reached Martinsburg, townspeople went wild with joy. The general had no choice but to admit part of the crowd to his temporary office. Lieutenant Douglas of his staff declared: "They came and swarmed about him. They all tried to get his hands at once. . . . They all talked at once with the disjointed eloquence of devotion . . . Blushing, bowing, almost speechless, [Jackson] stood in the midst of this remarkable scene, saying, 'Thank you, thank you, you're very kind.'"

A child asked for a button. Jackson cut one off his coat. Within moments almost all the buttons were gone. A request by a woman for a lock of his hair was more than Jackson could take. He fled the scene.[9]

Once in position at Harpers Ferry, the master gunner put his cannons in perfect position. At no time in the Civil War were Southern artillery at such a commanding elevation. Shortly after daylight on September 15, Jackson's guns opened a point-blank fire from three directions. Shells tore into homes, exploded among Union soldiers and horses, ripped holes in streets and storage areas, and created a hell-on-earth existence for the Federal garrison. A hapless Ohio colonel thought that Jackson's cannon fire "commanded every foot of the ground . . . producing terrible cross-fire . . . there was not a place you could lay the palm of your hand and say it was safe."[10]

The bombardment lasted less than an hour before white flags of surrender appeared over the Union works.

Confederates marched into the battered town. To their surprise, Union captors rushed to see the general who had defeated them. A Confederate soldier was guarding a group of Federals when Jackson came into view. "Almost the whole mass of prisoners broke over us, rushed to the road, threw up their hats, cheered, roared, bellowed, as even Jackson's own troops had scarcely ever done. . . . The general gave a stiff acknowledgement of the compliment, pulled down his hat . . . and went clattering down the hill, away from the noise."[11]

The twelve thousand and four hundred Federals seized at Harpers Ferry were the largest surrender of Union soldiers in the Civil War. Jackson had won one of the most complete victories in history.

Late that morning, he dashed off a quick note to Anna. "It is my grateful privilege to write that our God has given us

a brilliant victory at Harper's Ferry to-day. Probably nearly eleven thousand prisoners, a great number of small-arms, and over sixty pieces of artillery are, through God's blessing, in our possession. . . . Our Heavenly Father blesses us exceedingly."[12]

On the day before Jackson's great exploit, McClellan fought his way over South Mountain. Lee moved quickly to consolidate his army. Harvey Hill was to rejoin Longstreet; that portion of the army would move a dozen miles south to the village of Sharpsburg to shorten the distance Jackson would have to march to link up with Lee.

September 15–16 were frantic days of marching as elements of the Confederate army converged on Sharpsburg. Jackson restored Powell Hill to command (although the charges against him were left pending). Hill was ordered to secure Harpers Ferry and then march toward Lee's forces.

Jackson's other divisions struck out for Sharpsburg. A captured Vermont officer watched the Confederates march away. "They were silent as ghosts; ruthless and rushing in their speed . . . disheveled and devilish, as though keen on the scent of hot blood. . . . The shuffle of their badly shod feet on the hard surface of the Pike was so rapid as to be continuous like the hiss of a great serpent."[13]

Meanwhile, McClellan did little more in those two critical days but watch most of Lee's army come back together again.

The two opposing forces moved into final battle positions on the rainy night of the sixteenth. Sharpsburg was a sleepy little village of only thirteen hundred people. Yet it stood on high ground. Lee placed his army along the ridges. The Confederate line stretched in a semicircle for four miles. Lee's left anchored on the Potomac; his right curled back from Antietam Creek, which was substantial enough to be an obstacle to any troops wishing to cross it.

Much like Pope's army a month earlier, Lee's divisions were inside a large "V" formed by the two streams. McClellan had only to puncture the line at some point, and Lee faced a water trap. "An army of liberation was [now] an army of desperation," one authority wrote of Lee's command.[14] More remarkably, the two opposing generals had switched roles. McClellan was the attacker, Lee the defender.

Jackson's half of the army was the left of the line and almost at right angles to the other half. It faced woods and cornfields. The most prominent landmark was a white Dunker church standing on a small rise of ground inside the Southern lines. Jackson got only a glimpse of the terrain on September 16. Not having slept for two days, he used the short time before battle to get a little rest.

McClellan might have destroyed Lee's army at the Battle of Antietam if he had attacked with his superior numbers at every point of Lee's line. Instead, for reasons never quite clear, the Union commander chose to assault one sector at a time. The first onslaught that Wednesday, September 17, came against Jackson at 5:30 A.M.

For three hours, some of the most vicious fighting ever seen in America swirled around Jackson's position. Place-names such as the East Wood, The Cornfield, and the West Wood became monuments to gallantry. General Joseph Hooker's full Union corps, with heavy artillery support, attacked Jackson. Probably no more than fifty-five hundred Southerners were in line. (The famous old Stonewall Brigade, which had once numbered four thousand soldiers, counted barely three hundred men that day.) Hooker was attacking with nine thousand Federals.

By 7 A.M., one of Jackson's divisions was wrecked beyond recognition and commanded by a mere colonel. The other division had broken into fragments as if it had been a pane of glass dropped to a pavement. Units on both sides had melted in the heat of battle. The 12th Massachusetts lost 224 of 334 men—the highest proportion of casualties suffered by the Union army in the battle. The Louisiana brigade in Lee's army suffered 323 casualties among 500 men in action—and all of the losses came in a fifteen-minute period.

Jackson urgently called up the twenty-three-hundred-man division of General John B. Hood. They were greeted by what Jackson termed a "terrific storm of shell, canister and musketry."[15] A member of the 1st Texas in Hood's division wrote of the regimental flag: "Just as fast as one man would pick it up, he would be shot down. Eight men were killed or wounded trying to bring it off the field. I can't say we were whipped, but we were overwhelmed."[16]

Jackson rode to and fro along his line. If he was aware of shells exploding around him and bullets whizzing about him, he gave no sign. The general was horrified by his losses. All he could do was urge the survivors to stand firm.

John Hood was a giant Kentuckian who loved combat. Jackson once said of him: "Oh! he is a soldier!"[17] His troops felt the same way as their leader. Hood concluded amid the savage fighting that the best defense was an offense. He ordered his men to charge Federals then advancing through a mangled cornfield. Confederates raised the yip-yip-yip of the Rebel Yell and dashed forward.

The two sides collided in a bloody free-for-all. Union General Hooker reported: "Every stalk of corn in . . . the greater part of the field was cut as closely as could have been done with a knife, and the slain lay in rows precisely as they had stood in their ranks only a few moments before. It was never my fortune to witness a more bloody, dismal battle-field."[18] The 1st Texas, in the midst of the fighting, lost 186 of 226 men. This casualty rate of eighty-two percent was the highest of any Southern unit in any battle of the war.

A second Union corps soon entered the contest against Jackson. Yet Lee got enough troops in the area for Jackson to order a general advance. The tide of battle now swung to the Southerners. Confederates could only gain back the blood-drenched land they had held when the battle began. A combination of hours of high casualties, few officers left to command, and general confusion brought the fighting in Jackson's sector to a close at 9 A.M.

Jackson's ranks had taken a frightful

Union soldiers charging through a cornfield toward Jackson's lines at Antietam.

pounding. Half of his command was dead or injured. Somewhere close to three thousand of his men had been lost. The Stonewall Brigade—always a good measuring tool for battle losses—was the size of two companies rather than the fifty companies it was supposed to have.[19] That anyone was still alive was a miracle. Once again, "Stonewall" Jackson had earned his nickname.

He could only watch as the remainder of the most murderous one-day battle in American history ran its course. Parts of McClellan's army repeatedly attacked the center of Lee's line. This was Harvey Hill's front. His North Carolinians made such a brave and sacrificing stand in a sunken road at the bottom of a hill that the road has since been known as "Bloody Lane." Union soldiers gained control of the road but could go no farther.

In midafternoon the third stage of Antietam occurred when Federals fought their way across Burnside's Bridge and Antietam Creek. Up high ground they swept, pushing aside skeleton-thin elements of Lee's force. The Federals were turning Lee's right flank away from Virginia and toward doom at the Potomac River.

Then, in one of the most dramatic moments of the war, Lee escaped destruction. A. P. Hill, left behind at Harpers Ferry by Jackson and then summoned by Lee, double-timed his men seventeen miles to Sharpsburg. Fully a third of Hill's division was left panting along the roadside, but the three thousand men left slammed into the Union flank as it peeled back Lee's

line. Federals recoiled from the unexpected onslaught of Powell Hill, then slowly retraced their steps across the Antietam. Darkness mercifully brought the battle to an end.

Losses that day challenged belief. Some six thousand men were dead or dying; another seventeen thousand were wounded in every conceivable way. As many men were lost at Antietam as fell in three of America's wars: the War of 1812, the Mexican War, and the Spanish-American War. Four times as many Americans fell on September 17, 1862, as were casualties on D-Day in World War II.[20]

As after all battles, darkness at Antietam brought new sounds: screams of pain and cries of "Water! Water!" from wounded and dying soldiers on the field. Surgeons moved among the thousands of injured men to do what they could. Exhausted soldiers who had survived the battle made little campfires and cooked rations with dead companions sprawled all around them.

Jackson summed up the Battle of Antietam in a simple phrase: "God has been very kind to us today."[21] His devotion to duty shone three times at Antietam. With complete assurance that God was with his men, he fought with unbroken confidence. Then, twice in the hours following the battle, he sought to mount an attack against McClellan's army. Such thoughts illustrated the man's unyielding will—his desire always to drive ahead against the foe. Jackson never thought of defeat. To him, victory was ever close at hand.

In contrast, McClellan on September 18 had some thirty-three thousand troops who had seen no action. The Union general would not renew the attacks. That night Lee escaped across the Potomac with his army. Confederates had happily sang "Maryland, My Maryland" two weeks earlier when they had begun the Northern invasion. Now they gloomily recrossed the river to the music of "Carry Me Back to Old Virginny."

McClellan made a halfhearted pursuit. On September 20, Jackson unleashed A. P. Hill's division to hit the lead Union brigade. Hill routed the Federals, many of whom plunged for safety into the Potomac—only to be shot by Confederates from the heights above the river. It was "an appalling scene of destruction to human life," Jackson wrote.[22]

Lee's thinned and bloodied columns trudged slowly back to Virginia and went into camps north of Winchester. Jackson was pleased to be again in his beloved Shenandoah Valley. Yet much rebuilding of his command must be done. Ranks and morale had to be strengthened, discipline and faith increased. The end of the war was nowhere in sight.

The Federal attack on Jackson got only as far as the Dunker church before it faltered and fell apart.

✳ CHAPTER XIII ✳
CORPS COMMANDER

AS THE SUMMER days of September became the autumn weeks of October, Lee's army slowly came back to life. The waters of Opequon Creek in the Martinsburg-Winchester areas enabled men to emerge from the filth of marches and battles. Stragglers made their way back to regiments; new recruits appeared as well. Badly needed food and rest revived the Confederate forces. When the Union army showed no inclination to advance, the immediate future looked like a vacation from war.

Dealing with lax discipline was a major step in improvement insofar as Jackson was concerned. While reorganization took place, courts-martial worked overtime. Over one hundred soldiers went on trial for desertion and other offenses. Death sentences were rare, but punishments were severe. A deserter from the Stonewall Brigade was ordered to receive twenty-seven lashes on

In November 1862, Jackson surprised some dinner guests by agreeing to a request that he have his picture made. The resultant Winchester Photograph *is the most famous likeness of the general and the one his wife most liked.*

the bare back, have his head shaved, and be dishonorably dismissed from service.[1]

Jackson toiled equally hard to find shoes, clothing, and good campsites for his soldiers. Attending to little things built morale. The men could not complain of a lack of luxuries when their own general lived no better than they did. Jackson stood out among Lee's generals for his dirty uniform, plain hat, and lack of gold braid. His camp equipment could be carried in the back of a single wagon.

Lee used the October lull to reorganize his army. Battles were becoming too complicated, and armies too large, to try to maneuver two dozen or more brigades and divisions into combat. Following the example of the Union forces, Lee decided to divide the Army of Northern Virginia into two corps.

James Longstreet, the senior division commander, was an obvious choice to head one corps. Lee was convinced that Jackson should also be promoted. "My opinion of the merits of General Jackson has been greatly enhanced during the Antietam campaign," he wrote President Davis. "He is true, honest, and brave; has a single eye to the good of the service, and spares no exertion to accomplish his object."[2]

Promotion to lieutenant general came to Jackson on October 11 and with it official command of half of the army. The Second Corps had thirty-two thousand soldiers in ninety-two regiments, plus twenty-three batteries containing just under one hundred guns. The new corps leader was not openly joyful over his new rank. Too many duties needed to be performed. Among the most important was the ongoing feud with General Powell Hill.

Jackson believed that his arrest of Hill prior to Antietam had taught the division commander a lesson. Certainly Hill's gallantry in the battle made no further punishment necessary. Hill did not see it that way. He demanded a court of inquiry to investigate his being "treated with injustice and censured and punished at the head of my command."[3] Either Jackson must prove his case or apologize in public.

Lee tried to calm down the situation with tact and kind words. Hill became angrier. He not only demanded a hearing on Jackson's allegations; he filed charges of his own against Jackson.

At one point, after being assigned to patrol an isolated point on Lee's defense line, Hill told Jeb Stuart: "I suppose I am to vegetate here all the winter under that crazy old Presbyterian fool—I am like the porcupine, and all bristles, and all sticking out too, so I know we shall have a smash up before long."[4]

That did not occur because Lee grew weary of the whole episode and refused to allow either of two of his best generals to be the subject of a court-martial. Thereafter, Jackson and Hill exchanged only formal communications. When they met, they stiffly saluted one another and said little.

In spite of unhappy relations with his best division leader, some pleasant moments marked the time at Jackson's Bunker Hill encampments. One involved a gift from Jeb Stuart. The fun-loving cavalryman decided that Jackson ought to have a better uniform coat than the stained, soiled jacket that had no buttons because citizens of Martinsburg had taken them for souvenirs. So one day Stuart sent his giant Prussian aide, Major Heros Von Borcke, to Jackson's headquarters with a new coat shining from brass buttons and gold stripes.

Jackson was so confused by the lavish gift that he barely touched it. He folded it carefully and told Von Borcke: "Give General Stuart my best thanks. The coat is much too handsome for me, but I shall take the best care of it."

The burly Prussian would not be put off. Stuart would be insulted if Jackson did not wear it, he declared. The general donned the new coat as he and Von Borcke left the headquarters tent for supper. Word spread rapidly. In no time, Von Borcke observed, "soldiers came running by hundreds to the spot, desirous of seeing their beloved Stonewall in his new attire."

Laughter and cheers turned Jackson red with embarrassment.[5]

Stuart and Jackson continued their deep respect and affection for each other. One night the cavalry chief arrived at Jackson's headquarters after the general had gone to bed. Stuart climbed into Jackson's bed without removing anything but his sword. The next morning Stuart was warming himself by a campfire when Jackson emerged from his tent.

"Good morning, General Jackson!" Stuart beamed. "How are you?"

Jackson assumed an air of sternness and answered: "General Stuart, I am always glad to see you here. You might select better hours sometimes, but I'm always glad to see you." Then, rubbing his shins as if in pain, Jackson added: "But, General, you must not get into my bed with your spurs on and ride like [you were on] a cavalry horse all night!"[6]

How much of a Southern hero Jackson had become was evident when he led a detachment to destroy a section of the Baltimore and Ohio Railroad near Martinsburg. Jackson was astride Little Sorrel and peering through his telescope at the enemy's position. A young mother walked up to him, handed her eighteen-month-old son up to the general, and asked him to bless the child.

A staff officer noted that Jackson turned to the mother "with great earnestness and, with a pleasant expression on his stern face, took the child in his arms, held it to his breast, closed his eyes and seemed to be . . . occupied for a minute or two with prayer,

during which we took off our hats and the young mother leaned her head over the horse's shoulder as if uniting in the prayer."

When Jackson handed the child back to the mother, "she thanked him with streaming tears."[7]

Late in October, Lee shifted Longstreet's corps eastward to Culpeper to protect the central (piedmont) region of Virginia. Jackson remained in the Valley. Gifts of every description poured into his headquarters; visitors from near and from as far away as England flocked to meet the general. Politicians and foreign dignitaries who sought an audience were always disappointed with the results. Jackson distrusted people who wished to discuss the war. If the conversation moved to that subject, Jackson avoided questions and said little.

Going to church provided some relief for Jackson. One Sunday he attended morning worship at the church of his old friend, the Reverend Graham. A Winchester matron noted: "He sat quite near where I was. He had on a splendid new uniform, and looked like a soldier. He looked, too, so quiet and modest, and so concerned that every eye was fixed on him."[8]

When a religious revival swept through Jackson's corps that autumn, he eagerly moved into the middle of it. He would learn of a field service, leave his tent, and join the soldiers in a clearing or inside woods for prayer meeting. One night he spoke openly with his surgeon, Dr. McGuire. "I have no fears whatever that I shall ever fall under the wrath of God," Jackson said. "I am as certain of my acceptance, and heavenly reward, as that I am sitting here." He then declared that he would not "exchange one shade" of heavenly hope for all the reputation he had or might have in the future.[9]

On November 1, Jackson was having lunch at the McGuire family home in Winchester. Marguerite McGuire, the younger sister of Jackson's surgeon, boldly asked the general to have his picture taken. To the surprise of everyone, Jackson agreed. He and his hosts walked into town to the studio of Nathaniel Routzahn. The photographer took what many consider the best likeness of Jackson.

The weeks of relative quiet ended in mid-November. Lee summoned Jackson's corps to Fredericksburg. Early that month Union President Abraham Lincoln had fired McClellan. Lee expressed regrets at seeing the Union general leave. "We always understood each other so well," he told Longstreet. "I fear that they will continue to make these changes till they find someone whom I don't understand."[10]

McClellan's successor at the head of the Army of the Potomac was General Ambrose E. Burnside. The same age as Jackson, and a year behind him at West Point, Burnside was a stout and energetic man. He compensated for premature baldness with a fantastic set of whiskers that curved from in front of his ears, down over his jaws, and up across his mouth. Burnside was brave but not brilliant. He would move from disaster to disaster with a strange sense of dignity.

Knowing he had been appointed to fight—something McClellan had consistently shown a reluctance to do—Burnside moved at once. He pulled back from Lee's front and moved secretly eastward. Within a week, the Union army was opposite Fredericksburg and threatening to cross the Rappahannock River for a direct advance on Richmond.

Jackson got his columns on the road for the eighty-mile march to Fredericksburg. The Second Corps was a pathetic mass of men. Snow was falling. Many of the soldiers lacked shoes, or blankets, or both. "I tremble every time I look at some of our boys," a South Carolina captain wrote. A member of the 58th Virginia noted in his diary: "I fear I will freeze today."[11]

Union general Ambrose E. Burnside succeeded McClellan and led the Army of the Potomac in battle at Fredericksburg. His fantasic set of whiskers led to reversing the syllables of Burnside's name and calling such whiskers "sideburns."

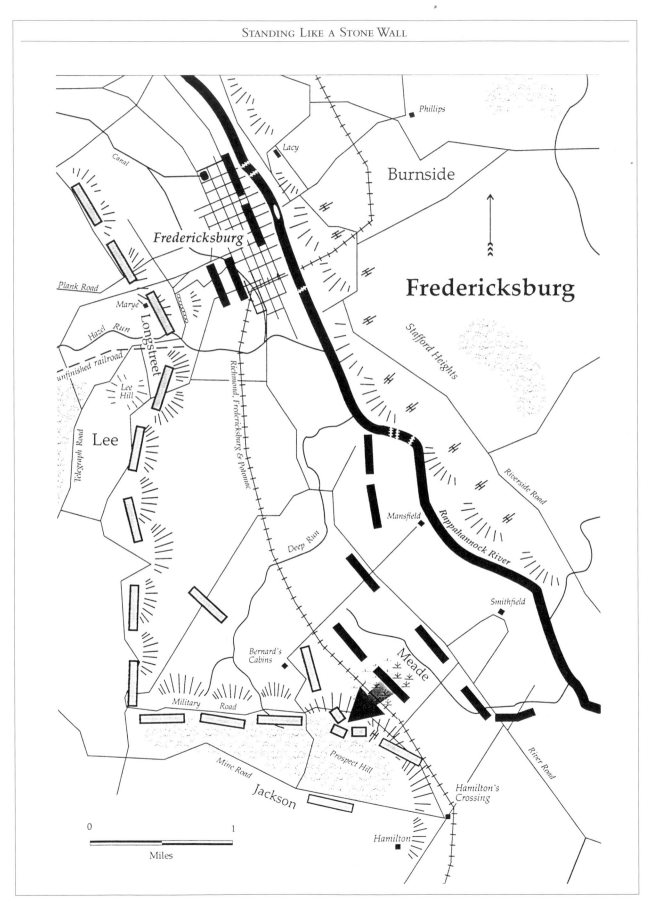

Phillips

Lacy

Burnside

Canal

Fredericksburg

Plank Road

Marye

Hazel Run

Longstreet

unfinished railroad

Lee Hill

Telegraph Road

Lee

Richmond, Fredericksburg & Potomac

Deep Run

Stafford Heights

Fredericksburg

Riverside Road

Mansfield

Rappahannock River

Smithfield

Meade

Bernard's Cabins

Military Road

Mine Road

Prospect Hill

Jackson

Hamilton's Crossing

River Road

Hamilton

0   1

Miles

Jackson paid no attention to the cold, for he received one of the happiest messages of his life.

During the months in which Jackson had fought in the Valley, Seven Days', Cedar Mountain, Second Manassas, and Antietam Campaigns, his pregnant Anna lived quietly in North Carolina.

The child was due sometime in November. Jackson was quite aware of this. Toward the end of November, he became anxious. Anna was far away, and he had not heard from her as he usually did. Jackson had already lost a wife and two children associated with childbirth. Death seemed to loom always nearby. Was it to strike again at his heart?

Then a short note arrived from Anna's sister, Harriet Irwin. Anna had given birth to a daughter. Mother and child were fine. The news sent Jackson to his knees in thanksgiving. A day or so later, Jackson received another letter (also in Mrs. Irwin's handwriting). The contents were different. It stated in part:

"My Dear own father, . . . I hope that God has sent me to radiate your pathway through life. I am a very tiny little thing. I weigh only eight and a half pounds, and Aunt Harriet says I am the express image of my darling papa . . . My hair is dark and long, my eyes are blue, my nose straight just like papa's . . . I was born on Sunday, just after the morning services at church . . . Your dear little wee Daughter."[12]

An excited father then wrote his beloved Anna: "Oh! how thankful I am to our Heavenly Father for having spared my precious wife and given us a little daughter! I cannot tell you how gratified I am, nor how much I wish I could be with you and see my two darlings." Jackson then suggested that the child be named Julia after his mother. This was done.[13]

All too quickly, Jackson began worrying about losing a family member whom he loved. Anna wrote of how totally she worshiped their daughter and how often she smothered the baby with love. Back from Jackson came a warning: "Do not set your affections upon her, except as a gift from God. If she absorbs too much of our hearts, God may remove her from us."[14]

Jackson's corps reached Fredericksburg early in December. The town had once been a charming and bustling community of forty-five hundred inhabitants. Situated at the falls in a sharp bend of the Rappahannock River, Fredericksburg had long been a river port for the Shenandoah Valley. It lay midway between Washington and Richmond.

By December 1862, rain and snow pricked the war-torn city. Two mighty armies stood poised for battle on opposite river heights. The town and the Rappahannock lay in the valley below.

Lee expected to be attacked. He established his lines with care. They extended seven miles along the crest of an almost unbroken ridge. Confederate soldiers were packed seven men to the yard. Never had the Army of Northern Virginia been so concentrated for battle.

Longstreet's corps formed the left half of Lee's position. Much of it was entrenched atop the area's highest terrain, called Marye's Heights. Jackson's corps, on the right, was on lower ground. The Second Corps would go to Longstreet's aid, if needed, or it could move swiftly downriver if Federals attempted to flank the Confederate position.

Guarding against a turning movement forced Jackson to spread his divisions over a twenty-mile area of river crossings below Fredericksburg. Yet his major defense line was solid. It ran along a ridge no more than forty feet high. It was an ideal defensive spot: low enough to invite attack, high enough to provide a clear field of fire.

A. P. Hill's division was in front, backed up by the divisions of Jubal Early and Harvey Hill. The better part of thirty-four thousand Southerners manned a two-mile front. All were concealed in woods.

Elements of Burnside's army fought their way across the river on December 11 and established a beachhead in downtown Fredericksburg. It took Burnside a day to get his massive army across the Rappahannock. Union brigades took position on a broad, open plain six hundred to one thousand yards wide in front of the hills where Lee's men waited.

Saturday, December 13, dawned foggy. Staff members stared in shock when Jackson walked from his tent. They were accustomed to seeing their general in the plainness of dress. This morning, he was wearing the new coat given him by Stuart, plus a new hat wrapped in gold braid—a present from Anna. New trousers and shiny boots completed the wardrobe.

As Jackson rode along his lines for a final inspection, shouts of approval came from his men. "The General is dressed up as fine as a Lieutenant of a Quartermaster!" one yelled. Another shouted in mock despair: "Old Jack will be afraid of his clothes and will not get down to work!" To many, it appeared that even Little Sorrel pranced more than usual because of the impressive-looking rider he was carrying.[15]

Lee's army stood silently as the hours of dense fog continued. Around 11 A.M., wind shredded the haze and then pulled it aside. There, in the chilly sunlight on the bare plain, stood the Army of the Potomac, one hundred and ten thousand strong and massed in battle formation. For Lee's seventy-seven thousand Confederates, it was a breathtaking view.

Jeb Stuart, scouting along the edge of the line, sent his Prussian aide to warn Jackson that the first attack would be against his line. Major Von Borcke expressed concern that Jackson might not be able to hold against so many Federals in his front. Jackson calmly replied: "Major, my men have sometimes failed to *take* a position, but to *defend* one, never! I am glad the Yankees are coming."[16]

A hush lay over the area. The roar of Union cannon shattered the quietness. Southern artillery answered just as long lines of Union infantry started forward.

Jackson thought he was ready, especially after the Union high command made a tactical mistake. Only a single division—five thousand men under General George G. Meade—charged against Jackson's line. Incredibly, the assault came at a swampy area Jackson had not bothered to defend because he thought it impassable.

Meade's soldiers struggled through the marsh, crossed railroad tracks, surged uphill through stubby thickets, and drove through Jackson's main line. The Union attack shattered three Confederate brigades and momentarily gave hope to the Northern soldiers. Yet Jackson calmly made adjustments. Soon Federals found themselves advancing into a giant "U" formed by Confederates firing on them from three directions.

The Union assault quickly lost its momentum. Federals fled back to their lines. In doing so, they took as many casualties on the return trip as they had fighting their way into Jackson's position.

Staff officer William Williamson was with Jackson when the Union assault collapsed in defeat. Williamson wrote of the general: "I saw him raise his hand & the expression on his face & the gesture so impressed me that I rode on behind him saying to myself, 'I will get the benefit of that prayer.'" Other Confederates who saw their praying general removed their hats and bowed their heads even as the battle was still raging.[17]

Lee watched the action from his command post near the middle of the Confederate line. When Jackson hurled back the Union columns with heavy loss, Lee turned to Longstreet. "It is well that war is

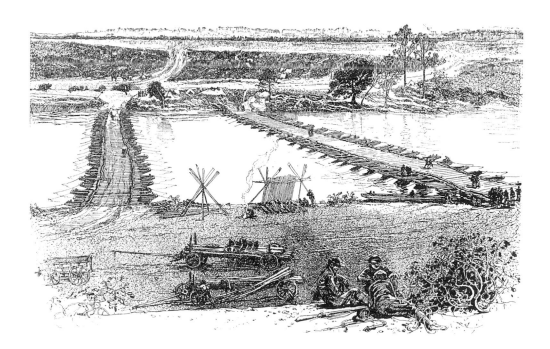

Two of the Union pontoon bridges stretching across the Rappahannock River. Federals used these bridges to attack Jackson's line. The Confederate position was on the high ground a quarter-mile in the distance.

Some of Jackson's men in battle position in the woods at Hamilton's Crossing.
This was the anchor of Lee's right flank at Fredericksburg.

so terrible!" he said. Otherwise, "we should grow too fond of it!"[18]

Artillery fire continued, but by 2 P.M. the infantry fighting in Jackson's sector had ended. Over on Longstreet's front were defensive works that simply could not be broken. Confederates repulsed thirteen separate attacks in a one-sided contest variously called a "massacre" and "slaughter pen."[19]

As could be expected, Jackson wanted to launch a counterattack that night. He made strong preparations for an advance that would "drive the enemy into the river."[20] Yet confusion of orders and heavy Federal cannon fire forced Jackson to cancel the assault.

In the cold darkness of night, rescue parties did what they could. Southern soldiers in need crept onto the battlefield, made their way among the dead, and secured blankets, clothing, and—especially—shoes. The next morning scores of dead and naked Yankees lay bloated on the ground. The sight reminded many Southern farm boys of hogs being slaughtered and cleaned.

The Union army had suffered twelve thousand six hundred losses. Lee's casualties were fewer than five thousand men. Nothing of military consequence had been achieved. Jackson had waged a masterful defensive battle. His losses were 3,415 men killed, wounded, and captured. Federal losses against Jackson were 3,787 troops.[21]

Jackson's high casualties were the result largely of the swampy ground in his front being left undefended. This oversight became a lingering controversy in the Fredericksburg campaign.

On December 16, Burnside abandoned the field. The Union army retired northward and went into winter quarters. Lee's forces likewise settled down for the winter. Confederates had much work to do. Earthworks must be constructed along the Rappahannock. Food and ammunition must be secured. Thinning ranks had to be reorganized and strengthened, for the Union army would surely return with the spring.

Bitterly cold weather and an earache forced Jackson to leave the spartan outdoor existence he customarily followed. His staff found comfortable shelter: "Moss Neck," the palatial Corbin mansion eleven miles downriver from Fredericksburg. The family welcomed Jackson eagerly and offered him an entire wing of their mansion as a headquarters. No, the general politely answered, the home was "too luxurious for a soldier, who should sleep in a tent."[22]

A few days spent in windy, subfreezing weather caused Jackson to catch cold.

Surgeon McGuire insisted that he seek indoor accommodations for the winter. The general moved into a small frame building fifty yards in front of the mansion. The structure had three rooms and served as a plantation office. Jackson's "home" for the next three months was one of the rooms. It contained a fireplace, a cot against one wall, a desk against the other, and two plain chairs. The room offered comfort and privacy, which was as much as Jackson required.

A restless spirit inside the general occasionally surfaced. In one of his informal conversations with mapmaker Jed Hotchkiss, Jackson talked about the suffering of his men in the cold weather and the destruction of proud old Fredericksburg. "War is the greatest of evils," he suddenly exclaimed.[23]

In a letter written at the same time to a friend in Lexington, Jackson observed: "I greatly desire to see *peace, blessed peace,* and I am persuaded that if God's people throughout our Confederacy will earnestly unite" in praying to God for peace, "that we may expect it."[24]

Equally pressing on Jackson's heart was a longing to be with his family. He especially wanted to see his daughter. "I tell you," he wrote Anna, "I would love to caress her and see her smile. Kiss the little darling for her father."[25]

CHAPTER XIV

CROSSING THE RIVER

THE WINTER OF 1862-63 for Jackson was busy but often pleasant.

While his brilliance as a field commander was established for all time, he hated the drudgery of paperwork. Yet duty required submission of reports and the like. Jackson therefore gave strong attention that winter to written details. Among his first actions was to appoint Charles J. Faulkner to his staff.

In his mid-fifties, Faulkner was a former congressman and diplomat. He was also a lawyer with gifted writing skills. Jackson had not submitted an official battle report since the March 1862, contest at Kernstown. He readily admitted an awkwardness when it came to writing such things. Faulkner soon demonstrated that he could transform Jackson's thoughts to readable—and occasionally exciting—prose.

The elder Faulkner did not get along cordially with members of the staff; Jackson's heavy editing of the manuscripts Faulkner submitted was irritating; army headquarters regularly clamored for reports that had not been prepared. Yet Faulkner worked diligently. All of the battle reports were finished by the end of winter.

Jackson's battle summaries were easily recognizable by the pious manner in which they ended. Examples: "For these great and signal victories our sincere and humble thanks are due unto Almighty God." . . .

"We can but express the grateful conviction of our mind that God was with us and gave us the victory, and unto His holy name be the praise."[1]

Meanwhile, the general spent a good part of each day poring over incoming and outgoing documents. His chief aide, "Sandie" Pendleton, was of great help in streamlining the normal daily schedule. Still, the workload was so heavy that Jackson would sometimes fall asleep at night while affixing the signature "T. J. Jackson" to a letter.[2]

Courts-martial handed out regular and severe punishments that winter, especially for desertion. Jackson had no sympathy for a man who abandoned his fellow soldiers. Death by firing squad was the appropriate penalty. If this seemed harsh, Jackson was quick to say that war was harsh. Fighting for country and God demanded both patriotism and faith. A violation of either was inexcusable.

Duty required one's presence. Jackson took no furloughs and granted none. Women were allowed to visit loved ones in camp—a practice that irritated bachelor General Jubal Early. He asked Jackson to declare the encampments off-limits to all females. Jackson replied: "I will do no such thing. I wish my wife would come to see me."[3]

Kyd Douglas, the youngest of Jackson's staff members, once worked up the courage to tell Jackson that he had not been out of the army since he had entered it.

"Very good," Jackson answered. "I hope you will be able to say so after the war is over."[4]

Jackson believed the key to good discipline to be subordinate officers. He demanded much of them because he demanded so much of himself. The worst personnel problem he had that winter was the still-smoldering tension with his best division commander, General A. P. Hill.

In January 1863, Hill pressed anew for a hearing on the charges Jackson filed against him prior to the Battle of Antietam. Jackson attempted to play down the whole incident; Lee wanted to forget it. Hill was insistent. "If the charges preferred against me by Genl. Jackson are true," Hill wrote Lee, "I do not deserve to command a division." On the other hand, "if they are untrue, than Genl. Jackson deserves a rebuke as serious as my arrest."

Meanwhile, Hill added, he intended to "preserve every scrap of paper received from Corps Hd. Qrs. to guard myself against any new eruption from this slumbering volcano [Jackson]."[5]

By March, Jackson had endured enough. He asked Lee to transfer Hill from his command. Two sterling officers had now filed court-martial charges against one another. Lee was faced with losing one of his best generals. The army commander understandably delayed taking any action.

Military problems continued to be worrisome, but Jackson found many periods of delight during the weeks at Moss Neck plantation. One area of pleasure, naturally, was religion. He often quoted the maxim: "Duty is ours; the consequences are God's."[6]

The army revivals of the previous autumn exploded with greater fervor in the Fredericksburg camps. Jackson took a leading role in all activities. "Time thus spent in genuine enjoyment," he told Anna.[7]

Morning prayers at headquarters

Union general Joseph Hooker developed an excellent battle plan against Lee. Yet Hooker lost confidence in himself when the action began at Chancellorsville.

marked the beginning of each workday. Evening prayer meetings were held at least twice weekly. Sunday afternoons were the time for full worship services. Jackson attended as many as circumstances permitted.

Mapmaker Jed Hotchkiss recalled the general being asked at a field service to give a prayer. Jackson moved to a position in the middle of the large crowd of soldiers. Hotchkiss wrote: "He devoutly prayed for all classes, orders, & conditions of the Confederate States, for success to our arms at all times, for confusion & defeat to our enemies, but for blessings to them in all right & proper things, especially that they might have the blessings of peace. He very earnestly prayed that this 'unnatural war' might speedily be brought to a close, and that blessing might come upon our absent dear ones."[8]

Jackson also worked to make religion a basic part of army life. Toward that end, the general organized the Chaplains Association for the Second Corps. Its functions were to coordinate religious activities inside the army and to recruit civilian ministers for regiments badly in need of chaplains. "Each Christian branch of the Church should send into the army some of its most prominent ministers," Jackson declared. It made no difference to him what denomination the cleric was. The only question should be: "Does he preach the Gospel?"[9]

Knowing that he did not have time to oversee all work with the ministers in the army, Jackson searched for someone who could be his "Chaplain General." He found such a servant in a roving minister and old friend, the Reverend B. Tucker Lacy. Able, energetic, and faithful, the Presbyterian clergyman began his duties with a zeal that warmed Jackson's heart.

Units such as the Stonewall Brigade built chapels. Prayer meetings increased in number. So did the soldiers who flocked to services in search of spiritual comfort. Jackson himself underwent a "total spiritual rebirth."[10] His corps and his God were moving steadily closer to one another. Increasingly, Jackson came to regard himself as a true servant of the Lord. Chaplain Lacy remarked afterward that Jackson's "interest, all along, was deep, constant, excessive; it cannot be exaggerated."[11] A Richmond clergyman-friend said of the general: "How anxious he was for his army! . . . To glorify God possessed all his thoughts."[12]

Anna and the daughter he had never seen occupied many of Jackson's thoughts at the Moss Neck home of the Corbin family. His deep love for children made it almost inevitable that he would acquire a close friend in those lonely months. Janie Corbin was six years old, with golden hair and large blue eyes that sparkled happily. She and the general developed an instant love for each other.

In the afternoons, when Jackson rested from paperwork, Janie would appear at his office. She would cut the Stonewall Brigade out of folded paper and delight in the long line of soldiers she had made. Jackson was not good at that sort of thing, but he could play games and tell the child fascinating stories.

The two spent hours together, cemented forever when Jackson saw how enamored Janie was with the gold braid adorning his cap. He took his pocketknife and removed the gilt band. After tying it around her curls, he took her cheeks in his hand and said: "Janie, it suits a little girl like you better than it does an old soldier like me."[13]

In March, Jackson had to shift his headquarters closer to the Fredericksburg lines. This meant saying good-bye to the Corbins in general and to little Janie in particular. Jackson did not get to see Janie; the child was down with scarlet fever but seemed to be improving. The general sent her an affectionate message. A day later he learned that Janie had taken a sudden turn for the worse. The child was dead. Jackson began weeping before falling to his knees in prayer. Death had claimed yet another loved one.

The ache in Jackson's heart became a stronger yearning to see Anna and his little Julia. When the weather turned wetter than usual and delayed the opening of the spring campaign, Jackson invited his family to join him for a brief visit. They arrived from North Carolina on April 20. Jackson met them at the Guiney Station railhead south of Fredericksburg. Soldiers cheered as the general in a carriage drove his wife and daughter to their temporary quarters in the Thomas Yerby home.

For the next week, "the general spent all his leisure time in playing with the baby."[14] General Lee and his staff called to pay respects to Jackson's family. Anna was panic-stricken at the thought of meeting the great chieftain. Yet, she said, "I was met by a face so kind and *fatherly,* and a greeting so cordial, that I was at once reassured and put to ease."[15]

On April 23 (Julia's five-month birthday), Jackson proudly held the baby as the Reverend Lacy performed the rite of baptism. The general had never seemed happier, Anna later noted. "His conversation

This Chancellorsville Photograph
of Jackson was taken only a week before his mortal wounding. According to Mrs. Jackson, blowing wind caused the general's hair to stick out.

was more spiritual than I had ever observed before. . . . He never appeared to be in better health than at this time, and I never saw him look so handsome and noble."[16]

At Anna's urging, Jackson agreed to have a Richmond photographic team take his picture. He wore the uniform coat that Jeb Stuart had given him as he sat in the entrance hall of the Yerby home. A strong breeze blowing in his face gave what Mrs. Jackson termed "a sternness to his countenance that was not natural."[17]

This likeness, often called the *Chancellorsville Photograph,* remains the most popular image of the general.

Jackson watched the rains stop and the roads dry. He was not surprised when a courier awakened him on the morning of April 29. The Union army was in motion. Another spring campaign was underway. Luckily there was time for a loving embrace and sweet kisses. Then, as Anna and Julia departed by train for North Carolina, Jackson turned back to war.

That winter the Army of the Potomac had gotten a new commander. General Joseph Hooker was then forty-eight, tall, handsome, and red-faced. He rode a snow-white horse despite the target it presented. Men called him "Fighting Joe." Hooker talked tough and drank hard, but he had proven himself a brave officer in combat. Yet Hooker was extremely vain and openly ambitious.

The plan that Hooker developed against Lee in the spring of 1863 was as good as any general ever made. Hooker had built up his army to 130,000 well-trained soldiers with 404 guns. He knew that Lee's army of 62,000 troops and 228 cannons was on open ground south of Fredericksburg.

Hooker (perhaps borrowing from Lee's favorite strategy) divided his forces. General John Sedgwick and fifty thousand

Federals were to stand at Fredericksburg and hold the Confederates in check. Hooker with seventy thousand Federals would march up the Rappahannock, cross the river at unprotected fords, and attack Lee's left flank. If the Southern commander retreated, he would move directly across Hooker's front. If Lee stood firm, Hooker and Sedgwick would close like a giant vise and squeeze the Confederate army into surrender.

Never known for modesty, Hooker boasted to one and all that he now had "the finest army the sun ever shone on." The only question, Hooker told President Lincoln, was not whether he took Richmond but when. "My plans are perfect, and when I start to carry them out, may God have mercy on General Lee, for I will have none."[18]

By the time Lee realized what the Union strategy was, Hooker's huge wing was across the Rappahannock and moving through a dense woodland known locally as the Wilderness. Twelve miles long and six miles wide, the Wilderness was a dark, tangled mass of stunted pines, hardwood trees, vines, and undergrowth. One could not see more than twenty yards in any direction. The whole area was no place for an army to be. Hooker needed to get in, and get out, as quickly as possible.

Another day, and Hooker would be in the open and threatening Lee's flank. Now came the first mistake in Hooker's plan: the expectation that Lee would do what Hooker thought he would do.

Lee's army was not up to strength.

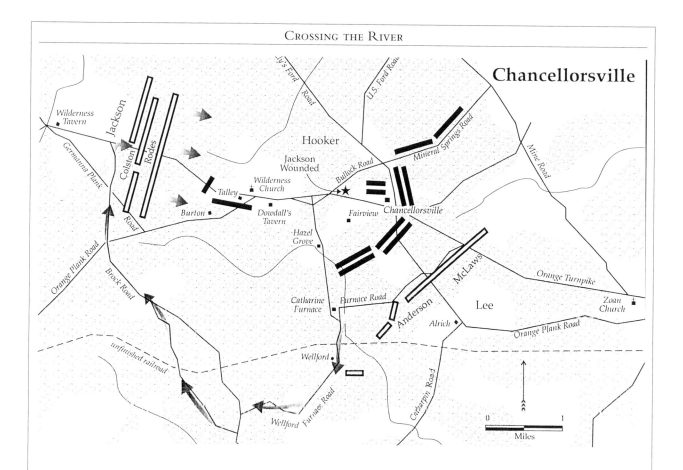

Chancellorsville

Longstreet and two divisions were on duty in southeastern Virginia. Nevertheless, the Southern commander saw that the real danger was not Sedgwick but was Hooker to the west. Lee quickly split his forces.

General Jubal Early and ten thousand Southerners would face Sedgwick from the hills Lee had used in the December battle. The bulk of the Confederate army—forty-two thousand soldiers—would hasten west to confront Hooker. Jackson would be in the lead.

As the march got underway, everyone seemed to notice Jackson. Officers at headquarters caught "a wondrous change" in the general. To Chaplain Lacy, "his bearing became quicker, energetic, more lofty. The whole man energized and inspired all else."[19]

On May 1, fog shrouded Jackson's early-morning advance. The metallic clank of canteens, muskets, and other equipment added a high pitch to the thud of thousands of marching feet. No other sound could be heard from the ranks. Meanwhile, a Union division commander wrote of that day: "All of the army . . . were in exuberant spirits . . . the general hilarity pervading the camps was particularly noticeable; the soldiers, while chopping wood and lighting fires, were singing merry songs and indulging in peppery camp jokes."[20]

Near noon, as the lead elements of Hooker's army were emerging from the Wilderness, Jackson's men slammed into the Federals. This totally unexpected attack completely unnerved Hooker. The Union general forgot all ideas of offense. He

*Lee and Jackson, seated on cracker boxes in the darkness
of the Wilderness, planned the next day's attack at Chancellorsville.*

ordered his army (over protests from his corps commanders) to return to the dense woods and take a defensive stand around an intersection of two country roads. The clearing was known as Chancellorsville.

That night Lee and Jackson sat on cracker boxes at another road intersection only a mile from the Union lines. A small campfire separated the two generals as they discussed what to do. They knew that Hooker's line curled in a wide arc, with its left resting on the Rappahannock at U.S. Ford. Where to attack was the question the two Confederate generals pondered.

Then cavalryman Jeb Stuart arrived with exciting news. Hooker had made another mistake. Stuart had ranged far to the west and discovered that Hooker's right flank was "in the air." It was not anchored

on any firm piece of land, nor was it bent back to provide strength. The Union line simply extended west to the last Union soldier and then stopped.

Lee's army was badly outnumbered. Lee had already divided it once. Now he would divide it again. The attacked would become the attacker, he concluded. While he occupied Hooker's attention in front, Jackson and the bulk of the forces at hand would make a wide march around the Union right. Then Jackson would assail the Union flank and rear while Lee assaulted from the front.

Numbers showed the danger Lee faced. Jackson was leading twenty-eight thousand men on a flanking movement. Lee and fourteen thousand Confederates would be all that stood between Hooker and

Richmond. If the Federal commander learned what the Confederates were doing, the campaign—and possibly Southern hopes for independence—were doomed.

From another viewpoint, Lee was not endangering the Southern cause. It was already in danger. Lee was badly outnumbered; and because he was, he was free to take enormous chances. The odds against him were so long that lengthening them further would do little harm.

For Jackson, the flank march was ideal strategy. Secrecy and speed were the ingredients. He would take the offensive with a rapid advance. Then would come an onslaught against inferior numbers at the edge of the enemy army.

Jackson got an hour's nap on wet ground. He awakened chilled, a sure sign that a cold was developing. A quick cup of coffee, then he mounted Little Sorrel for perhaps the most important movement of his military career. Shortly after 7:30 A.M. on May 2, Jackson's long column started down a single-lane country road.

The general had ridden only a short distance when he met Lee by the roadside. A brief conversation followed. Then Jackson, eyes ablaze, pointed to the west. Jackson saluted; Lee did the same as his lieutenant rode down an incline in the woods. The two generals had seen each other for the last time.

Throughout that warm Saturday, Confederates four abreast wound and turned as they made their way through forests and clearings. Local guides used deserted wagon trails and overgrown paths. Sometimes it seemed to the men that no trails existed at all.

One "foot cavalryman" remembered that the long line "went swiftly forward through the Wilderness, striking now and then a dim path or road. Strict silence was enforced, the men being allowed to speak only in whispers. Occasionally a courier would spur his tired horse past us as we twisted through the brush. For hours at the time we neither saw nor heard anything."[21]

A North Carolina soldier added: "One thing we did know and know for a certainty was that Old Jack was going around the bulls horn and unless the bull kept his tail twitching very fast the old hero would have a grip on it before the sun went down."[22]

South, west, north, northwest, the long line snaked. One stream provided the only water in the twelve-mile journey. Confederates marched at an excited, almost eager pace. In their front, a grim Jackson carefully watched terrain. An air of determination became denser with each passing mile.

By the middle of the afternoon, a third of Jackson's force had reached the Orange Turnpike. This was the main east-west thoroughfare through the Wilderness. Jackson quietly spread his force into battle position in the woods a few hundred yards from Hooker's right flank.

Now was the time to inform an anxious Lee of the situation. Jackson took out a wrinkled piece of paper and, using his saddle as a desk, wrote hastily:

Near 3 P.M.
May 2d, 1863

General,
The enemy has made a stand at Chancellor's
which is about 2 miles from Chancellorsville.
I hope as soon as practicable to attack.
I trust that an Ever Kind Providence will bless
us with great success.

Respectfully,
T. J. Jackson

Lt. Genl.
Genl. R. E. Lee
The leading division is up & the next two
appear to be well closed.
T. J. J.[23]

Jackson had done it! By 5 P.M. two full divisions, each a mile and half long, stretched in two lines through the Wilderness on either side of the Orange Turnpike. His orders were clear. Once the command to charge was given, "under no circumstance . . . was there to be any panic in the advance."[24]

Minutes passed while Jackson waited for stragglers in the lead division to catch up and take their places in line. He looked around at the officers standing in front of their men. Familiar faces of former cadets at VMI stared back in pride. Emotion momentarily swept through the general. "The Institute will be heard from today," Jackson said with a firm expression.[25]

A look at his watch—it was 5:15—and Jackson gave the order. Slowly, but gaining momentum as they moved, the line surged through the woods. Deer, rabbits, and other wildlife fled toward the Union camps. Most Federal soldiers were cooking supper over their campfires. Here and there a Union band was playing. One song had the appropriate title: "Won't You Come Out of the Wilderness?"

The attack was dramatic in every respect. An artillery officer in Jackson's corps wrote: "The surprise was complete. A bolt from the sky would not have startled [the Federals] half as much as the musket shots in the thickets . . . and then a solid wall of gray, forcing their way through the timber and bearing down upon them like an irresistible avalanche. There was no stemming such a tide. . . . The shock was too great; the sense of utter helplessness was too apparent. The resistance offered was speedily beaten down. There was nothing left but to lay down their arms and surrender, or flee. They threw them away, and fled. Arms, knapsacks, clothing, equipment, everything, was thrown aside and left behind. . . . Men lost their heads in terror, and the roads and woods on both sides [of the turnpike] were filled with men, horses and cattle, in one mad flight."[26]

For three miles Jackson's men drove the shattered Union line. Growing darkness, the tangled blindness of the Wilderness, and attacking lines breaking into bits and pieces because of terrain or resistance caused the advance to wear down.

Jackson had accompanied his artillery on the Orange Turnpike. Now, at the action, he was a picture of boundless energy. Never had victory been so sweet! The great Union host was on the verge of being destroyed. Powell Hill's division was moving in as support. A full moon had replaced the sun. A night attack, Jackson was convinced, would be the crushing blow. The Lord is with us! One more onslaught will bring triumph!

Disregarding everything, Jackson took some of his aides and rode through black woods to determine where the new Union position was. It was 9:15; darkness had enveloped the earth. Sandie Pendleton felt deep concern. "General," his chief of staff asked, "don't you think this is the wrong place for you?"

Jackson gave no thought to personal safety. Sweeping success was at hand. "The danger is all over!" he shouted. "The enemy is routed! Go back and tell A. P. Hill to press right on!"[27]

It did not take long to find the Union lines. The sound of axes and spades told Jackson where Federals were preparing hasty earthworks. He turned Little Sorrel and started with his staff back to his own lines. The party rode at a trot. It sounded like a troop of cavalry, and the horses were approaching from the direction of the Union army.

Men in the 18th North Carolina could hear riders coming straight at them. Jackson had always taught his soldiers to shoot first and then ask questions. The

Jackson's sudden flank attack sent part of the Union army
reeling for three miles and resulted in high casualties among the Federals.

horsemen were barely twenty yards away when an officer shouted: "Pour it into them, boys!"[28]

A sheet of musketry lit the woods for an instant, six of Jackson's staff members escaped injury; seven of the nine horses were not hit. Yet Jackson himself was struck, and for the first and only time in the war Little Sorrel bolted in panic. The general barely managed to stay in the saddle as branches cut his face and tore at his clothing. Finally two staff officers stopped the horse and eased Jackson to the ground. General A. P. Hill reached the area, dismounted at once, and gently held Jackson's head in his lap while others rushed to find medical aid.

Three bullets had struck Jackson. One ball entered the left forearm an inch below the elbow and passed out near the wrist. The second struck his right palm, broke two fingers, and lodged against the skin at the back of his hand. The third ball plowed through the bone and muscle of his left arm just below the shoulder. All three wounds were bleeding heavily.

Much time passed before two Confederates with a stretcher found Jackson. They placed the general on the canvas litter. The painful journey through dense woods and thick underbrush to a field hospital took two hours and was torturous for Jackson. Twice the bearers tripped, hurling Jackson both times to the ground. A wagon was secured for the last half-mile of the three-mile trip.

Surgeon McGuire rushed to his chieftain and knelt down as Jackson was placed on the ground. "I hope you are not much hurt," McGuire said as he began to examine the wounds.

Jackson answered evenly but feebly: "I am badly injured, Doctor. I fear I am dying."[29]

Sometime after midnight, with Jackson unconscious from the effects of chloroform, a team of surgeons amputated the general's left arm. Jackson endured the operation in amazingly good form, in the face of fatigue and loss of blood.

The next morning he felt strong enough to talk with members of his staff. A message arrived from Lee: "Could I have directed events, I should have chosen for the good of the country to have been disabled in your stead. I congratulate you upon the victory which is due to your skill and energy."[30]

For the first and only time, Jackson disagreed with his commander. "General Lee is very kind," he said, "but he should give the praise to God."[31]

Throughout May 3, Confederates moved into action with battle cries of "Revenge Jackson! Revenge Jackson!" The fighting that Sunday became the second bloodiest day of the Civil War, ranking only behind Antietam. Lee's forces swept forward to one of the great victories in American military history.

That afternoon, as fighting raged over a thirteen-mile area, Jackson had a conversation with Chaplain Lacy. The minister could not conceal his regrets over Jackson's loss of an arm. The General reassured his friend. "I would not replace my arm if I

Union artillery try desperately to stop the long lines of Confederates bearing down on them at Chancellorsville.

could," he told Lacy. "This is a blessing from God that I do not understand. Yet I shall know what it means either in this world or the next. I am perfectly content."[32]

After dark, Surgeon McGuire made a visit. Jackson asked for news of the battle. McGuire watched Jackson as he told of the hard-won victory. "His face would light up with enthusiasm and interest when I told him how this brigade acted, and that officer displayed conspicuous courage, and his head gave a peculiar shake from side to side, as he uttered his usual 'good, good' with unwonted energy when I spoke of the Stonewall Brigade."

The men of that brigade, he told McGuire, "will be proud one day to say to their children: 'I was one of the Stonewall brigade.' I have no right to the name

'Stonewall.' It belongs to the brigade and not at all to me."[33]

With fighting at Chancellorsville continuing into the next day, Lee became concerned for Jackson's safety. His lieutenant must be moved from the battle area and closer to the military hospitals near Richmond. The site selected was Guiney Station on the Richmond, Fredericksburg and Potomac Railroad. Transferring Jackson there involved a twenty-seven-mile ride over rough roads in a wagon that lacked springs. Although Jackson complained little during the ordeal, the trip exhausted him.

It was nighttime on May 4 when the party reached Guiney Station and "Fairfield," the estate of Thomas Coleman Chandler. So many wounded soldiers were in the main house that McGuire canceled

Following his surgery, and for safety reasons, Jackson was taken twenty-seven miles to the estate of Thomas Coleman Chandler at Guiney Station. His bedroom in the little office building was behind the door on the right-hand side of the porch.

plans to put the general there. Instead, Jackson was placed in a small building similar to his headquarters at Moss Neck. All seemed to be going well with Jackson's recovery. He was in good spirits and talked freely.

Shortly after midnight on May 7, Jackson awakened with fever, pain, and nausea. McGuire knew immediately what was wrong: dreaded pneumonia. At that time, no cure existed. Treatment for the most part was to control discomfort. Jackson's condition steadily worsened.

Anna and the baby arrived to find the general in a stupor from opiates. The change in Jackson from ten days earlier was shocking, Anna noted. "His fearful wounds, his mutilated arm, the scratches upon his face, and, above all, the desperate pneumonia, which was flushing his cheeks, oppressing his breathing, and benumbing his senses,

wrung my soul with such grief and anguish as it had never before experienced."[34]

Jackson awakened to see his frightened wife standing over his bed. He managed to say: "My darling, you must cheer up, and not wear a long face."[35] Then he slipped back into unconsciousness. Physicians, family, and staff could do nothing but watch life ebb away.

From the day he embraced God as his closest friend, Jackson had expressed the hope that he might be blessed to die on the Lord's day. Sunday, May 10, was spring-like and beautiful. Jackson's faith remained firm as his strength failed. He was in a drugged and heavy sleep most of the day. Then, at 3:15 P.M., he opened his eyes, stared upward, and said in a clear voice: "Let us cross over the river and rest under the shade of the trees."[36]

A moment later, Jackson completed his earthly duties and joined heaven's army.

*The bedroom and furnishings where Jackson died
on Sunday afternoon, May 10, 1863.*

EPILOGUE

THE NEWS OF Jackson's death spread throughout the South and struck hard. This was especially true inside the ranks of the Army of Northern Virginia. General Raleigh Colston noted that "the sounds of merriment died away as if the Angel of Death himself had flapped his muffled wings over the troops. . . . Many were the veterans . . . whose bronzed cheeks were now wet with burning tears, and whose dauntless breasts were heaving with uncontrollable sobs."[1]

An emotional Lee told his son: "It is a terrible loss. I do not know how to replace him."[2] In Lexington a young girl exclaimed that Jackson's passing "was the first time it had dawned on us that God would let us be defeated."[3]

From Guiney Station, Mrs. Jackson, several officers, and a military escort accompanied the general's body to Richmond. There his remains were embalmed and a death mask was made. A few days earlier, the Confederate Congress had adopted a new Confederate emblem (known as the Third National Flag). The first banner made was draped over Jackson's metallic casket.

For a day the body lay in state in the governor's mansion. Then it was moved to the hall of the House of Representatives in the Capitol. The largest crowd ever assembled in Richmond stood in line for hours to get a glimpse of the coffin containing the Confederacy's most popular hero.

Public expressions of grief were usually not made in nineteenth-century America. Yet Jackson's death was different. So deep was the shock, so intense the loss, that people filing by his remains literally covered the coffin with flowers.

Anna and a small group were on the train that conveyed the body to Lynchburg. There the party boarded a barge for the final stage of the journey. The canal boat *Marshall* slowly made its way up the James River. At day's end, the boat reached Lexington. Cadets waited at attention.

"The Major" lay in state that night in his old classroom. It was "just as he left it

The death mask of General Jackson, made in Richmond the day after his passing.

The general's binoculars with case and haversack. Jackson was wearing these items at the time of his wounding.

two years before," one man wrote. When the casket was placed in front of his favorite chair, it "brought tears to many eyes."[4] Throughout the night, two cadets stood hour-long shifts at either end of the coffin.

Full military honors prevailed at the Friday, May 15, funeral service. Jackson's coffin rested on a caisson draped in black as it moved from VMI to the Presbyterian church and then up South Main Street to the cemetery. Cannons fired every half-hour in honor of the departed commander. Jackson was buried beside his first daughter and not far from his first wife.

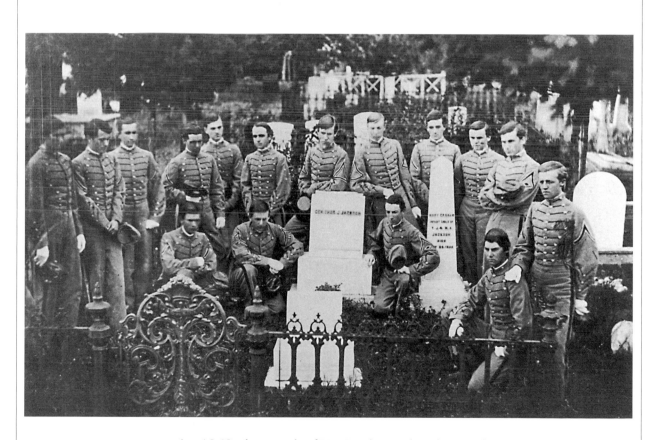

An 1868 photograph of VMI cadets gathered around the general's grave in Lexington.

Anna Jackson returned to Charlotte, North Carolina, and enjoyed a full, honored life. Known as the "Widow of the Confederacy," she devoted her postwar years to her family, Southern patriotic groups, and writing her memoirs of life with the immortal Stonewall. She traveled widely and had the distinction of meeting five presidents. Anna died March 24, 1915. The cause of death was pneumonia, the same illness that took the life of her husband. She was buried beside Jackson in Lexington.

Julia Jackson, an infant when her father died, had but a brief sojurn on earth. From childhood, she had been frail. At the age of twenty-two, Julia married William E. Christian in Richmond. Their union produced two children. On August 30, 1889, Julia died of typhoid fever at the age of twenty-six.

If Laura Jackson Arnold ever had remorse over the permanent separation from her brother, she never expressed it publicly. Laura remained a Unionist to the end of her life. She made no effort to associate with any member of the Jackson family. Divorced from her husband, Jonathan Arnold, and a victim of poor health, she spent nineteen years in an Ohio sanitorium. Laura died September 24, 1911, at the West Virginia home of a daughter-in-law.

Jackson undoubtedly would have preferred to spend eternity in an inconspicuous grave. His legions of admirers would not have it so. On July 21, 1891, the thirtieth anniversary of the Battle of First Manassas and the creation of the name

"Stonewall," a new grave for the general was dedicated. It would become the centerpiece of the Stonewall Cemetery in Lexington. A life-size bronze statue of Jackson looks south from atop a tall stone column. Over twenty-five thousand people attended the unveiling ceremonies in what has been called "the greatest day that Lexington saw or will probably ever see again."[5]

That was not the first statue erected to Jackson's memory. A move to place a

The Virginia Orphan *is what artist Mort Künstler entitled this drawing of Jackson in a relaxed pose.*

metal likeness in Richmond's Capitol Square began two weeks after the general's death. Today at least eight memorial statues exist. They are located from Manassas and Richmond to Clarksburg, and New Orleans, Louisiana.

In addition, dozens of metal or stone markers stand along roadsides to show where he was or what he did at a given moment. His name adorns schools, buildings, cemeteries, highways, museums, parks, and postage stamps.

In 1906 the all-black congregation at the Fifth Avenue Presbyterian Church in Roanoke, Virginia, dedicated a stained-glass window in memory of Jackson. The minister was the son of slaves who had found hope and love in the major's Sunday school class. The Fifth Avenue Presbyterian Church is still in existence; the altar window to Jackson's memory remains in place.

Jackson's Mill, the estate where Tom Jackson passed his youth, is now a West Virginia state park. The only home he ever owned is preserved in Lexington, Virginia, as a museum, archives, and sponsor of conferences. The little outbuilding at Guiney Station where he died is likewise preserved. It is known appropriately as the Jackson Shrine.

In mid-August 1862, a Georgia lieutenant wrote his wife that Jackson "is one of the greatest men living. So brave, so pleasant in his intercourse and kind to the soldiers. . . . You never hear a word against

him unless, by chance, some weary fellow will say that he is marched too hard; but he will invariably add, 'I reckon old Stonewall knows what is best, don't think he would march us so hard unless it was necessary.'" [6]

"Old Jack's" qualities—honesty, courtesy, modesty, dedication to duty—combined with his personal faith and military brilliance—make him a truly extraordinary individual in his or in any age. For countless men in the Union armies, fighting against Jackson became a right of passage into manhood. It was the real test of a soldier. Many historians support the belief of hundreds of Johnny Rebs and Billy Yanks that had Jackson been at the Battle of Gettysburg (only two months after his death), the results would have been a smashing victory that might have won the Civil War for the Confederacy. [7]

Almost thirty years later, a group of admirers were standing in front of the Jackson monument at Lexington. One visitor asked a former Confederate soldier in the group the secret of Jackson's success. "He made his soldiers believe he was invincible," the old veteran replied. Then, with tears in his eyes and his voice breaking, he added: "He *was* invincible; and as God has decreed that the South should not succeed, he had to take Stonewall away." [8]

His gifts are a legacy. Jackson was a man we did not know—but one we can never forget.

NOTES

INTRODUCTION

1. *London Times,* May 11, 1863.

2. Thomas J. Jackson book of maxims, George and Catherine Davis Collection, Tulane University.

3. Austin C. Stearns, *Three Years with Company K* (London: Associated University Presses, 1976), 92–93.

4. Maria Lydig Daly, *Diary of a Union Lady* (New York: Funk and Wagnalls Company, 1962), 171.

5. James I. Robertson, Jr., *Stonewall Jackson: The Man, The Soldier, The Legend* (New York: Macmillan Publishing USA, 1997), 753.

6. Thomas J. Jackson to Anna Jackson, August 5, 1861, Charles W. Dabney Papers, University of North Carolina.

CHAPTER I

1. The original Lewis County has since been divided into six separate counties.

2. Robertson, *Stonewall Jackson,* 7.

3. Mary Anna Jackson, *Memoirs of Stonewall Jackson by His Widow* (Louisville, Ky.: The Prentice Press, 1895), 16–17. Jackson and his stepbrother, William Wirt Woodson, were never close friends.

4. Robertson, *Stonewall Jackson,* 10, 166, 169–70. Woodson quickly married again but died only a year after Julia Jackson Woodson.

5. Thomas J. Jackson to Laura Arnold, July 6, 1850, Thomas J. Jackson Papers, Virginia Military Institute.

6. J. H. Diss Debar, "Two Men: Old John Brown and Stonewall Jackson of World-wide Fame," typescript, West Virginia Department of Archives and History, 6.

7. Roy Bird Cook, *The Family and Early Life of Stonewall Jackson* (Charleston, W.Va.: Charleston Publishing Co., 1924), 52–53.

8. Robertson, *Stonewall Jackson,* 17.

9. Thomas J. Arnold, *Early Life and Letters of General Thomas J. Jackson— "Stonewall" Jackson, by His Nephew* (New York: Fleming H. Revell Co., 1916), 305.

10. Cook, *Family and Early Life,* 64–65.

11. Robertson, *Stonewall Jackson,* 19.

12. Ibid., 20–21.

13. Mrs. Jackson, *Memoirs,* 27.

14. John Milton, "Paradise Regained," Book IV, lines 220–21, in Merritt Y. Hughes (ed.), *John Milton: Complete Poems and Major Prose* (New York: Macmillan Publishing Co., 1957), 520.

CHAPTER II

1. Robertson, *Stonewall Jackson,* 25, 795.

2. Cook, *Family and Early Life,* 86–88.

3. James L. Morrison, Jr. *"The Best School in the World": West Point, The Pre-Civil War Years, 1833–1866* (Kent, Ohio: The Kent State University Press, 1986), 27.

4. Dabney H. Maury, *Recollections of a Virginian* (New York: Charles Scribner's Sons, 1894), 22–23.

5. John C. Waugh, *The Class of 1846* (New York: Warner Books, 1994), 12.

6. Lloyd Lewis, *Captain Sam Grant* (Boston: Little, Brown and Co., 1960), 89.

7. Robertson, *Stonewall Jackson,* 28–29.

8. Ibid., 29.

9. Frank E. Vandiver, *Mighty Stonewall* (New York: McGraw-Hill Book Co., 1957), 15.

10. G. F. R. Henderson, *Stonewall Jackson and the American Civil War* (London: Longmans, Green and Co., 1898), I, 20.

11. Stephen W. Sears, *George B. McClellan: The Young Napoleon* (New York: Ticknor & Fields, 1988), 7.

12. Mrs. Jackson, *Memoirs,* 35.

13. For the full text of Jackson's book of maxims, see Robertson, *Stonewall Jackson,* 154–56.

14. Arnold, *Early Life and Letters,* 13.

15. Ibid., 66.

16. Robertson, *Stonewall Jackson,* 41.

17. Ibid.

18. Thomas J. Jackson to Laura J. Arnold, February 10, 1845, Thomas J. Jackson Papers, Virginia Military Institute.

19. Robertson, *Stonewall Jackson,* 43–44.

20. Ibid., 44.

21. Robert L. Dabney, *Life and Courage of Lieut.-Gen. Thomas J. Jackson* (New York: Blelock & Co., 1866), 36.

22. Henderson, *Jackson,* I, 20.

23. The highest ranking cadets in a graduating class were assigned to the army's elite branch, the engineers. The next highest group went into the artillery. Those in the middle of the class were usually appointed to the cavalry, while graduates at the bottom of the standing went into the infantry.

24. Arnold, *Early Life and Letters,* 74.

CHAPTER III

1. David Nevin, *The Mexican War* (Alexandria, Va.: Time-Life Books, 1978), 6, 17, 19.

2. Ibid., 22, 150.

3. Robertson, *Stonewall Jackson,* 46.

4. Ibid., 52.

5. Ibid., 52, 799.

6. Allan R. Millett and Peter Maslowski, *For the Common Defense: A Military History of the United States* (New York: The Free Press, 1984), 147–48.

7. Arnold, *Early Life and Letters,* 82.

8. Thomas J. Jackson to Laura J. Arnold, March 30, 1847, Thomas J. Jackson Papers, Virginia Military Institute.

9. James W. Anderson, "With Scott in Mexico: Letters of Captain James W. Anderson in the Mexican War, 1846–1847," *Military History of the West,* 28 (1998): 23.

10. Ibid., 38.

11. Nevin, *Mexican War,* 146.

12. Robertson, *Stonewall Jackson,* 57. Captain Taylor reported that the guns were brought up at night "through the great exertions of Lieut. Jackson."

13. Elizabeth Preston Allan, *The Life and Letters of Margaret Junkin Preston* (Boston: Houghton, Mifflin Co., 1903), 83.

14. Waugh, *Class of 1846,* 101.

15. Thomas J. Jackson to Laura J. Arnold, May 1, 1847, Thomas J. Jackson Papers, Library of Congress.

16. Thomas J. Jackson to Laura J. Arnold, May 25, 1847, Thomas J. Jackson Papers, Virginia Military Institute.

17. Arnold, *Early Life and Letters,* 129–30.

18. Robertson, *Stonewall Jackson,* 61.

19. Waugh, *Class of 1846,* 104.

20. Ibid., 111.

21. Robertson, *Stonewall Jackson,* 63–64.

22. Ibid., 64.

23. Nevin, *Mexican War,* 211.

24. Arnold, *Early Life and Letters,* 130.

25. Roberton, *Stonewall Jackson,* 66–67.

26. Ibid., 67.

27. Ibid.

28. Millett and Maslowski, *For the Common Defense,* 149.

29. Robertson, *Stonewall Jackson,* 70.

CHAPTER IV

1. Robertson, *Stonewall Jackson,* 72.

2. Arnold, *Early Life and Letters,* 128.

3. Mrs. Jackson, *Memoirs,* 48.

4. Robertson, *Stonewall Jackson,* 80.

5. *Clarksburg Sunday Exponent-Telegram,* April 20, 1930.

6. Robertson, *Stonewall Jackson,* 82.

7. Ibid., 83.

8. Vandiver, *Mighty Stonewall,* 48.

9. Thomas J. Jackson to Laura J. Arnold, July 2, 1849, Thomas J. Jackson Papers, Virginia Military Institute.

10. Robertson, *Stonewall Jackson,* 92.

11. Lenoir Chambers, *Stonewall Jackson* (New York: William Morrow & Co., 1959), I, 150.

12. Maury, *Recollections,* 71.

13. Thomas J. Jackson to Laura J. Arnold, March 1, 1850, Thomas J. Jackson Papers, Library of Congress.

14. Virginia Bergman Peters, *The Florida Wars* (Hamden, Conn.: Archon Books, 1979), 267, 274.

15. Canter Brown, Jr., *Fort Meade, 1849–1900* (Tuscaloosa: The University of Alabama Press, 1995), 4–7.

16. Edward M. Coffman, *The Old Army: A Portrait of the American Army in Peacetime, 1784–1898* (New York: Oxford University Press, 1986), 57–58.

17. Thomas J. Jackson to Laura J. Arnold, April 2, 1851, Thomas J. Jackson Papers, Virginia Military Institute.

18. Robertson, *Stonewall Jackson,* 108.

CHAPTER V

1. Robertson, *Stonewall Jackson,* 114.

2. For a modest but proud account of the school's first years, see Francis H. Smith, *The Virginia Military Institute: Its Building and Rebuilding* (Lexington: Virginia Military Institute, 1912).

3. Robertson, *Stonewall Jackson,* 111.

4. Differing accounts exist of this episode. For example, see ibid., 140–41; Willie Walker Caldwell, *Stonewall Jim: A Biography of General James A. Walker, C.S.A.* (Elliston, Va.: Northcross House, 1990), 1–5.

5. Ibid., 120.

6. Ibid., 119.

7. Vandiver, *Mighty Stonewall,* 78.

8. Robertson, *Stonewall Jackson,* 124.

9. William Couper, *One Hundred Years at V.M.I.* (Richmond, Va.: Garrett and Massie, 1939), 1:263.

10. *Southern Historical Society Papers,* 38 (1910): 271.

11. Thomas J. Jackson to Laura J. Arnold, August 20, 1851, Thomas J. Jackson Papers, Virginia Military Institute.

12. Couper, *V.M.I.,* 1:236.

13. Edwin L. Dooley, "Lexington in the 1860 Census" (Lexington: Rockbridge Historical Society, 1979, typescript), 4.

14. Mrs. Jackson, *Memoirs,* 68.

15. Robertson, *Stonewall Jackson,* 130.

16. Ibid., 130-31.

17. Ibid., 131.

18. John W. Wayland, *Stonewall Jackson's Way* (Dayton, Ohio: Morningside Bookshop, 1984), 7.

19. Ernest T. Thompson, *Presbyterians in the South, 1607–1861* (Richmond, Va.: John Knox Press, 1963), 362, 433.

20. Mrs. Jackson, *Memoirs,* 57.

21. Ibid., 58.

22. Robertson, *Stonewall Jackson,* 135.

23. Arnold, *Early Life and Letters,* 182.

24. Romans 8:28 (King James Version of the Bible). Jackson, remembering the sadness of his youth, was also fond of Revelation 21:4: "And God shall wipe away all tears from their eyes; and there shall be no more death, neither sorrow, nor crying, neither shall there be any more pain . . ."

25. H. M. White (ed.), *Rev. William S. White, D.D., and His Time, 1800–1873: An Autobiography* (Harrisonburg, Va.: Sprinkle Publications, 1983), 138–39.

26. See Robertson, *Stonewall Jackson,* 136–38.

27. Ibid., 137.

28. Ibid., 138.

29. Thomas J. Jackson to Laura J. Arnold, September 7, 1852, Thomas J. Jackson Papers, Library of Congress.

CHAPTER VI

1. Vandiver, *Mighty Stonewall,* 90.

2. Robertson, *Stonewall Jackson,* 145.

3. Ibid.

4. Mary P. Coulling, *Margaret Junkin Preston: A Biography* (Winston-Salem, N.C.: John F. Blair, Publisher, 1993), 65–72.

5. Vandiver, *Mighty Stonewall,* 98.

6. Thomas J. Jackson to Laura J. Arnold, October 19, 1853, Thomas J. Jackson Papers, Virginia Military Institute.

7. Robertson, *Stonewall Jackson,* 157.

8. Ibid., 160.

9. Allan, *Life and Letters*, 72.

10. Ibid., 77.

11. Arnold, *Early Life and Letters*, 220.

12. White, *Dr. White*, 158.

13. Robertson, *Stonewall Jackson*, 169.

14. See Coulling, *Margaret Junkin Preston*, 65–72.

15. Robertson, *Stonewall Jackson*, 171.

16. Thomas J. Jackson to Anna Morrison, April 25, 1857, Charles W. Dabney Papers, University of North Carolina.

17. Thomas J. Jackson to Anna Morrison, May 16, 1857, ibid.

18. William C. Chase, *Story of Stonewall Jackson* (Atlanta: D. E. Luther Publishing Co., 1901), 142.

19. Robertson, *Stonewall Jackson*, 179, 183.

20. Ibid., 191.

21. Ibid., 183.

22. Mrs. Jackson, *Memoirs*, 107.

23. See Robertson, *Stonewall Jackson*, 191–92.

24. Anna Jackson to Robert L. Dabney, Autumn, 1863, Charles W. Dabney Papers, University of North Carolina.

25. James D. McCabe, *The Life of Thomas J. Jackson, By an Ex-cadet* (Richmond, Va.: James E. Goode, 1864), 26.

26. Robertson, *Stonewall Jackson*, 195.

27. Mrs. Jackson, *Memoirs*, 111.

28. Arnold, *Early Life and Letters*, 273.

29. Robertson, *Stonewall Jackson*, 200.

30. Ibid., 197.

31. Ibid., 199.

32. Mrs. Jackson, *Memoirs*, 132.

33. Ibid., 133–34.

34. Robertson, *Stonewall Jackson*, 204.

35. Thomas J. Jackson to Thomas J. Arnold, January 26, 1861, Thomas J. Jackson Papers, West Virginia University.

36. Robertson, *Stonewall Jackson*, 205–6.

37. Couper, *V.M.I.*, 2:81–82.

38. Ibid., 86.

39. James H. Wood, *The War: "Stonewall" Jackson, His Campaigns and Battles; The Regiment, As I Saw It* (Gaithersburg, Md.: Butternut Press, 1984), 11.

40. Robertson, *Stonewall Jackson*, 210–11.

41. Abraham Lincoln, *The Collected Works of Abraham Lincoln* (New Brunswick, N.J.: Rutgers University Press, 1953), 4:332.

42. See George Ellis Moore, *A Banner in the Hills: West Virginia's Statehood* (New York: Appleton-Century-Crofts, 1963), 33–46, 195–207.

43. For Laura's subsequent years, see Robertson, *Stonewall Jackson*, 690–91, 760.

44. Mrs. Jackson, *Memoirs*, 145.

CHAPTER VII

1. Robertson, *Stonewall Jackson*, 219.

2. Chase, *Jackson*, 222.

3. Robertson, *Stonewall Jackson*, 226–27.

4. Mrs. Jackson, *Memoirs*, 168.

5. See Vandiver, *Mighty Stonewall*, 138–40, 149.

6. Robertson, *Stonewall Jackson*, 241–42.

7. Mrs. Jackson, *Memoirs*, 159.

8. Robertson, *Stonewall Jackson*, 245.

9. C. A. Fonerden, *A Brief History of the Military Career of Carpenter's Battery* (New Market, Va.: Henkel & Company, 1911), 7.

10. Robertson, *Stonewall Jackson*, 261.

11. John Newton Lyle, "Sketches Found in a Confederate Veteran's Desk," typescript, Washington and Lee University, 204.

12. Ibid., 206–7.

13. Robertson, *Stonewall Jackson*, 263.

14. Ibid.

15. Ibid., 264, 835–36.

16. *Confederate Veteran*, 31 (1923): 275.

17. Robertson, *Stonewall Jackson*, 267.

18. Hunter McGuire and George L. Christian, *The Confederate Cause and Conduct in the War between the States* (Richmond: L. H. Jenkins, 1907), 197.

19. Alexandra Lee Levin, *"This Awful Drama": General Edwin Gray Lee, C.S.A., and His Family* (New York: Vantage Press, 1987), 29.

20. U.S. War Dept. (comp.), *War of the Rebellion: A Compilation of the Official Records of the Union and Confederate Armies* (Washington: U.S. Government Printing Office, 1880–1901), Ser. 1, Vol. 5, 500. Cited hereafter as *Official Records,* with all references being to Ser. 1.

21. Thomas J. Jackson to Anna Jackson, July 22, 1861, Charles W. Dabney Papers, University of North Carolina.

22. Mrs. Jackson, *Memoirs,* 181–82.

23. Robertson, *Stonewall Jackson,* 241.

24. Thomas J. Jackson to Anna Jackson, August 22, 1861, Charles W. Dabney Papers, University of North Carolina.

25. Mrs. Jackson, *Memoirs,* 194.

26. Henry Kyd Douglas, *I Rode with Stonewall* (Chapel Hill: The University of North Carolina Press, 1940), 14.

27. Robertson, *Stonewall Jackson,* 282–83.

Chapter VIII

1. Vandiver, *Mighty Stonewall,* 178.

2. In a twenty-four-hour period, Winchester changed hands four times. Robertson, *Stonewall Jackson,* 840. The city that came closest to matching Winchester was Romney, but it underwent change-of-possession "only" forty times during the war.

3. Ibid., 290–91.

4. Mrs. Jackson, *Memoirs,* 218.

5. Ibid., 295.

6. George M. Neese, *Three Years in the Confederate Horse Artillery* (Dayton, Ohio: Morningside, 1988), 10.

7. Douglas, *I Rode with Stonewall,* 19.

8. Robertson, *Stonewall Jackson,* 301, 843.

9. Vandiver, *Mighty Stonewall,* 189.

10. Lyle, "Sketches," 348.

11. Champ Clark, *Decoying the Yanks: Jackson's Valley Campaign* (Alexandria, Va.: Time-Life Books, 1984), 52.

12. Robertson, *Stonewall Jackson,* 306, 310–11.

13. Clark, *Decoying the Yanks,* 55.

14. *Official Records,* 5:1033.

15. Mrs. Jackson, *Memoirs,* 212.

16. *Official Records,* 5:1053.

17. For a full account of the resignation crisis, see Robertson, *Stonewall Jackson,* 315–22.

18. Ibid., 322.

19. Thomas M. Rankin, *Stonewall Jackson's Romney Campaign, January 1–February 20, 1862* (Lynchburg, Va.: H. E. Howard, 1994), 147.

20. Robertson, *Stonewall Jackson,* 323.

21. James R. Graham, "Some Reminiscences of Stonewall Jackson," *Things and Thoughts,* 1 (1901): 124, 198–99.

22. Jackson made this statement at least twice to Alexander R. Boteler, his closest friend in the Confederate Congress. See Robertson, *Stonewall Jackson,* 321, 330.

23. *Official Records,* 5:1095.

24. *Southern Historical Society Papers,* 25 (1897): 97.

25. Robertson, *Stonewall Jackson,* 338–39.

26. Mrs. Jackson, *Memoirs,* 249.

27. Robertson, *Stonewall Jackson,* 343.

28. Ibid.

29. Robert G. Tanner, *Stonewall in the Valley* (Mechanicsburg, Pa.: Stackpole Books, 1996), 132–33.

30. Ibid., 136.

31. Vandiver, *Mighty Stonewall,* 210.

32. Robertson, *Stonewall Jackson,* 353.

33. Mrs. Jackson, *Memoirs,* 248.

34. *Southern Historical Society Papers,* 11 (1883): 129.

35. Clark, *Decoying the Yanks,* 86.

36. Robertson, *Stonewall Jackson,* 357.

37. Robert E. Lee, *The Wartime Papers of R. E. Lee* (Boston: Little, Brown and Company, 1961), 156–57.

38. *Official Records,* 12: Pt. 3, 111, 118.

Chapter IX

1. *Official Records,* 12: Pt. 1, 119.

2. Robertson, *Stonewall Jackson,* 377.

3.   Richard S. Ewell, *The Making of a Soldier: Letters of General R. S. Ewell* (Richmond: Whittet & Shepperson, 1935), 108.

4.   Robertson, *Stonewall Jackson,* 338.

5.   Vandiver, *Mighty Stonewall,* 232.

6.   Robertson, *Stonewall Jackson,* 386.

7.   *Southern Historical Society Papers,* 9 (1881): 189.

8.   Lucy R. Buck, *Shadows on My Heart: The Civil War Diary of Lucy Rebecca Buck* (Athens: University of Georgia Press, 1997), 81.

9.   Robertson, *Stonewall Jackson,* 400.

10.   Clark, *Decoying the Yanks,* 131.

11.   James B. Avirett, *The Memoirs of General Turner Ashby and His Compeers* (Baltimore: Selby & Dulany, 1867), 196–97.

12.   Douglas, *I Rode with Stonewall,* 59. Mrs. Jackson, *Memoirs,* 261, had Jackson shout: "Forward! After the enemy!"

13.   Ibid., 265.

14.   Cornelia McDonald, *A Diary with Reminiscences of the War and Refugee Life in the Shenandoah Valley, 1860–1865* (Nashville: Cullom & Ghertner, 1935), 163.

15.   Miscellaneous Manuscripts: Thomas J. Jackson Papers, New York Historical Society.

16.   Lincoln, *Collected Works,* 5:232.

17.   *Official Records,* 12: Pt. 3, 267.

18.   Richard Taylor, *Destruction and Reconstruction* (New York: Longman, Green and Co., 1955), 72.

19.   Neese, *Three Years,* 64. Jackson's account of the movement to Anna was a typical expression of faith. "I am again retiring before the enemy. They endeavored to get in my rear by moving on both flanks of my gallant army, but our God has been my guide and saved me from their grasp." Mrs. Jackson, *Memoirs,* 268–69.

20.   James K. Edmondson, *My Dear Emma (War Letters of Col. James K. Edmondson, 1861–1865)* (Verona, Va.: McClure Press, 1978), 97.

21.   Robertson, *Stonewall Jackson,* 429.

22.   See ibid., 431–32, 867.

23.   Clark, *Decoying the Yanks,* 161.

24.   Wood, *The War,* 63-64.

25.   *Official Records,* 12: Pt. 1, 690, 717–18.

26.   Robertson, *Stonewall Jackson,* 438.

27.   *Official Records,* 12: Pt. 3, 221.

28.   Robertson, *Stonewall Jackson,* 446.

29.   Robert U. Johnson and C. C. Buel (eds.), *Battles and Leaders of the Civil War* (New York: The Century Co., 1884–1887), 2:297.

30.   Mrs. Jackson, *Memoirs,* 283.

31.   Philip Slaughter, *A Sketch of the Life of Randolph Fairfax, A Private in the Ranks of the Rockbridge Artillery* (Baltimore: Innes and Company, 1878), 34. Field Marshal Viscount Garnet Wolseley of the British army wrote after meeting Jackson in the field: "I believe that, inspired by the presence of such a man, I should be perfectly insensible to fatigue and reckon upon success as a moral certainty." Garnet Joseph Wolseley, *The American Civil War: An English View* (Charlottesville: University Press of Virginia, 1964), 36.

32.   Mrs. Jackson, *Memoirs,* 283–84.

33.   Vandiver, *Mighty Stonewall,* 287–88.

34.   Johnson and Buel, *Battles and Leaders,* 2:296–97.

35.   Robertson, *Stonewall Jackson,* 457.

36.   Susan Leigh Blackford (comp.), *Letters from Lee's Army* (New York: Charles Scribner's Sons, 1947), 84–85.

CHAPTER X

1.   Robertson, *Stonewall Jackson,* xiv.

2.   Douglas, *I Rode with Stonewall,* 98.

3.   William Stanley Hoole, *Lawley Covers the Confederacy* (Tuscaloosa, Ala.: Confederate Publishing Co., 1964), 31.

4.   John Esten Cooke, *A Life of Gen. Robert E. Lee* (New York: D. Appleton and Co., 1871), 264.

5.   For the conference with Lee, Jackson rode ninety miles in thirty-three hours. Robertson, *Stonewall Jackson,* 467.

6.   The full text of Lee's message to Jackson is in ibid., 469.

7.   Douglas, *I Rode with Stonewall,* 100.

8.   William W. Blackford, *War Years with Jeb Stuart* (New York: Charles Scribner's Sons, 1945), 71.

9.   Dabney, *Life and Campaigns,* 444.

10. Alexander Hunter, *Johnny Reb and Billy Yank* (New York: Neale Publishing Co., 1905), 170–71.

11. Robertson, *Stonewall Jackson,* 481.

12. James Huffman, *Ups and Downs of a Confederate Soldier* (New York: William E. Rudge's Sons, 1940), 52. For a similar statement on the Union side, see *Official Records,* 12: Pt. 2, 301.

13. *Southern Historical Society Papers,* 10 (1882): 151.

14. Robertson, *Stonewall Jackson,* 485.

15. Mrs. Jackson, *Memoirs,* 298.

16. Robertson, *Stonewall Jackson,* 493.

17. Mrs. Jackson, *Memoirs,* 302.

18. McHenry Howard, *Recollections of a Maryland Confederate Soldier and Staff Officer under Johnston, Jackson, and Lee* (Dayton, Ohio: Morningside Bookshop, 1975), 149.

19. Dabney, *Life and Campaigns,* 466–67.

20. George M. Vickers (ed.), *Under Both Flags* (St. Louis: People's, 1896), 136.

21. Johnson and Buel, *Battles and Leaders,* 2:394.

22. Douglas, *I Rode with Stonewall,* 108.

23. Robertson, *Stonewall Jackson,* 503.

24. Ibid., 507, 880.

25. Ibid., 510.

26. *Official Records,* 12: Pt. 2, 176; Pt. 3, 915.

27. Thomas J. Jackson to Anna Jackson, July 14, 1862, Thomas J. Jackson Papers, Library of Virginia.

CHAPTER XI

1. Douglas, *I Rode with Stonewall,* 120–21.

2. Robertson, *Stonewall Jackson,* 670.

3. Howard, *Recollections of a Maryland Confederate Soldier,* 181.

4. Heros Von Borcke, *Memoirs of the Confederate War for Independence* (Edinburgh, Scot.: W. Blackwood and Sons, 1866), 1:104.

5. Robertson, *Stonewall Jackson,* 570.

6. Vandiver, *Mighty Stonewall,* 335.

7. Lee, *Wartime Papers of R. E. Lee,* 239.

8. Ibid., 248.

9. Robertson, *Stonewall Jackson,* 523.

10. See ibid., 523–25.

11. George H. Gordon, *Brook Farm to Cedar Mountain in the War of the Great Rebellion, 1861–62* (Boston: James R. Osgood and Company, 1883), 277.

12. Robertson, *Stonewall Jackson,* 525, 883.

13. *Official Records,* 12: Pt. 2, 181.

14. James I. Robertson, Jr., *General A. P. Hill: The Story of a Confederate Warrior* (New York: Random House, 1987), 100.

15. *Official Records,* 12: Pt. 2, 183.

16. Robertson, *Stonewall Jackson,* 531, 884.

17. Blackford, *Letters from Lee's Army,* 105.

18. Douglas, *I Rode with Stonewall,* 124.

19. Thomas J. Jackson to Samuel Cooper, August 10, 1862, Thomas J. Jackson Papers, Museum of the Confederacy.

20. *Official Records,* 12: pt. 2, 139, 183–85.

21. Robertson, *Stonewall Jackson,* 536.

22. George B. McClellan, *The Civil War Papers of George B. McClellan* (New York: Ticknor & Fields, 1989), 393.

23. Mrs. Jackson, *Memoirs,* 317.

24. Robertson, *Stonewall Jackson,* 549.

25. Johnson and Buel, *Battles and Leaders,* 2:533.

26. Dabney, *Life and Campaigns,* 517.

27. Wayland F. Dunaway, *Reminiscences of a Rebel* (New York: Neale, 1913), 38.

28. *Official Records,* 12: Pt. 2, 644, 723.

29. Robertson, *Stonewall Jackson,* 557.

30. Ibid.

31. William W. Blackford, *War Years with Jeb Stuart* (New York: Charles Scribner's Sons, 1945), 118.

32. Robertson, *Stonewall Jackson,* 561.

33. Blackford, *War Years,* 121.

34. *Official Records,* 12: Pt. 2, 657.

35. Buel and Johnson, *Battles and Leaders,* 2:510.

36. Robertson, *Stonewall Jackson,* 62.

37. *Official Records,* 12: Pt. 3, 721.

38. J. F. J. Caldwell, *The History of a Brigade of South Carolinians, Known First as "Gregg's," and Subsequently*

as "McGowan's Brigade" (Dayton, Ohio: Morningside Press, 1992), 63–64.

39. Douglas, *I Rode with Stonewall*, 137–38.

40. McGuire and Christian, *Confederate Cause*, 210.

41. Robertson, *Stonewall Jackson*, 571.

42. John O. Casler, *Four Years in the Stonewall Brigade* (Dayton, Ohio: Morningside Bookshop, 1982), 112–13.

43. Henderson, *Stonewall Jackson*, 2:179.

44. Robertson, *Stonewall Jackson*, 576.

45. Edward A. Moore, *The Story of a Cannoneer under Stonewall Jackson* (New York: Neale, 1907), 123.

46. Charles Royster, *The Destructive War* (New York: Alfred A. Knopf, 1991), 44.

47. Robertson, *Stonewall Jackson*, 576.

47. Douglas, *I Rode with Stonewall*, 142.

CHAPTER XII

1. Lee, *Wartime Papers*, 293.

2. *Southern Historical Society Papers*, 10 (1882): 507.

3. For the Hill-Jackson blowup, see Robertson, *General A. P. Hill*, 131–35; Robertson, *Stonewall Jackson*, 584–85.

4. Robertson, *Stonewall Jackson*, 586–87.

5. Ibid., 587–88.

6. Ibid., 590; Mrs. Jackson, *Memoirs*, 346.

7. Caldwell, *Brigade of South Carolinians*, 69.

8. The best treatment of the "Lost Order," as it is called, is in Stephen W. Sears, *Landscape Turned Red: The Battle of Antietam* (New York: Ticknor and Fields, 1983), 91–92, 112–14, 349–56.

9. Douglas, *I Rode with Stonewall*, 157–58; Robertson, *Stonewall Jackson*, 595, 597.

10. Robertson, *Stonewall Jackson*, 604.

11. Caldwell, *Brigade of South Carolinians*, 72–73.

12. Mrs. Jackson, *Memoirs*, 338.

13. Edward H. Ripley, *Vermont General: The Unusual War Experiences of Edward Hastings Ripley, 1862–1865* (New York: Devin-Adair Company, 1960), 34–35.

14. Douglas Southall Freeman, *Lee's Lieutenants: A Study in Command* (New York: Charles Scribner's Sons, 1942–1944), 2:204.

15. *Official Records*, 19: Pt. 1, 956.

16. Robertson, *Stonewall Jackson*, 615.

17. Ibid., 609.

18. *Official Records*, 19: Pt. 1, 218.

19. Robertson, *Stonewall Brigade*, 159–60.

20. James M. McPherson, *Ordeal by Fire: The Civil War and Reconstruction* (New York: Alfred A. Knopf, 1982), 285.

21. Robertson, *Stonewall Jackson*, 617.

22. Robertson, *General A. P. Hill*, 148–50.

CHAPTER XIII

1. Robertson, *Stonewall Jackson*, 625.

2. *Official Records*, 19: Pt. 2, 643.

3. Robertson, *General A. P. Hill*, 152.

4. Robertson, *Stonewall Jackson*, 627–28, 639.

5. Von Borcke, *Confederate War*, 1:295–97.

6. Douglas, *I Rode with Stonewall*, 196.

7. Blackford, *Letters*, 130–31.

8. McDonald, *Diary*, 105.

9. Robertson, *Stonewall Jackson*, 635.

10. Johnson and Buel, *Battles and Leaders*, 3.70.

11. Robertson, *Stonewall Jackson*, 640. See also ibid., 642–43.

12. Mrs. Jackson, *Memoirs*, 360–61.

13. Ibid., 361–63.

14. Ibid., 363.

15. Johnson and Buel, *Battles and Leaders*, 3:114; Vandiver, *Mighty Stonewall*, 425–26.

16. Von Borcke, *Confederate War*, 2:117.

17. Robertson, *Stonewall Jackson*, 659.

18. Ibid., 659, 905.

19. Vandiver, *Mighty Stonewall*, 432.

20. John B. Hood, *Advance and Retreat: Personal Experiences in the United States and Confederate States Armies* (New Orleans: Hood Orphan Memorial Fund, 1880), 50.

21. Robertson, *Stonewall Jackson*, 661.

22. Ibid., 666.

23. Jedediah Hotchkiss, *Make Me a Map of the Valley: The Civil War Journal of Stonewall Jackson's Topographer* (Dallas: Southern Methodist University Press, 1973), 102.

24. Allan, *Preston,* 153.

25. Mrs. Jackson, *Memoirs,* 372.

CHAPTER XIV

1. Robertson, *Stonewall Jackson,* 697.

2. *Southern Historical Society Papers,* 43 (1920): 40.

3. Robertson, *Stonewall Jackson,* 682.

4. Douglas, *I Rode with Stonewall,* 217.

5. Robertson, *General A. P. Hill,* 172. See also Robertson, *Stonewall Jackson,* 678–80, 693.

6. Robertson, *Stonewall Jackson,* 683; Mrs. Jackson, *Memoirs,* 395, 408.

7. Mrs. Jackson, *Memoirs,* 401.

8. Robertson, *Stonewall Jackson,* 689.

9. Mrs. Jackson, *Memoirs,* 384–85.

10. Vandiver, *Mighty Stonewall,* 445.

11. Robertson, *Stonewall Jackson,* 684.

12. Ibid., 685.

13. *Confederate Veteran,* 20 (1912): 26.

14. Mrs. Jackson, *Memoirs,* 413.

15. Ibid., 412.

16. Ibid., 411.

17. Robertson, *Stonewall Jackson,* 696–97; Mrs. Jackson, *Memoirs,* 413–14.

18. Robertson, *Stonewall Jackson,* 701.

19. Ibid., 699.

20. Johnson and Buel, *Battles and Leaders,* 3:157.

21. Robertson, *Stonewall Jackson,* 717.

22. Ibid.

23. Jackson Papers, Library of Virginia.

24. *Official Records,* 25: Pt. 1, 940–41.

25. Couper, *V.M.I.,* 2:171.

26. Robertson, *Stonewall Jackson,* 722. A North Carolina soldier observed of the Federals: "They did run and make no mistake about it—but I will never blame them. I would have done the same thing and so would you and I reckon the Devil himself would have run with Jackson in his rear." Ibid.

27. Bean, *Pendleton,* 115.

28. Robertson, *Stonewall Jackson,* 728.

29. Ibid., 734–35.

30. Lee, *Wartime Papers,* 452–53.

31. Johnson and Buel, *Battles and Leaders,* 3:214.

32. Robertson, *Stonewall Jackson,* 918–19.

33. Ibid., 741; Robertson, *Stonewall Brigade,* 189.

34. Mrs. Jackson, *Memoirs,* 451.

35. Ibid., 452.

36. Mrs. Jackson, *Memoirs,* 457; McGuire and Christian, *Cause and Conduct,* 229.

EPILOGUE

1. Robertson, *Stonewall Jackson,* 754–55.

2. Lee, *Wartime Papers,* 484.

3. Allan, *A March Past,* 152.

4. Robertson, *Stonewall Jackson,* 760–61.

5. *Lexington Gazette,* July 30, 1891.

6. Ujanirtus Allen, *Campaigning with "Old Stonewall": Confederate Captain Ujanirtus Allen's Letters to His Wife* (Baton Rouge: Louisiana State University Press, 1998), 145.

7. For example, see *Confederate Veteran* 21 (1913): 494; Moore, *Cannoneer,* 127.

8. Withrow Scrapbooks, Washington and Lee University, 18:18.

SOURCES CITED

Allan, Elizabeth Preston. *The Life and Letters of Margaret Junkin Preston.* Boston: Houghton Mifflin Co., 1903.

Allen, Ujanirtus. *Campaigning with "Old Stonewall": Confederate Captain Ujanirtus Allen's Letters to His Wife.* Baton Rouge: Louisiana State University Press, 1998.

Anderson, James W. "With Scott in Mexico: Letters of Captain James W. Anderson in the Mexican War, 1846–1847," *Military History of the West,* 28 (1998).

Arnold, Thomas J. *Early Life and Letters of General Thomas J. Jackson— "Stonewall" Jackson, By His Nephew.* New York: Fleming H. Revell Co., 1916.

Avirett, James B. *The Memoirs of General Turner Ashby and His Compeers.* Baltimore: Selby & Dulany, 1867.

Blackford, Susan Leigh (comp.). *Letters from Lee's Army.* New York: Charles Scribner's Sons, 1947.

Blackford, William W. *War Years with Jeb Stuart.* New York: Charles Scribner's Sons, 1945.

Borcke, Heros von. *Memoirs of the Confederate War for Independence.* 2 vols. Edinburgh, Scot.: W. Blackwood and Sons, 1866.

Brown, Canter, Jr. *Fort Meade, 1849–1900.* Tuscaloosa: University of Alabama Press, 1995.

Buck, Lucy R. *Shadows on My Heart: The Civil War Diary of Lucy Rebecca Buck.* Athens: University of Georgia Press, 1997.

Caldwell, J. F. J. *The History of a Brigade of South Carolinians, Known First as "Gregg's," and Subsequently As "McGowan's Brigade."* Dayton, Ohio: Morningside Press, 1992.

Caldwell, Willie Walker. *Stonewall Jim: A Biography of General James A. Walker, C.S.A.* Elliston, Va.: Northcross House, 1990.

Casler, John O. *Four Years in the Stonewall Brigade.* Dayton, Ohio: Morningside Bookshop, 1982.

Chambers, Lenoir. *Stonewall Jackson.* 2 vols. New York: William Morrow & Co., 1959.

Chase, William C. *Story of Stonewall Jackson.* Atlanta: D. E. Luther Publishing Co., 1901.

Clark, Champ. *Decoying the Yanks: Jackson's Valley Campaign.* Alexandria, Va.: Time-Life Books, 1984.

Clarksburg Sunday Exponent-Telegram. 1930.

Coffman, Edward M. *The Old Army: A Portrait of the American Army in Peacetime, 1784–1898.* New York: Oxford University Press, 1986.

Confederate Veteran [magazine]. 40 vols. Nashville: A. S. Cunningham, 1892–1932.

Cook, Roy Bird. *The Family and Early Life of Stonewall Jackson.* Charleston, W. Va.: Charleston Publishing Co., 1924.

Cooke, John Esten. *A Life of Gen. Robert E. Lee.* New York: D. Appleton and Co., 1871.

Coulling, Mary P. *Margaret Junkin Preston: A Biography.* Winston-Salem, N.C.: John F. Blair, 1993.

Couper, William. *One Hundred Years at V.M.I.* 4 vols. Richmond: Garrett and Massie, 1939.

Dabney, Charles W. Papers. University of North Carolina.

Diss Debar, J. H. "Two Men: Old John Brown and Stonewall Jackson.," typescript, West Virginia Department of Archives and History.

Dooley, Edwin L. "Lexington in the 1860 Census," typescript, Rockbridge Historical Society, 1979.

Douglas, Henry Kyd. *I Rode with Stonewall.* Chapel Hill: University of North Carolina Press, 1940.

Dunway, Wayland F. *Reminiscences of a Rebel.* New York: Neale Publishing Co., 1913.

Edmondson, James K. *My Dear Emma (War Letters of Col. James K. Edmondson, 1861–1865).* Verona, Va.: McClure Press, 1978.

Ewell, Richard S. *The Making of a Soldier: Letters of General R. S. Ewell.* Richmond: Whittet & Shepperson, 1935.

Fonerden, C. A. *A Brief History of the Military Career of Carpenter's Battery.* New Market, Va.: Henkel & Co., 1911.

Freeman, Doulas Southall. *Lee's Lieutenants: A Study in Command.* 3 vols. New York: Charles Scribner's Sons, 1942–1944.

Gordon, George H. *Brook Farm to Cedar Mountain in the War of the Great Rebellion, 1861–62.* Boston: James R. Osgood and Company, 1883.

Graham, James R. "Some Reminiscences of Stonewall Jackson," *Things and Thoughts,* 1 (1901).

Guernsey, Alfred H., *Harper's Pictorial History of the Civil War.* 2 vols. New York: Harper & Bro., 1866–1868.

Henderson, G. F. R. *Stonewall Jackson and the American Civil War.* 2 vols. London: Longman, Green and Co., 1898.

Hood, John B. *Advance and Retreat: Personal Experiences in the United States and Confederate States Armies.* New Orleans: Hood Orphan Memorial Fund, 1880.

Hoole, William Stanley. *Lawley Covers the Confederacy.* Tuscaloosa, Ala.: Confederate Publishing Co., 1964.

Hotchkiss, Jedediah. *Make Me a Map of the Valley: The Civil War Journal of Stonewall Jackson's Topographer.* Dallas: Southern Methodist University Press, 1973.

Howard, McHenry. *Recollections of a Maryland Confederate Soldier and Staff Officer under Johnston, Jackson, and Lee.* Dayton, Ohio: Morningside Bookshop, 1975.

Huffman, James. *Ups and Downs of a Confederate Soldier.* New York: William E. Rudge's Sons, 1940.

Hughes, Merritt H. (ed.). *John Milton: Complete Poems and Major Prose.* New York: Macmillan Publishing Co., 1957.

Hunter, Alexander. *Johnny Reb and Billy Yank.* New York: Neale Publishing Co., 1905.

Jackson, Mary Anna. *Memoirs of Stonewall Jackson By His Widow.* Louisville, Ky.: The Prentice Press, 1895.

Jackson, Thomas J. *Book of Maxims.* New Orleans: Tulane University.

———. Papers. Library of Congress.

———. Papers. Library of Virginia.

———. Papers. The Museum of the Confederacy.

———. Papers. Virginia Military Institute.

———. Papers. West Virginia University.

Johnson, Robert U. and C. C. Buel (eds.), *Battles and Leaders of the Civil War.* 4 vols. New York: The Century Company, 1884–1887.

Lee, Robert E. *The Wartime Papers of R. E. Lee.* Boston: Little, Brown and Company, 1961.

Levin, Alexandra Lee. *"This Awful Drama:" General Edwin Gray Lee, C.S.A., and His Family.* New York: Vantage Press, 1987.

Lewis, Lloyd. *Captain Sam Grant.* Boston: Little, Brown and Co., 1960.

Lexington Gazette. 1891.

Lincoln, Abraham. *The Collected Works of Abraham Lincoln.* Edited by Roy P. Basler. 9 vols. New Brunswick, N.J.: Rutgers University Press, 1953–1955.

Lyle, John Newton. "Sketches Found in a Confederate Veteran's Desk," typescript, Washington and Lee University.

McCabe, James D. *The Life of Thomas J. Jackson, By an Ex-cadet.* Richmond: James E. Goode, 1864.

McClellan, George B. *The Civil War Papers of George B. McClellan.* New York: Ticknor & Fields, 1989.

McDonald, Cornelia. *A Diary with Reminiscences of the War and Refugee Life in the Shenandoah Valley, 1860–1865.* Nashville: Cullom & Ghertner, 1935.

McGuire, Hunter, and George L. Christian. *The Confederate Cause and Conduct in the War between the States.* Richmond: L. H. Jenkins, 1907.

McPherson, James M. *Ordeal by Fire: The Civil War and Reconstruction.* New York: Alfred A. Knopf, 1982.

Maury, Dabney H. *Recollections of a Virginian.* New York: Charles Scribner's Sons, 1894.

Millett, Allan R., and Peter Maslowski. *For the Common Defense: A Military History of the United States.* New York: Free Press, 1984.

Moore, Edward A. *The Story of a Cannoneer under Stonewall Jackson.* New York: Neale Publishing Co., 1907.

Moore, George Ellis. *A Banner in the Hills: West Virginia's Statehood.* New York: Appleton-Century-Crofts, 1963.

Morrison, James L., Jr. *"The Best School in the World": West Point, The Pre-Civil War Years, 1833–1866.* Kent, Ohio: Kent State University Press, 1986.

Mottelay, Paul F. *The Soldier in Our Civil War.* 2 vols. New York: J. H. Brown Publishing Co., 1884–1885.

Neese, George M. *Three Years in the Confederate Horse Artillery.* Dayton, Ohio: Morningside, 1988.

Nevin, David. *The Mexican War.* Alexandria, Va.: Time-Life Books, 1978.

Official Records—see U. S. War Department (comp.).

Peters, Virginia Benjamin. *The Florida Wars.* Hamden, Conn.: Archon Books, 1979.

Randolph, Sarah Nicholas. *The Life of Gen. Thomas J. Jackson ("Stonewall" Jackson).* Philadelphia: J. B. Lippincott, 1876.

Rankin, Thomas M. *Stonewall Jackson's Romney Campaign, January 1-February 20, 1862.* Lynchburg, Va.: H. E. Howard, 1994.

Ripley, Edward H. *Vermont General: The Unusual War Experiences of Edward Hastings Ripley, 1862–1865.* New York: Devin-Adair Company, 1960.

Robertson, James I., Jr. *Civil War! America Becomes One Nation: An Illustrated History for Young Readers.* New York: Alfred A. Knopf, 1992.

———. *General A. P. Hill: The Story of a Confederate Warrior.* New York: Random House, 1987.

———. *The Stonewall Brigade.* Baton Rouge: Louisiana State University Press, 1963.

———. *Stonewall Jackson: The Man, The Soldier, The Legend.* New York: Macmillan Publishing USA, 1997.

Sears, Stephen W. *George B. McClellan: The Young Napoleon.* New York: Ticknor & Fields, 1988.

———. *Landscape Turned Red: The Battle of Antietam.* New York: Ticknor & Fields, 1983.

Slaughter, Philip. *A Sketch of the Life of Randolph Fairfax, A Private in the Ranks of the Rockbridge Artillery.* Baltimore: Innes and Company, 1878.

Southern Historical Society Papers. 52 vols. Richmond: Southern Historical Society, 1876–1952.

Tanner, Robert G. *Stonewall in the Valley.* Mechanicsburg, Pa.: Stackpole Books, 1996.

Taylor, Richard. *Destruction and Reconstruction.* New York: Longmans, Green and Co., 1955.

Thompson, Ernest T. *Presbyterians in the South, 1607–1861.* Richmond: John Knox Press, 1963.

U.S. War Department (comp.). *War of the Rebellion: A Compilation of the Official Records of the Union and Confederate Armies.* 128 vols. Washington: U.S. Government Printing Office, 1880-1901.

Vandiver, Frank E. *Mighty Stonewall.* New York: McGraw-Hill Book Co., 1957.

Vickers, George M. (ed.). *Under Both Flags.* St. Louis: People's, 1896.

Waugh, John C. *The Class of 1846.* New York: Warner Books, 1994.

Wayland, John W. *Stonewall Jackson's Way.* Dayton, Ohio: Morningside Bookshop, 1984.

White, H. M. (ed.). *Rev. William S. White, D.D., and His Times, 1800-1873: An Autobiography.* Harrisonburg, Va.: Sprinkle Publications, 1983.

Wolseley, Garnet Joseph. *The American Civil War: An English View.* Charlottesville: University Press of Virginia, 1964.

Wood, James H. *The War: "Stonewall" Jackson, His Campaigns and Battles; The Regiment as I Saw It.* Gaithersburg, Md.: Butternut Press, 1984.

INDEX

Photographic Credits

Grateful acknowledgment is made for the use of the following illustrations:

Laura Arnold (p. 13), Jackson (p. 35), and Margaret Preston (p. 53), courtesy of the Stonewall Jackson Foundation, Lexington, Virginia.

D. H. Hill (p. 46), "Jackson at First Manassas" (p. 71), W. W. Loring (p. 79), and Jackson equipment (p. 165), courtesy of The Museum of the Confederacy, Richmond, Virginia.